CHILD OF THE RIVER

BOOK 1 IN THE PROPHESIED PRINCE SERIES

ANNA BUSHI

Library of Congress Control Number: 2024901542

ISBN 978-1-7364103-8-7 (paperback) — ISBN 978-1-7364103-9-4 (hardback)

Cover designed by Getcovers.

To my grandmother, who told me the most delightful stories.

MAGADHA
RAIDAK MOUNTAINS
TIPTI
SINGALILA
SUNKOSH RIVER
NIRA SEA
JALPAIGURI
SATARA SEA
PUNE SEA
N
W E
S
0 50 100 150 200 250
miles
KASHGAR

CHARACTERS

MALLA KINGDOM

- King Jay
- Queen Aranya, wife of Jay, princess of Saral
- Sudha, wife of Jay, daughter of Chief Mani Vindhya
- Queen Mother Meera, sister of Jay
- Crown Prince Atul, son of Meera, presently in Kashgar

Vindhya House

- Chief Mani
- Sudha, daughter of Mani, wife of King Jay
- Rish, guard of Queen Mother Meera, cousin of Mani

PADI KINGDOM

- King Naladeva, son of Queen Kayal and former King Nala
- Queen Mother Kayal, wife of former King Nala, princess of Malla
- Princess Yamini, daughter of Queen Kayal and former King Nala
- Queen Mother Meera, wife of former King Atul, mother to Nala, Amar, Atul, and Priya
- Prince Amar, brother of Nala, regent to the young king
- Prince Atul, brother of Nala, presently in Kashgar

KASHGAR KINGDOM

- Former King Rajasuriya
- Prince Aggabodhi, son of Rajasuriya
- Princess Malathi, sister of Rajasuriya
- Chief Vikramasinha of Singalila, husband of Princess Malathi
- Parvati, daughter of Vikramasinha and Princess Malathi
- Chief Jeevahatta of Jalpaiguri
- Gowri, daughter of Jeevahatta

PROLOGUE

On that dreary day, the sea was choppy and gray. Powerful waves crashed against the rocks, spraying water in a mist. The tall, steep cliffs at the ocean's edge loomed large and dark.

All day, her grandfather had seemed weary and distracted. Sugandha had wondered what troubled him. When he cautioned her to stay home and left hurriedly, Sugandha followed her grandfather to the beach and now stood partially hidden behind a sandstone boulder.

She wriggled her toes, wishing she could be home, eating her meal. Her fingers grazed the rough edge of the rock. She shifted to one side to view the bumps on the surface and found a carving of a boat. It had weathered in time, but the image remained clear. With the sails fluttering in the wind, she could almost imagine the raft afloat. She wondered if the sculptor had used his imagination or if a real craft had loomed in front of him like the one before her eyes.

A large ship tossed on the waves, and she could see people moving on its deck. The howling wind sounded like a cry for help from the ship's passengers.

Her uncle cleared his throat, and she peeked around the rock to view him. "Curse them, Father," her uncle commanded. He stood on the shore facing the ocean, tugging the sacred thread worn across his chest.

Her grandfather gazed at his son, his shoulders slumped. "These men are messengers. Cursing them is an act of war," he said gravely.

Her uncle laughed. "Don't tell me you have gone soft in your old age. Magadha is harboring Prince Aggabodhi. We must send a strong message that we will not tolerate their interference in our affairs." He spread his legs wide apart and placed his hands on his hips. "I need that boy to rule this land."

Harboring Aggabodhi? She thought the prince had died along with his father, their last king.

"Rule? Ori, we are priests, not rulers. And you know about the curse on this kingdom," said her grandfather.

Curse? Their splintered kingdom had no ruler. Instead, several contenders clashed with each other for the right to wear the crown. *Did a curse cause this ruin?*

Sugandha imagined a flicker of irritation passing on her uncle's face, though she could not see him well. He shifted to face his father. "Yes, I remember the curse. It seems like you have forgotten the past. While I am setting right the wrong committed, you continue to believe we should be passive observers. If you don't aid me, I will find others who will." His icy tones caused a tremor in her heart.

Her grandfather sighed. "King Jay is not a man who is easily frightened, but I will curse the ship." He sat cross-legged on the sandy shore, facing the floating vessel. She watched him as if it were entertainment, not understanding what was about to happen.

"Spare the life of the one boy holding my message till he passes it on," her uncle said, turning to gaze at the ship.

In a solemn ritual, her grandfather summoned the god of fire, chanting an ancient *mantra* that resonated through the air.

"With the essence of my life, I curse the passengers on board the ship to meet their end when they reach the shores of Magadha. The lad bearing Ori's message shall meet his demise after the message is relayed," he proclaimed the curse in an eerily high-pitched voice.

Then, he took water from his jug and washed his palm. An unsettling scent of smoldering wood permeated the air, though no flames appeared from the arcane invocation. An unknown dread gripped her throat.

With a pounding heart, Sugandha watched a whorl of dust depart her grandfather and reach the large craft. As she craned her neck to watch the ship, she heard a noise closer to her. Before Sugandha determined the source, silence reigned.

Peering through the fading light, she scanned the beach. She spotted a pair of feet belonging to a man lying on the sand. Her heart thudded louder as she recognized them. Her grandfather had collapsed on the beach. Childishly, she thought he would rise. But she was wrong.

"Take him home," Ori ordered, walking away from his father without a backward glance. Two men carried her grandfather. With her stomach knotted in worry, she followed them at a distance.

The sun dipped into the ocean, and the sand shimmered gold, but anxiety shrouded Sugandha. A cart rode past on the opposite side, and a lantern under the carriage cast gloomy shadows.

In the fading light, she reached her home with a primeval fear gnawing at her bones. A dog growled in the distance. She found her grandfather lying on a cot in his room. With trembling hands, she touched his arms. Cold! She turned to fetch a blanket, but a movement caught her attention.

He flexed his right hand.

"Grandfather?"

His eyes fluttered open, and he peered at her. "Sugandha, I was waiting for you. I have enough life force left to offer you a blessing." His breath came in gasps as if he were struggling to climb a mountain peak.

Horror struck her anew. "Grandfather, please, spare your life force," she pleaded, her voice trembling with anguish. "The only blessing I seek is more time by your side. I fear the thought of facing this world alone without you."

"Child, bring me my water jug." She edged toward the shelf that held the jug without taking her eyes off him. When she handed the vessel to him, he clasped the handle tightly.

Tears flowed down her chin as he whispered a haunting *mantra*, invoking the river Goddess for protection. "Conceal her from Ori," he beseeched the divine, sprinkling sacred water upon her head. "Your uncle poses a grave danger to your very existence. Depart swiftly to find Purohit Parivan, the revered priest dwelling within the temple of the moon," he murmured, his weakening voice laden with urgency and concern.

"Grandfather," she cried, but the god of death claimed his victim.

She collapsed on top of his chest and sobbed. Time stood still while twin streams flowed down her chin. A sound penetrated her sorrow—bells tied to oxen pulling her uncle's cart. Something stirred inside her. Her uncle was arriving home, and her heart fluttered with uncertainty.

Her grandfather's intentions remained veiled, yet his ominous caution echoed in her mind. Aware of the looming threat her uncle posed, Sugandha steeled herself. She rose and wiped her eyes roughly. With trembling hands, she gathered a few belongings, each holding a fragment of cherished memories. Limping across the familiar threshold for what might be the last time, she glanced back at the solemn figure of her departed grandfather.

Emotions welled within her as she bid an unspoken farewell to the sanctuary that had cradled her throughout her life. With a heavy heart and a mixture of fear and determination, Sugandha stepped into the unknown, leaving behind the comforting embrace of the only home she had ever known.

SUGANDHA

WINTER YEAR 1

I hid behind a tree on the side of the road, waiting for the familiar cart to pass. My uncle rode in front, and I could see some figures in the back. My grandfather had blessed me to hide me from Uncle Ori's eyes, but I did not know if it would hide me from the men with my uncle, so tendrils of fear rose in my throat.

I stood frozen till the carriage receded from my sight. Many questions swirled in my head. *Why did my grandfather say my uncle was a threat to my life? What* would *he gain by my death?*

Sorrow and grief filled my heart when I realized I would receive no more guidance from my grandfather. I had never known my parents, and my grandfather had raised me from birth.

Usually, I would stir into wakefulness at this time of day. From my cot, I would hear my grandfather in the kitchen, pulling down pots, grinding an array of herbs, and brewing them.

Those small sounds would bring me peace, and I would snuggle into my sheets and close my eyes. Moments later, our neighbor's rooster would crow. Reluctantly, I would rise and push my hair back from my face.

"You are awake," he would say when I stumbled into the main room. He would grin at me as if I brightened his day just by existing, his wrinkled face glowing. "Now I can have some milk for my prayers," he would say gently, reminding me of my duty to milk the cows. I would lean my head briefly on his stooping shoulders and allow him to pull me into a hug.

Tears stung my eyes as I realized my grandfather was not around to offer me comforting words or a loving embrace. I was alone, bereft of all that gave me solace and support. I felt like a ship adrift in a sea of troubles. I had loved my grandfather dearly.

My grief slowly turned to anger. A tempest of hatred brewed in my stomach at my uncle for killing my grandfather. In one night, I had lost everything. All because of my uncle.

Something crawled up my leg, and I nearly screamed. Biting my lips, I lifted my skirt, spotting a caterpillar on my lower leg. I swiped it off my skin and watched the insect curl into a tiny ball. I wanted to curl up and go to sleep to rest my aching feet and sore heart. But the temple of the moon was still miles away. Light shimmered on the horizon, chasing away the night.

Not wanting to leave the king's road, I walked alongside the path, hiding behind trees and shrubs. A flock of birds flew overhead, looking like the head of an arrow.

Why did my grandfather ask me to find Purohit Parivan?

Almost every night, my grandfather would narrate a story to me after he had finished his duties for the day. As the sun set, I would hurry to complete all my chores. After our evening meal, I would sit cross-legged on the floor next to his feet. He would clear his throat and weave a remarkable tapestry of characters filled with courage, wisdom, and generosity. With my heart pounding, I had imagined the divine and noble people embarking on one adventure after another.

Sadness pooled in my heart as I realized my grandfather would never tell me any more stories. I roughly blotted the tears I spilled while I searched my memory for any tales of this priest. But I remembered none.

The sound of running water reached me, and my parched throat begged me to stop for a drink. Leaving the road, I walked toward the gentle babbling noise and found a creek flowing over small rocks and roots of nearby trees.

Across the stream, I saw a deer lower its head and use its lips to lap up the water. As I knelt on the shore, it raised its head to look in my direction and then disappeared into the bushes, flashing its rump. I plunged my hands in to gather some water. I brought my palms to my lips, and the cold water trickled down my neck.

A tiredness from walking all night swept over me. I climbed a nearby tree and tied myself to a thick branch. The sun rose and warmed my body, and sleep claimed me.

Shrouded in a mist, I walked behind a tall man as he knocked on the door of a house. The wind whipped his clothes, but mine remained stationary. I could hear a faint whimpering sound coming from him. Darkness swirled around us, with a half-moon reluctantly peeking out of the clouds.

"Purohit Parivan," greeted a man who opened the door. He looked remarkably like my grandfather but years younger, with no wrinkles marring his face.

The man, whom my *grandfather* addressed as Purohit Parivan, entered the house holding a cloth bundle to his bare chest. He had gathered his long dark hair in a top knot. The door shut behind us, but neither man took notice of me. He held out his hands. "Take care of her. I will reveal all when the time is right."

Parivan handed the bundle to my grandfather. The cloth

moved to reveal a tiny foot. *A baby?* My grandfather accepted the baby reverently.

~

A soft chirping sound reached my mind, and I shifted and nearly slid off the tree. A wave of weariness rolled over me. Grabbing the branch with both hands, I sat up with a frown. A sharp pain pounded my head. I shut my eyes tightly but found no relief. I waited for the agony to subside and then opened my eyes. Two monkeys sat on a trunk across from me, one grooming the other while cooing to each other. I massaged my temple. *Did I dream of my grandfather and Parivan? Why did it feel unlike any of my other dreams? Who was the baby he held?* A tiny knot twisted my stomach.

Before I could ponder the piling mysteries, I heard voices floating from below. I hid among the leaves and peeked through a small gap.

"Ori is searching for his niece," said a woman holding a clay pot.

"What happened to Sugandha?" asked another as she filled her vessel with water from the stream. I peered at her to see if I recognized the woman who knew my name.

"Ori said someone killed his father and abducted the girl. He had promised his sister he would marry her daughter. Now he is worried someone intent on thwarting his efforts to bring peace to this land is behind the kidnapping."

They moved away from the creek, and I sat stunned. *Uncle Ori's sister?* That would be my mother. She died years ago. *How could he have promised her to marry me?* My grandfather never mentioned any marriage, let alone to my uncle. I would rather die than wed my uncle. I remembered my grandfather had perished to protect me.

Shame coiled around me for thinking callously about my

death. My grandfather wanted me to survive, and I would find a way. Whatever game my uncle played, I would not let him win. I resolved to find Purohit Parivan before I fell into my uncle's clutches.

I untied myself and slid down the tree. Before I took a few steps, a loud grumble erupted from my stomach, reminding me that I had not eaten since midday yesterday. Further away, I saw an irrigation canal leading away from the creek. I followed it to a banana grove. Sneaking in surreptitiously, I searched for ripe bananas among the lush green leaves that grew taller than me. Finding a promising bunch, I used a small knife I carried on me to cut a dozen. A sweet smell filled the air. I peeled one to take a bite.

"Hey, thief!" An angry voice shattered the serene atmosphere.

I was a crook stooping to steal from others to keep myself alive. Before shame overwhelmed me, I heard the pounding of rapid footsteps that signaled a relentless pursuer headed my way. Panic surged through me like a thunderbolt. Hastily, I crammed the stolen fruit into my mouth, munching it down in a single gulp. Throwing the peel behind me, I took off at a run.

"Catch him," shouted a voice.

Still holding the uneaten bananas in one hand and the knife in the other, I ran with my mouth open, taking abrupt left and right turns to evade my pursuers.

"It is a girl." That sound came from someone nearby. My feet pounded the ground with each step. As I turned a corner, I nearly collided with a man. I spun on my heels and darted in the opposite direction, my heart thundering.

My skinny frame allowed me to weave between the thick tree trunks. I could feel the leaves brushing against my skin, but that did not slow me down. I leaped over fallen branches and dodged trees. I heard shouts and curses behind me, but I kept moving.

After an eternity, I burst out of the grove into an open meadow. With no place to hide, I ran, the sound of my breathing filling my ears. Near a small clump of trees, I stumbled to a stop, gasping for air. I scanned the horizon for any pursuers. Seeing no one, I sighed in relief. Sweat trickled down my neck.

Then, a new fear caught hold of me. *What if word reached my uncle that I was spotted near the banana grove?* I imagined being married to him, and horror clamped my throat. I had overheard two older girls talk about their marriages. They mentioned sharing a bed with a stranger and allowing him to touch parts they usually kept covered even while bathing. I recoiled when I imagined my uncle's lips brushing mine. Hurriedly, I removed my braid and gathered it into a top knot at the crown of my head. I stole a boy's clothes from the ones laid out to dry along a lake shore. Hiding behind a large tree trunk, I wore the dhoti—a long piece of cloth wrapped around one's waist and legs—and the loose-fitting upper garment. Looking down at my chest, I took the upper garment off and tightened the band around my breast to flatten it. Satisfied with the results, I put on the garment again. I checked myself in the reflection in the water. I was fifteen, and in these clothes, I could pass for a thirteen or fourteen-year-old boy.

The longer I lingered near my home, the more chance for one of my uncle's acquaintances to stumble upon me. It would take me days on foot to put distance between us. As I pondered what to do, I saw two men loading a cart with coconut leaves.

"When we drive past the temple of the moon, I have to stop to make an offering to God Chandra. When my son fell ill last month, I prayed that if the boy were cured, I would donate a dozen coconuts," said one of them.

The other nodded. "I will fetch our food, and then we can leave." One man stood fitting the yoke to the bulls while the other moved away.

I saw no way to sneak past him to the back of the cart. Before I risked it, a woman hailed him. "Do you want me to deliver some of your pickles to your daughter?" he asked, walking toward her. Using this opportunity, I moved to the side of the cart facing away from the street. Making sure no one noticed, I climbed in among the coconut leaves. The serrated edges scratched my skin as I settled in a corner, covering myself with the fronds. The light filtered between the long blade-like leaves.

Humming a song, one of the men from earlier tied a rope around the coconut branches. I held my breath, fearful of being caught. Soon, the cart swayed gently, and the wheels rolled forward. Releasing my breath, I relaxed. *What would I do when I reached the temple? Would Purohit Parivan recognize my name?*

My folded legs started to feel numb and tingly, and I had no room to stretch them. Potholes the size of a curled-up snake lurked on the road. The constant jostling and bouncing of the cart added to my discomfort. Cramped and surrounded by coconut leaves, I was sticky and sweaty, even though summer was months away. I shifted my hips to find a comfortable position and pondered about the events of the past.

Uncle Ori had left our home a few years ago to go to Tipti, the capital of Kashgar. King Rajasuriya had died in an uprising nearly two years ago. Ordinary folks had risen in protest of the heavy taxation while they starved due to our severe drought. Since then, a fierce clash had erupted among the nobles on who should rule Kashgar.

Was Uncle Ori siding with one of the clans in this fight? What was the reason behind his request to Grandfather to curse the ship bound for Magadha, especially if they had provided shelter to Prince Agga-bodhi? I had heard of Magadha as a prosperous land to our east, but I did not know its connection to Kashgar. I only had questions and no answers. The rocking motion of the carriage put me to sleep.

Smoke oozed through the cracks into a room, flooding it as a man dragged an object across it. Leaning it against the wall, he stepped back, muttering, "That ought to give me some time." Shrouded in smoke, I could not determine what he had placed in the chamber.

I gazed at the back of the man. With his long gray hair piled into a top knot, he moved with a hunch. Sweat dripped down his neck.

"Sugandha," he murmured as he gathered his belongings. The crackling of flames nearly drowned his voice. *Who was he? How did he know my name?* "My child, don't seek me. Stay hidden," he said as the orange glow of fire cast eerie shadows on the wall. He moved through the flying sparks and embers and disappeared from my view.

A jolt knocked me against the cart, and I surfaced into wakefulness with a gasp. A splitting headache thundered through my skull. Sweat trickled down my chin. I took several deep breaths to dampen my agony. Darkness surrounded me. *Who was the man in my dreams?* There was something familiar about him, but my pain-addled brain could not place him. *Why did he think I was seeking him?* I sought Purohit Parivan. *Did I dream about Purohit Parivan again?*

When light filtered in through the cracks in the leaves, the cart stopped. I wanted to stand up and stretch my legs, but the voices floating around me kept me imprisoned in the cart. The bananas I had stolen had squashed in the tight quarters, but I peeled two and ate them. Our cart rolled forward again. Soon, the sun rose higher in the sky, and I sweltered in the heat. *How far were we from the temple of the moon?*

I heard the word fire and sat up. Our cart halted again. "It burned down," said a man's voice. I rose on my knees and pushed aside some of the leaves covering me to better hear the conversation.

"When did it happen?" asked one of the cart drivers.

"Last night," answered a voice beside the cart.

"What happened to Purohit Parivan?"

"We found his charred bones. We believe the priest met his demise amidst the raging flames."

I dropped down, realizing Purohit Parivan had not only known my name but, through his yogic powers, could send vivid visions into my mind. However, like my grandfather, this man had also met an untimely death.

My eyes brimmed with tears. I seemed to harbor ill luck that spilled into the lives of people associated with me. Isolated and surrounded by a world of terror, I had nowhere to go. Like a tortoise withdrawing into its shell, I had no other option but to remain concealed from the prying eyes of the outside world.

ATUL

WINTER YEAR 2 (OCCURS A YEAR AFTER CHAPTER 1)

"Stop," I said to my captain. "If we go any nearer, they will spot us from the shore. Drop the rafts, and we will use those to reach land."

The half-moon cast an eerie glow over the ocean, illuminating its vast expanse in an ominous light. The distant stars in the dark sky appeared cold and indifferent. The veteran captain nodded and ordered the sailors to drop the rafts. "I will go back to the island we spotted a few hours ago and anchor there," he said to me.

I went looking for Aggabodhi and found him leaning on the wooden railing and staring at his home, Kashgar. He faced the land as if he awaited instructions from it. "I have been away for two years. What if there is no one left to support my attempt to regain my kingdom?" asked the prince.

I understood Aggabodhi's emotions—more than he knew. I feared that the men who revered me as the Heir to Malla would abandon me if they knew the truth about my birth. That was the reason I had urged my uncle, King Jay of Malla, to send me on this mission. Uncle Jay wanted me to wait until our soldiers had secured Kashgar, but I itched to prove myself.

I wanted to be worthy of being king by my deeds because I was no prince by birth. My ships that sailed west across the Nira Sea carried not only Malla men but also men from the other two kingdoms of Magadha—Padi and Saral. With their help, I hoped to seat Aggabodhi on the Kashgar throne and return to Magadha as a victorious prince.

I set aside my musing and attempted to lighten Aggabodhi's feelings of isolation. "What am I? Deadwood?" He straightened and grimaced at my poor quip. At sixteen years of age, he reached my chin.

"Prince Atul, while I have called you by several names, dead is not one of them. You are very much alive. And thank Buddha for that. I would not have endeavored on this voyage without you by my side."

"You have to stop calling me prince and giving away my identity," I said.

"I will call you brother then. I can be the younger brother you never had," said Aggabodhi. Images of my cousin Vikram floated into my mind. Vikram—son of Uncle Jay—was more than a brother to me. We grew up together and had remained inseparable till his death two years ago, but the hole in my chest left by his void never filled.

Aggabodhi read the emotions flitting through my face and winced. "I apologize. I know you and your cousin grew up as brothers," he said kindly.

"I hope I can protect you better than I protected him." I had been unable to save Vikram. Guilt ate my stomach.

"Brother, no one holds you accountable for his death," he said to assuage me.

I smiled weakly. I was partly responsible for Vikram's death. If I hadn't abandoned him, he would still be alive. I pulled myself away from these gloomy thoughts. "Bodhi, I can be your older brother and impart my knowledge. You have a lot to learn from my wisdom gathered over the last nineteen years. First, let us set foot on your kingdom before sunrise."

Plop. Four boats plonked onto the sea. "I might be younger than you, but there is one thing I can teach you. How to dive into the water." With that, Aggabodhi ran onto the deck and flew off the vessel. Before his feet launched into the sky, he tugged my arm, causing me to fly with him.

I could hear Aggabodhi's excited laughter as I awkwardly jumped off the edge. The wind ruffled my hair, and the sound of the waves rose to greet me as I plunged in head first. The cold water rushed to engulf my body and shocked my senses. I disappeared into the dark, swirling water. As my body adjusted to the chill, I surfaced and wiped salt water out of my eyes.

"Here," shouted Aggabodhi, and I swam to his craft.

As I pulled myself up, he grabbed an oar and started rowing. "Bodhi, our guards!" I exclaimed, squeezing water out of my dhoti.

"They can follow us in another boat," he said.

In the middle of the sea, our small vessel seemed insignificant. I picked up the other oar and joined him. The waves emerged to breathe in and out as they rolled. As we approached the shore, a thick fog enveloped us like blankets obscuring the ship from our view. The land dissolved into the mist. I peered through the dense air that reeked of salt and fish. Indistinct shapes arose before us, and I felt like I had fallen into a nightmare.

A huge wave crashed into the raft and overturned us. The current tried to yank my legs out of my body. With a strong kick, I came up, gasping for air, the cold waves drenching my face. Memories swept through the dark: returning to Magadha with Uncle Jay, another overturned boat, and losing my cousin to the sea. I had utterly failed in my mission to save my cousin.

At that moment, an awful thought crept into my head. *Was I doomed to repeat my mistakes from the past?* I swam frantically, searching for Aggabodhi. I yelled his name, and water entered my mouth, causing me to gag. Shame gripped my heart that I had failed to teach Aggabodhi caution, that I had failed to tell him what to do in these circumstances, that I had failed to predict that such a thing might occur.

A dark object bobbed up. I swam to it—a plank. I grabbed onto it. "Aggabodhi," I screamed. I was not going to let Aggabodhi drown. I could not lose him before he could stake his claim for his throne. Before our mission even began. It could not end like this.

The turbulent sea tossed me around, and I lost my sense of direction. Sky and sea merged into one dark storm bent on destroying me. I battled the choppy waves, scanning the murky waters.

An arm flailed in the distance.

"Bodhi," I whispered and swam feverishly to it.

It did not take long to see him, his short hair plastered to his head. I grabbed his shoulder roughly from behind. He made no sound. Panic seized me as I lowered my grip to his chest. I felt a faint heartbeat. "Stay with me," I said, holding him as I swam. *Which way was land?* I floated on the water, letting it support our weight. I could not wait for daylight if Aggabodhi were hurt.

Moonlight cascaded into the fog like milk, helping me find our direction. I moved forward again. An old ship at anchor loomed suddenly, barnacled and dirty. Carefully, I navigated around the vessel. Weeds wrapped my legs, and waves shattered onto rocks, signaling the nearness of land.

My arms hurt from bearing Aggabodhi's weight, but I pulled him along. The fog was so thick that, at first, I did not see anything. Then, slowly, a dark cliff took shape. The edge of the night pulled away as we came around the bend. In waist-deep water, I stood up and hauled him onto my shoulders.

On the shore, I placed Aggabodhi on the sand and knelt beside him. As a child, I grew up with my cousins, my life filled with laughter and companionship. As we grew older, one left to rule a kingdom, and another perished in a madman's revenge.

Aggabodhi arrived in Magadha at the right time to save me from loneliness. These past two years, we had trained together and learned how to rule from the greatest king of Malla, Uncle Jay. I felt nauseated at the thought of losing Aggabodhi.

The sun peeked out of the ocean. In the faint dawn, I saw a visible cut on his forehead. Blood oozed out of the wound. Our boat must have hit him as it capsized. I turned him gently to his side and rocked him back and forth to force water out of his body. *Don't let him die.* After a few moments, he coughed, expelling water.

Until then, I did not realize I had held my breath. I sighed and rocked on my heels.

He peered at me as though I had sprouted wings. "Bodhi?" He blinked twice and then tried to rise. I pushed him down gently. "Let me check you first." Apart from the bruise and swelling on his forehead, he appeared fine. I nodded at him.

He sat up to grab the sand with his hands and rubbed it between his palms. I kept my gaze on him as I rose and inhaled the crisp air.

"What happened?" he asked in a dazed voice.

You nearly died, I thought. "Nothing. The boat hit you as it capsized, so I helped you to swim to the shore," I said, minimizing my panic-filled moments.

Aggabodhi nodded distractedly, his attention grabbed by the land around him. With gleaming eyes, Aggabodhi looked at me. "Home." I sensed terror and exhilaration in his voice.

The sun climbed out of the ocean as a fireball, and the water glittered like gems. Beyond the beach rose the cliffs dotted with dwarf trees—no sign of the other boats.

I scanned the horizon. I had no supplies with me. "Aggabodhi, we can wait here for our men to find us or head to the village." A Magadha contingent had arrived a few weeks ago to establish contacts with men loyal to the former king, Rajasuriya. They were a few miles from this port.

"Village," he said. I stretched my hand to him, and he grasped it and stood up. My guards would find me. I turned to Aggabodhi.

"Ready?" I asked, letting go of him. He moved without a limp.

We picked our way along the cliffs, the sun driving out the fog. The turquoise sea broke against the rocks. Aggabodhi paused now and then to point out edible fruits. I plucked a few for us to eat.

"If you call me brother, what do I call you?" I asked, not knowing if calling him Bodhi would reveal his identity.

"You can continue to use Bodhi. It was the name of one of our ancient Buddhist monks and hence a common name for boys in this land."

The ground turned rocky, and Aggabodhi nearly stumbled. I caught his arm, steadying him. "I am fine," he said, shaking me off. I felt a momentary knot in my stomach, a panic that I would lose him too, like I had lost my cousin. I released him slowly, watching him like a hawk. We started down the trail again and walked in silence for several moments.

"This is a mistake," said Aggabodhi in a loud voice.

I sensed the panic reverberating from him. "Were you expecting elephants lined up to welcome you home? Girls showering flower petals on you?"

He shot me a withering look.

"Bodhi, we are here to gather support for your campaign to take the throne. And my presence here shows Magadha's willingness to fight for you. First, we will find your aunt, who can confirm your identity as her brother's son. Then, we will stealthily meet with men who are loyal to you. And gain their pledges." I glanced at Aggabodhi.

He scowled. "Brother, why would they back an unknown prince?"

"Because you are the heir of the last king of Kashgar," I answered.

A rock settled in my stomach as I uttered the word heir. My cousin, Vikram, groomed to rule, died at the hands of an old foe. With no other sons, my uncle anointed me as the Crown Prince of Malla, but I had no claim to the throne. While my mother—older sister of Uncle Jay—was an esteemed queen, I was her baseborn son. Not many knew of the truth about my birth, and I masqueraded as a trueborn prince. Every day, I worried that a reckoning would arrive for this deceit.

"My father was killed—not by invaders—by his own people." Aggabodhi looked grim as if he contemplated something unpleasant.

"You will be a better ruler than him," I said.

That was what I told myself. I would strive to serve my people tirelessly so that even if they find out about my illegitimacy, they would continue to support me rather than plan to overthrow me.

Aggabodhi stood with his fists at his sides. "Some days, I want to let this Ori run the kingdom and spend my days growing crops."

I laughed with no mirth. "I think of raising cows." I knew this was wishful thinking on my part.

He looked at me sharply. Before he could reply, we heard the sound of approaching men and animals. I signaled to Aggabodhi, and we huddled near a tree. Heralds bearing a mud-stained banner came around the bend. Behind them came men carrying spears, ox-drawn carts, and soldiers on foot.

"Is that your banner?" I whispered, staring at the large eye depicted on the fluttering cloth.

"It is Chief Jeevahatta's banner," Aggabodhi whispered, his spine rigid. Jeevahatta, a ruler of the House of Jalpaiguri in the

South of Kashgar, was one of the men we sought to support our cause.

"May fortune embrace you," said Aggabodhi when the first people came near and glanced at us.

"Chief Jeevahatta has called young men like you to join his fight to save this kingdom," said one of them. "Once the land is taken, you will have your pick of gold or silks."

"Or girls," added another man with missing front teeth.

A broad man twisted his mustache. "Those who don't join us will turn to stone."

"If you don't fall to a stray arrow," said another, clutching his bow.

SUGANDHA

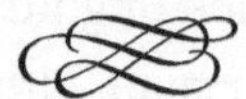

WINTER YEAR 1

I stepped back and looked at the painted backdrop hung on stage. A light wind rustled the cloth, depicting a forest.

"Is it straight? Can I tie it?" Bheema asked impatiently.

"Lift it a finger length," I instructed.

The villagers started to arrive and sat on the ground in front of the makeshift platform. As I stepped off the stage, Bheema followed me. Indra, the king of Gods, wearing golden armor and wielding a thunderbolt, stood in front of us in his resplendent orange silk dhoti. Holding weapons in both hands, he stood with his eyes shut, waiting for the music to begin.

"I want to play the lead like him," Bheema whispered in my ear, his warm breath caressing my skin.

Ignoring the flutters in my stomach, I glanced at the lanky young man who normally played the female characters. "You are a talented singer and dancer. I am sure you will be offered the lead role soon," I said sincerely.

Bheema smiled, put his arm around my shoulders, and pulled me along. "No time to dither. We have many things to move." His hip brushed mine as we walked, and a strange sensation between fear and desire rose in my body. I felt too young to understand the emotion.

Behind us, Indra jumped onto the stage. "Who stole my cattle?" he thundered. I imagined him twisting his mustache as he paced.

Bheema and I helped rearrange the stage between scenes, working well together. When I joined the theater a month ago, I gravitated toward him because he played female characters. His lean look blended well with mine. After being lost and lonely, this group offered me shelter. Among the men in costume, I felt safe. He vanished in the middle of the play to get dressed while I continued to help backstage.

Holding a long bow, Bheema halted in front of me. "Nanda, my dhoti has come undone," he called, gesturing toward his stomach with his chin. "Tuck it in the middle. My scene is next."

Swallowing, I viewed his slender frame, and a tremor ran through me. *Don't be foolish*, I chided myself. A normal boy would not shake like a wind-blown leaf at the sight of a bare chest. Unfortunately, I was only pretending to be a boy. I approached him tentatively and slid my fingers across his lower abdomen to push the cloth in. His coarse hair caused me to tremble, but the actor was distracted by the sound of cymbals and drums that rose from the other side.

I tightened the sash around his waist, trying to breathe normally. "Time to make my grand entrance. I will see you after the play," he said, moving away.

"Nanda, go adjust the flaming torch so the light falls on his face," whispered another actor in my ears. Grateful to do something, I ran around the stage to fix the light. Then, I went hunting for the actor playing the cow, whom I found in an alley, grinning idiotically at a girl.

"You are late for the play," I hissed.

He threw the cow mask at me. "I don't even have words to

utter, and my face is hidden inside this ridiculous costume. No one will miss me."

I had seen him prance on stage the last few days. *How hard could it be to play a cow?* I ran back, put the mask on, and stepped on stage. The bright light blinded me, and I staggered like a drunken cow. Indra held my neck gruffly, halting my motion, and belted out his song, nearly deafening my ears.

The audience showered us with flower petals as the play concluded. My grandfather, if he had lived, would hardly recognize me. A month had passed since I fled my home. I was nearly sixteen now and no longer looked like the girl who had left her home in the middle of the night.

"Boy, go and collect offerings from them," said the narrator. I took off my mask, tucked it under one arm, and walked toward the dispersing crowd. Other actors and musicians mingled with them, too.

"Today was our last show," I said. "We welcome your gifts." I accepted their bundles of grains with an eager smile.

I heard the name Ori and paused. "I heard Guru Ori is joining Chief Jeevahatta."

"What claim does either have to the throne?"

"With King Rajasuriya and Prince Aggabodhi dead, it is open season."

They walked away, and my mind spun like the wheel of a chariot. *Why did my uncle align with a nobleman? Was he still hunting for me?* With my mind occupied, I went about collecting the offering rather grimly.

Some handed me a coin or two. One man presented me with ten yards of cotton. "Before the wars and the drought, the village elders would host the entire troupe for a feast. Those days are gone. Now we barely get enough to eat," lamented one of the older men. After loading all the things into a cart, I walked quietly, listening to others chatter about their performance.

"You brayed like a donkey," someone said, shoving another.

"Better than you standing still having forgotten your lines."

"What is our next play?" asked the man who played Indra.

"Let us rest from this before we start rehearsing the next."

"We should perform Ramayana," said Bheema.

"Why, Bheema? Are you itching to wear a sari and become Princess Sita?" Chuckles floated around us. I glanced at him in a supporting manner, wishing I could do more. He gave me a rueful smile.

I heard someone step close to me. "I want a house, a field to farm in, and a wife," whispered the man who failed to play the cow. "None of which will be mine if I travel from village to village in this drama troupe." He picked at his nose while I stared at him.

"What will you do?"

"Leave," he said, staring at the moon. I wanted none of what he wished for. I wanted to be hidden. Wearing masks suited me fine.

A rooster crowed loudly, waking me from my disturbed sleep. As I wiped the remnants of the night away from my eyes, the sun sneaked in like a stealthy thief. No visions last night. None since the temple burned down. The feeble hope I had harbored that Purohit Parivan had survived the fire perished.

I cursed myself for staying asleep until dawn. I usually crawled into the fields in the dark to relieve myself. Now, I would have to walk several yards away from my troupe to do my morning duties. After the temple of the moon burned down, I found these actors and musicians enacting their play in a nearby village. Passing myself as a boy, I joined them as a helper.

"Nanda, wake up, you lazy donkey," scolded the lead performer of my drama troupe. He narrated our plays, and his voice carried for several yards. I rose before he started practicing his curses on me. Across the sky, bright spring clouds danced with haste, their movements mirroring the voyage of ships traversing a vast, ever-changing sea.

I grabbed a clay pot and walked to the stream to fetch water for our morning meal. A group of boys from our acting group splashed in the waist-deep water.

"Nanda, the water is refreshing. Come join us," hailed one.

"If I fooled around, who would cook your meals?" I pretended to be angry to hide my self-consciousness at seeing their near-naked bodies.

I waded into the cool water and filled my pot. One of the boys pushed another into the stream, laughing loudly, and I moved to avoid their tangle. As I straightened and stepped out of the water, a voice I recognized called, "Do you need help with that?"

Bheema stood in front of me in just his loincloth. Water dripped down his chest in tiny rivulets, and I lowered my eyes, embarrassed for noticing. Shouts and laughter from behind reached me. I shook my head vigorously and rushed back to our campground. I could feel his eyes burning a hole into my back.

Soon, I had a fire going and cooked our rice with yellow lentils. As I stirred the rice, my mind wandered to the incident earlier that morning. I had sought refuge among men who painted their faces. For the most part, my disguise worked. As a cook and helper, I enjoyed the work and the easy rapport. But on days like today, when there were no shows to perform at night and the other boys idled around, I worried someone would detect I was a girl.

I picked up a grain of rice and squashed it between my fingers. It had cooked to a soft consistency. I sprinkled water on the wood to extinguish the fire.

I served the porridge on lotus leaves and handed them to the actors, musicians, and helpers.

One of the men who played the animal skin drum said, "I see a tiny hair sprouting on your upper lip." He reached to touch my face, and I shrank from him. He dropped his hand and broke into laughter. "Nope. You are still beardless." Tears stung my eyes, and I blinked them rapidly. Taking a deep breath, I continued serving the food, but my fingers shook slightly. *How long could I pretend to be a thirteen-year-old boy?*

Sensing my distress, Bheema admonished his fellow artist. "Leave him alone." I felt a lump choking my throat at his unexpected kindness. Clearing it away, I gazed at him, grateful for his support. His eyes met mine. There was a question in them that I had not noticed before.

As the sun rose overhead, I carried the dirty clothes to wash in the stream. While scrubbing the clothes, I cleaned myself discreetly. I spread the clothes to dry on bushes and shrubs and sat on the sand. A gray crane with a redhead stood on one leg in the water.

I heard the crunch of dry leaves and glanced up to see Bheema. He stared at me, and there was a flash in his eyes I did not recognize. But I did not want his energy directed at me, so I dropped my gaze. Bheema sank down beside me, his hip touching mine. I slid back a little to move away from him. A sudden fear gripped me as his hand crawled underneath my upper garment and up my spine. I sat frozen in panic as his fingers touched the cloth band I wore around my chest.

Bheema leaned in, and I could smell betel leaves on his breath. Many actors chewed it to freshen their breath because they worked in close quarters with others. "Just as I suspected. You are a girl," he said as his fingers reached the base of my neck.

He pulled his hand out, draped it around my shoulders and drew me close to him. "I can protect you," he said, his lips grazing my ear. I kept my eyes on the tiny waves, afraid to meet his eyes. "For a payment. Share my mat at night."

Voices floated in as two villagers brought their donkeys to the water. Bheema rose abruptly and stretched his hands overhead with a yawn. I heard his steps recede, but I dared not turn to look.

I felt chilled as pain ambushed me. Like a fool, I had let my guard down and made myself vulnerable. A sob erupted in my throat, and I fought the temptation to fall to the ground and cry. Instead, I bit my lips to quash the sound while twisting my dhoti into a ball in my fist. I knew I could not let fear overwhelm me, not now. I waited for the sun to begin its descent and then bundled some of the dry clothes and slipped away into the twilight.

ATUL

WINTER YEAR 2

e marched with about a hundred men of all ages. Farmers and cowherds surrounded me with their pitchforks and scythes. They appeared to come from small neighboring villages and the countryside. I did not know if fear for their lives or loyalty to their liege lord motivated them to join this army. I could sense they had little military or weapons training. Any army fighting with these men would have to rely on brute force rather than complex formations.

I pulled Aggabodhi aside. "Bodhi, act like them to blend in with them."

Pointing with his chin, Aggabodhi retorted, "More like that?"

I followed his gaze to look at a man inspecting the sharp edge of his spear within a palm length of his eyes. A quick shove would cause him to lose his sight. Suppressing my grin, I answered, "Act like a novice around weapons. Not a complete fool."

"But I feel like a fool. Why is Jeevahatta gathering an army? Is he planning to claim the throne for himself?" Aggabodhi pouted.

"They believe you have perished along with your father.

With no lion to rule the forest, every jackal will try to claim the throne," I whispered, scanning the area for curious ears.

"What are you brothers talking about? Plotting your escape?" A broad man stroked his mustache with one hand while the other patted the knife hung on his waist. He was the commander of this chaotic bunch of men.

Aggabodhi and I could kill him in the blink of an eye and take another dozen down. But that would not serve our purpose.

"Why would we think of leaving you, my lord?" Though Aggabodhi had taught me his native tongue, I worried my accent would still betray me as a foreigner to this land.

The broad man sensed nothing amiss in my intonation. He exposed all his yellowing teeth in a terrifying grin at my calling him lord.

"You promised us wealth and girls," I said while my mind traveled to Malla. Images of my two wives floated into my head. I missed Rukmini's laughter, which sounded like raindrops on a silver plate. She had an easy way about her, allowing me to talk to her about things I loved. Vibha loved Malla as fiercely as I did and did nothing in half measures. I missed our long rides together, my arms around her waist, breathing in her jasmine-scented hair, moving as one.

The broad man with the mustache said something I did not hear, my mind lingering back home. Aggabodhi nodded in vigorous agreement.

"March on," the commander instructed and moved forward. I fell in step with Aggabodhi. This man and his two trusty aides appeared to be the only men in their company who had undergone any battle training. I decided to keep an eye on them to avoid any unpleasant surprises.

When we arrived in the village square, the commander ordered, "Go find food."

I paused to observe how the others accomplished it. They

knocked on doors and demanded to be fed. One young man tried to shut the door on a soldier asking for food. "He is resisting Chief Jeevahatta's orders," cried the soldier. Two others rushed to his aid, and they dragged the young man out and kicked him.

"They are stealing from my people and attacking them," Aggabodhi ranted and moved forward.

I snatched his arm and pulled him back. "Don't you dare move, or I will stab you myself," I whispered furiously.

"What?" asked Aggabodhi, sweating with rage.

"The ones attacking are also your people," I muttered. He swatted my arm away. Before he did anything foolish, I warned him, "Listen closely, for the fate of your kingdom hangs in the balance. Should you storm and lose your head, your kingdom will suffer a fate far worse than any enemy could inflict upon it. Keep your wits about you, for the welfare of your people depends on it."

With a swift pivot, I spun around and let my eyes roam over the surroundings. Every sense on high alert, I scoured the area for any signs that someone heard our conversation, my muscles tensed and ready for action. While I faced away, Aggabodhi yelled, "Enough."

Curse this prince and his impulsiveness. I turned to gaze at what Aggabodhi witnessed. One of our misfits dragged a woman by her hair to giggles and jeers. I also noticed the commander watching Aggabodhi with a long, calculating look—a look that asked how he might turn this to his advantage.

I pushed Aggabodhi behind me and shouted, "Leave her alone." It was not the voice Uncle Jay had trained me to use to lead my men. In my effort to conceal my identity, I sounded squeakier than I wanted.

The man dragging the woman glanced at me. "What will you do if I don't?"

I took a step forward. "Our fight is not with her."

"It is. These people helped King Rajasuriya enslave us." I heard Aggabodhi gasp. I hoped he had enough sense to stay out of this.

"I have no ties to kings," cried the woman clutching the back of her head.

The other villagers looked on in horror, too afraid to intervene. The man clasped her throat and started choking her. I charged toward him and used the hard part of my head to strike his stomach. Losing his balance, he stumbled back, and I kicked his knees, causing him to fall hard on his back. I fought like a thug rather than a prince.

"Run," I whispered to the woman, who took off.

"How dare you attack one of my men?" asked the commander in a menacing voice. "Teach him a lesson," he ordered, and about a half-dozen men surrounded me.

I shot a warning glance at Aggabodhi to stay in place. Using a crude defensive posture, I fended off the poorly aimed attacks but pretended they landed on me. I staggered dramatically and allowed a blow to land on my face. My lips tore, and I sensed a wet liquid trickling down. The sight of blood seemed to please the commander. "Please stop," I begged in a pathetic voice.

He waved the men off of me. "I will not tolerate such behavior in the future. As punishment, you will unload the carts at night, load them in the morning, and fetch water to fill our water pots." With slumped shoulders, I dipped my head.

Shrinking my size, I hobbled to Aggabodhi. He handed me a piece of cloth to wipe my face. "Let us go find some food," I said, limping toward an alley.

Aggabodhi followed along. "I apologize," he began.

"I hear someone," I said, halting him.

A young boy peeked at us from a street corner. Curious, I waited. He approached us cautiously. "My mother thanks you for saving her," he said, handing us a lotus leaf bowl. It held day-old rice. Before I could utter a word, he scurried away.

The boy brought back memories of my son. A year ago, when my uncle had placed my baby son in my palms, my emotions surprised me. I was not expecting the overflowing love that poured out of me and my overwhelming urge to protect the boy. My son had recently started walking while clutching my index finger. After a few steps, he would extend his hands to look at me with his huge eyes and let out a piercing cry to indicate he wanted me to carry him. I had no willpower to resist him. He would giggle when I threw him in the air. I let out a deep breath to suppress my longing to hold my child in my arms. I would return in time to teach him how to ride, fight with a sword, and battle his fears.

"Let us leave this company tonight, Brother," said Aggabodhi as we shared the meal.

"Till we find my men, this group offers us cover. And allows you a glimpse into the lives of your people."

Aggabodhi's eyes clouded at my words. "It is like looking into a mirror and finding I have sprouted horns."

I chuckled. "I can see the two tiny bumps." More seriously, I added, "Patience is a virtue that we young do not appreciate. To save these people, you need to reclaim the throne. Curb any action that jeopardizes that."

That night, the commander kept us busy unloading the camping and cooking equipment from the wagons. I used this as an opportunity to strengthen my various muscles by carrying the load on one shoulder and then the other. His sidekicks bumped into me a few times, trying to provoke a reaction. While my face remained a mask, I stayed vigilant.

Later, I kept first watch while Aggabodhi slept in the open field. The fires cast flickering shadows on the handful of tents. Most soldiers huddled around the campfires, their voices dying down as the moon rose.

The smell of burning wood pervaded the air. I saw two men patrol the perimeter, their steps echoing softly in the night. I drew circles on my thigh as my eyes roamed around, alert for any sign of danger.

At midnight, I nudged Aggabodhi. "Wake up." He murmured sleepily. I shook his shoulder while calling his name in a low voice. He yawned while opening his eyes a slit. "Your turn." He sat up and stretched his hands overhead. I lay on the ground with uneven stones digging into my back. I curled up, dreaming about my four-poster bed with silk sheets.

"Brother!" A hand shook my arm roughly. I rolled onto my other side and tried to return to my dream. Something sharp poked my ribs, and I opened my eyes with a groan. A palm covered my mouth. My gaze fell on Aggabodhi. He was gesturing to something out of my sight.

I rose to lean on my elbows and scanned the surroundings. In the faint light of the dawn, I glimpsed a man partially hidden behind a tree. I recognized him as one of my guards. The camp stirred to life with murmuring voices.

Under the guise of fetching water, Aggabodhi and I carried pots to the nearby stream. My guard followed us.

"This stream is a tributary of the Sunkosh River," said Aggabodhi as we entered the water to wash ourselves.

"**Find the girl**," echoed a voice in my ear.

"What girl?" I asked, spinning around to find the source of the sound.

"**Sugandha**." The name appeared to swirl in the mist hovering above the water.

"Did you hear that?" I whispered.

"Hear what, Brother?" Aggabodhi narrowed his eyes to gaze at me.

Was I dreaming? I splashed cold water on my face to clear my head. Then, I scanned the area again. No one was around but us.

"Nothing," I muttered, stepping out of the stream. Then, I stopped abruptly. "Do you know anyone named Sugandha?"

Aggabodhi shook his head, and we joined the guard waiting

patiently for us.

"I am glad to see you alive, my pr—" started the guard in the Malla language.

"No titles," I replied in the Kashgar language. I smiled at him to soften my rebuke for reverting to our native tongue. We all needed practice, and speaking in the local language minimized the risk of exposing ourselves as strangers. "What news do you have for us?"

"Princess Malathi is dead," he said in the local dialect.

"My aunt is dead?" Aggabodhi asked with trembling lips. We had relied on her to come to her nephew's aid.

The guard nodded.

"Cause of death?" I asked, drawing lines on my stomach.

"A storm capsized her boat on the Sunkosh River. She drowned."

Drowned? Could the Kashgar sages summon a storm? "Did someone use magic to cause the storm?"

My guard shook his head. "The storm brewed in the sea and moved inland, wreaking havoc along the way. Her death is likely due to natural causes. However, Chief Vikramasinha of Singalila did blame Chief Jeevahatta of Jalpaiguri for using Guru Ori to cast a curse on their vessel to kill his wife. Chief Jeevahatta has denied this vehemently. Also, rumors swirl that Jeevahatta has found Prince Aggabodhi, and he will head to Tipti with him to lay claim to the throne."

"Chief Jeevahatta has found Aggabodhi?" I asked stupidly. *How could that be?* We had just arrived on this land.

"The rumors are at least a month old," said my guard. *Who was this lad with Chief Jeevahatta?*

In shock, I stared at the boy I had known as Aggabodhi for the past two years and had grown fond of. Uncle Jay and I had assumed he was the prince based on a signet ring he had produced with the royal emblem. I felt a confusing pang of genuine distress. *Who was real, and who was fake?*

SUGANDHA

SPRING YEAR 1

I scratched my itchy scalp as I waited for the night to descend. Using my fingers, I tried to untangle the many knots but gave up halfway and piled the greasy hair into a top knot. The temple bells tolled for the evening pooja. Afterward, one of the priests handed out the day's offering. He twisted his nose and turned his head sideways while he dropped the ball of rice into my extended palm. I knew I smelled unpleasant.

Without glancing at me, he said, "There is a stream not far from here to wash yourself clean."

I bowed to him deeply and sought a quiet corner, away from the thronging temple goers, to eat my food. I gobbled up the rice like a starving beggar, which I was in many ways. Then, I walked to the creek to wash my hands.

The water reflected my wary eyes and youthful face, a sharp contrast. I plunged my hands into the stream, distorting the image. I caught a tiny fish in my hand, and it tried desperately to swim out of my fingers. In the fading light, its fin rippled with each motion. I opened my palms to release it, and it darted out of sight.

With a sigh, I quenched my thirst. I glanced around to ensure that there was no one around me. I waded into waist-high water and untied my dhoti. I removed the rag tucked between my legs and washed it in the stream, thankful for the darkness that hid the swirling blood. My monthly courses happened regularly, and being on the run made it harder to stay clean. I washed my legs, hands, and other body parts, leaving my hair dirty. My foul odor kept people away from me. I was in no hurry to lose that protection.

Draping the wet clothes on one shoulder, I set out. I felt like a snail, carrying all my belongings with me. I had no one to talk to on my solitary journey, but my legs were used to covering long distances.

I loved being outside, hearing the nocturnal creatures singing as I walked through the woods and smelling the blooms as they cascaded over the hedges. I loved the lush meadows underneath my feet, soft and silky like a carpet.

Spring had arrived in Kashgar. That meant I had completed sixteen years on this land. Last year, to celebrate my name day, my grandfather had taken me to the market to buy me new yards of cloths. A sudden yearning for his presence twisted my stomach. The moon rose high over my head as if to give me company while a wind moved the grass.

The sky grew pale as the first birds tentatively sounded out their notes. I came across fat cows with their heads down, munching the grass. I saw strips of farmland with neat rows of crops. I could find work as a farmhand and stay here for a few weeks. This was a busy time for the farmers. I saw a man working in the fields.

"Do you need any help today?" I asked.

"I cannot pay you," he said, looking me up and down. I no longer looked like a soft and plump girl. My lean body spoke of familiarity with hard labor.

"I only ask to be fed," I said.

"One mid-day meal."

I nodded gratefully. I spent the rest of the morning cutting hay that would be dried for feed. Nearby, barley stood tall in the fields. Carts and peddlers passed along the road as I bent over in labor.

I heard a commotion around the corner. Horses appeared around the bend with banners fluttering in the wind. I noticed a large eye painted on the silk cloth. A man wearing a blue silk turban adorned with gold embroidery rode in front.

"Who is he?" I asked, straightening.

"That is Chief Jeevahatta."

That is when I noticed the man riding beside him. In contrast to the nobleman, Uncle Ori wore a simple cotton garment. His saffron-colored robes symbolized spiritual purity. Foolishly, I gazed at him, and he turned and looked straight into my eyes.

Panic rose into my throat. It was too late for me to duck out of sight. But he turned around with no sign of recognition. *Was I invisible to him? Or did he see a different figure when he glanced at me?*

The blessing from my grandfather must keep me hidden from my uncle. Thinking about my grandfather brought forth a wave of rage. That kindly man was gone from my life forever because of my uncle. Suddenly, I wanted to grab his throat and strangle him. My breath came in gasps.

"The chief has a castle not far from here. That is where they are headed," said one of the farmers, not recognizing my fury. I clenched my fists. I should not be foolish and waste the boon from my grandfather. I could not stay in this village so close to my uncle, worrying about one of his men discovering me or me losing my mind and attacking him.

When the sun rose overhead, we took shelter under a tree. The man who hired me handed me rice with dried pickle. After I ate, I slipped away from others. I needed to put distance between my uncle and me. However, my body asserted its greater need for rest. At an orchard of fruit trees, I climbed up a tamarind tree and tied myself to the trunk. Overwhelming tiredness swept over me, and I fell asleep.

~

"The time is ripe for the reveal," a male voice said.

"No, she cannot bear the burden," responded another.

~

Something ran over my legs, and I sat up abruptly. A shiver ran down my spine as I tried to grasp something half-lost, vanishing around a corner like a thief, something I could never describe. It felt like holding the entire Sunkosh River in my cupped hands—a futile exercise.

Then, the voices I heard in my dream faded from my memory as I noticed the sun beginning its descent. The stars appeared against the twilight sky. I climbed down the tree and walked away from this village.

The moon painted my surroundings in shades of gray and silver during my lonely journey. I marched to the sound of dry leaves crunching underfoot. No breeze swirled around the trees today. An eerie feeling of being watched stirred in my stomach. I scolded myself for letting fear take hold after being alone for nearly two months.

A different challenge lodged in my head. With Purohit Parivan dead, I had only one goal. Survive. For that, I had to remain hidden from Uncle Ori. Whatever distance I covered on foot, he could easily cover on his horse. Stealing a horse would be impossible.

I remembered the Sunkosh River flowed not far from here. I could take a boat across the river. As the idea took root, a calmness settled over me. Instead of meandering to an unknown future, I had a destination. When I stopped at a pond, I washed my hair this time, not wanting to subject boat passengers to my dreadful smell.

I came across crows fighting for position on the ribs of a wild boar, causing a racket. Whatever predator had killed the boar had cleaned the animal, leaving only scraps clinging to the bones. As the sun hid behind the clouds like a girl on the run, my weary legs stumbled. Cowbells jingled, and a voice called out from a cart. "You look tired. Do you want a ride?" asked a boy about my age. He sat on top of bundled hay in the back of the wagon, his legs dangling.

With effort, I straightened my shoulders and shook my head. The boy grew smaller as the cart moved forward, but I could sense his eyes on me. Being alone suited me fine. My stomach groaned in protest at the lie, and my torn clothes mocked my pretense. Better hungry than dead, I consoled myself.

That afternoon, the Sunkosh River came into view. The rising tide created tiny waves that splashed on the shore. A kite bird cried and wheeled above my head, its reddish-brown wings bright as coral in the sunshine.

I looked around and spotted a nearly full wooden boat. I ran toward it, splashing through knee-high water. Suddenly, I felt the water swirl around my feet, and the river appeared to buoy me toward the vessel. The wind caressed me gently with the touch of a mother. In my sleep-deprived state, my imagination ran like a wild horse. I shook my head to clear it.

"Do you have room for one more?" I asked, sounding out of breath.

"There is room," answered a boy stretching his hand to me. I grabbed it, thankful for my calloused palms. As I gazed up, I recognized the boy from the cart that morning. He made room for me on the plank, and I sat beside him and placed my sack on my lap.

The boatman steered the boat with a long wooden pole as the currents moved us forward. "This is the first time I have left my home," the boy said, glancing around the boat in a mixture of wonder and fear.

I made no immediate reply as I gazed at his anxious baby face. "I am away from home for the first time, too," I said in a moment of genuine compassion. *And survived for nearly two months with my uncle on my tail*, I thought.

Hope leaped up in his trusting face. "Selva," he said, his chin dipping down. I gathered he was telling me his name.

"Nanda," I said. No one had called me Sugandha in nearly two months.

"Across the river lives a distant cousin of mine. He is a swordsmith. I am going to join him as an apprentice. If all works well, I might inherit his workshop and marry his daughter."

Envy at his simple life rose in my throat. Without waiting for my reply, he continued, "I have never met the father or the daughter. As long as all her limbs are present, I cannot say no to the match. My father died a few weeks ago, and my brother has a large family to feed. He would not welcome me back."

I longed for a roof over my head and an occupation to keep my mind engaged. My grandfather had taught me to read and schooled me on Kashgar's history and the geography of the kingdom. I found no use for all the learning. A dark mood settled in my mind, and matching dark clouds flitted across the sky. Lightning and thunder boomed miles away while we stayed dry.

"It is raining upstream. We must hurry. Able men, grab an oar," shouted the boatman.

Monsoon season was behind us, so the rain surprised me. I looked around and found a spare oar. I grabbed it and moved to the side of the boat. Ignoring my tired muscles, I pushed the water away with each stroke. The Sunkosh River seemed to part itself willingly when I plunged the flat blade in. I shook my head to clear my hallucinations. As he predicted, the calm river soon turned into a raging fury. The water level rose sharply, and the boat spun around like a top. The boatman steered the boat, cursing and praying, but the strong currents seemed intent on ripping us apart.

The old and weak huddled in the middle of the boat. Selva still remained in the same place, paralyzed. "Hold onto something," I shouted at him over my shoulders.

Suddenly, a large wave crashed into the side of the boat, causing it to sway widely. People screamed, trying to seize anything for support. The deluge soaked me, and my wet clothes clung to my skin. I gripped the oar tightly and dipped it into the water, desperate to stabilize the boat. However, the craft tipped into the churning water, sending us all under. I held onto the oar and kicked my legs. Some force pushed me up, and as I broke the surface, the gray clouds hung overhead, dropping rain into the swirling river.

"Help." I turned toward the sound. A woman clutching her baby to her chest wailed. I swam to her and thrust the oar at her.

"Grab it," I said.

She looked at me wildly, and I worried she would ignore my order. Thankfully, she gripped the oar tightly, nearly draping her upper body over it. I swam with a strength I did not know I possessed while others around me struggled against the current that tried to sweep them downstream. Reaching waist-high water, I stood and pulled the woman and her child to the land. She collapsed on the sand, kissing her baby, tears flowing down her face.

"Move to higher ground," I warned. "The water level is rising."

After ensuring her safety, I went looking for other survivors. The boatman dragged a limp body, and I ran to aid him. As I laid him on the wet shore, I noticed his face: Selva, the boy who sat beside me. Frantically, I kneeled and rolled him from side to side.

"He is gone, boy," cried the boatman.

I pumped his chest and placed my ear on his heart. No sound of a beating heart reached me. My grandfather had taught me many prayers, but I remembered none at that moment. I stood frozen with horror, and my breathing sounded like gulping sobs. The sand beneath me felt as cold as my scraped hands. Selva was a young man starting a fresh life, and he wilted before he took root. I rose and moved away.

"Does he have family in this village?" asked the boatman.

I remembered him speaking of a cousin whom he had never met before. "He has no one," I muttered.

The boatman shook his head in pity. "Help me drag him back into the water, then. The river will purify him and send him to his next life." While I helped him, the thought that was a wisp earlier took shape. Apprentice with a swordsmith. Roof overhead. More than a meal a day. A mat for a bed instead of a tree trunk. Maybe Selva still had a purpose in death.

"What is your name?" the boatman asked, letting the corpse sink.

"Selva," I said, making a decision. I would take on the guise of Selva.

ATUL

WINTER YEAR 2

"Fake Aggabodhi? Who can it be, Brother?" asked Aggabodhi, the color drained from his face. At that instant, his face appeared fragile and vulnerable, and I felt shameful for doubting him earlier, for thinking the boy I had trained with for the past two years could be fake.

I muttered helplessly, "I don't know, Bodhi." My brain furiously sought the reason for using a fake prince. "Aligning with the son of the former king gives Chief Jeevahatta legitimacy and influence."

"How can they crown an impostor in violation of our sacred lineage?" he asked disbelievingly.

"Maybe the chief does not intend to crown the boy, so it matters little whether the boy is the real prince." I did not ask him to elaborate on which deity his ancestors claimed to descend from. It mattered not whether they traced their origin to the sun or the moon.

Uncle Jay taught me to view such beliefs with suspicion. He never sought legitimacy through the divine right to rule. Instead, my uncle believed his authority rested in his ability to protect the realm. However, being the illegitimate son of a queen, I sensed that a mythical being bestowing her blessing on me would solidify my position.

Aggabodhi dropped his head into his hands. "What do we do? I cannot win support for my cause if the noblemen parade around impostors."

I glanced around to see if we were alone. My guard stood alert, his eyes scanning the surrounding area. "Do not prepare for defeat before we even start. King Jay, the finest king of Magadha, trained you to rule. Don't betray his trust in you," I said.

He looked up at me, his eyes shining with unsplit tears. "With my aunt dead, how can I prove my identity?"

I drew a circle on my chest. "Is there a trusted servant who knows you or your father well?"

He straightened his shoulders. "My father's servant knew his plans to send me to Magadha."

"We will find him," I assured him.

"I apologize for losing my composure. I am afraid all the time," confessed the boy prince.

I understood his fear better than he knew. Two years ago, my cousin Vikram, the heir to the Malla kingdom, had perished to the blade of a man my uncle had banished to Kashgar. I could still see Vikram smile confidently at me from the depth of time. In a twist of fate, I—a boy with two older brothers and no claim to any throne—was crowned the heir. Wearing the crown, I felt naked and exposed because I did not have the protection of my royal birthright to wrap around me.

I patted Aggabodhi's shoulder and offered him comfort. "What is there to fear, Bodhi? Especially with me and the mighty Magadha army by your side. Let us learn more about this sham prince, and then we can decide what to do."

Aggabodhi nodded solemnly. "I want to see the charlatan myself. Maybe it is an old acquaintance."

I reflected on his words as I turned slowly and took a couple of steps. "We need to find a way to get close to Chief Jeevahatta." I spun around. "We can set a trap for him and then rescue him."

Aggabodhi glanced at me, nodding in agreement. "Your men can help," he affirmed.

I dipped my head in concurrence. "Guard, take us to my men," I demanded. "Before our newly acquired commander misses us and sends a search party."

"I doubt his men can find their backs, let alone us," sniggered Aggabodhi.

I smiled, glad he had regained his confidence. We slipped away quietly, with the guard leading the way and me bringing up the rear. Within a few yards from the campsite, another member of my guards joined us. About a mile away, I smelled smoke.

"Stop," I whispered and scanned the surroundings.

"The smoke is coming from the direction of our campsite," said Aggabodhi.

"The idiots recruited to Jeevahatta's army have set fire to either farms or houses or both," I said, heat coating my words.

Aggabodhi wheeled around. "I will teach them a lesson."

I barred his way. "I have a better idea. You sit on the throne and punish them." He stomped his feet in anger but abandoned the idea of returning to the camp.

"I will be ruling a cremation site rather than a kingdom," he muttered, turning back. I made no reply.

We walked through a forest filled with towering trees brimming with flowers. Among the living giants, I could see signs of the recent drought in dead trees infested with insects. Knee-high barley swayed gently in distant fields. Thick roots criss-crossed our path, and we hopped over them. I spotted a crumbling building overgrown with climbing creepers.

"That is an old tomb," Aggabodhi remarked. "This was the site of a great battle." Judging from the size of the trees around me, I guessed this land had not seen any bloodshed in a hundred years.

Soon, we reached the ruins, and one of my men hooted like an owl. An answering song came from inside, followed by a dark head that peaked at us over the wall. When his eyes landed on me, they lit up. I found a dozen or so of my men inside. They bowed to greet me, and I clapped their backs.

"Are we safe from curious eyes here?" I asked, looking around as the rays of sunlight penetrated through cracks in the wall. Echoes of the past lingered on the weathered stones, and tendrils of roots pried their way into the worn-out floor.

"The locals fear that ghosts haunt this place, so no one ventures out here," replied one of my men. I scanned the cobwebs strung from the sinking ceiling. *If I were a spirit stuck in this life, I would prefer a cheery haunt to this desolate tomb.*

"The men who fought here over a century ago betrayed their king. On his deathbed, the king cursed the treacherous men to remain in limbo in this life," said Aggabodhi, his eyes gazing at a decaying pillar as if he could see the ghosts of the past.

"A king with power over the dead and the living is one mighty ruler," I jested to lighten the mood. A monarch with such powers could use fear to coerce loyalty.

"It cost the king his last breath," said Aggabodhi, glancing at me. "To cast a powerful curse requires a great sacrifice."

I felt a chill in my bones despite the warm weather. Nearly a year ago, I remembered boarding a Malla ship that had returned from Kashgar. Inside, men with no battle wounds had been found dead. Rats had feasted on the corpses as I had gazed at their exposed skeletons in horror. Aggabodhi had whispered reverently in my ear, "Sorcery at work." I had not understood what he meant until my eyes landed on a boy about Aggabodhi's age. The messenger who had carried Ori's message had dropped dead shortly after he had delivered the message. Gazing at his young face twisted into something dark and insidious, I had imagined wraiths circling me like flames and hissing loud enough to snap one of the giant trees outside.

Today, a similar sensation rose in my chest. I felt someone pluck me by the skin of my neck, ready to toss me into an abyss. I clutched the hilt of my sword tightly as if I might float up into the air and sail back to that ship of death. I blinked rapidly, and the paralyzing fear from earlier retreated into the pit of my stomach, where it curled up like a viper, ready to strike when I let my guard down.

"Let us leave the haunted alone and focus on earning Chief Jeevahatta's trust," I said, masking my tremors.

The men huddled around me as if they, too, were eager to return to the world of the living. "The best way to earn a man's trust is to save his life. If we stage an attack on him, Aggabodhi and I can arrive in time to liberate him."

"He visits his mistress several times a fortnight, with only a guard or two. He leaves his castle after darkness and returns before dawn," said one of the Malla soldiers. A couple of the young guards snickered.

"Mistress? Why doesn't he marry her?" In Magadha, royal men took on many wives. My two wives came from two powerful Malla houses. With our union, I gained the support of these houses for my rule.

"She is a young widow, my lord. Chief Jeevahatta's father-in-law is funding his son-in-law's campaign for the throne. He would be displeased if he learned about the chief's errant ways." Magadha tradition also frowned upon widow remarriage. My mother, a widow, had remarried my father in secrecy, so I sympathized with the chief and his lover.

I traced a circle on my hip, lost in contemplation. A sudden surge of thoughts flooded my mind. Uncle Jay's relentless preaching about sacrificing for the sake of the kingdom echoed in my thoughts. Then, there was my mother, the embodiment of sacrifice, relinquishing her love for the greater duty. Chief Jeevahatta, on the other hand, seemed to revel in his pleasures without restraint. His indulgence made him an easier target for our plans. But a perplexing notion struck me: *Could a ruler who saw themselves as a sacrifice become a better leader?*

The shuffling feet of men brought me back to the present. "Should we ambush him at dawn as he comes back to his castle?" I asked. A chorus went up, and a plan took shape.

A few days later, Aggabodhi and I hid among the trees, watching the road below us. A pale light crept from the horizon like a prisoner sneaking out of a dungeon. The dew-laden leaves above our heads glistened like diamonds. A gentle breeze rustled them, causing the water droplets to fall gracefully to the ground. Some landed on my bare arms and slid down, leaving a sparkling trail.

Dust rose in the distance, and a horse-drawn carriage sped toward us. My eyes darted to the trees across us, waiting for the ambush to start. With a loud cry, two of my men leaped from the tall branches onto the cart, causing the horse to rear its head.

In the commotion that followed, two more men emerged from the shadows. One kicked the charioteer off the cart, and the other held the reins to calm the frightened animal. The charioteer rolled for a few feet on the ground and then stopped. From our distance, I could not tell if he moved.

A lone guard jumped from the covered wagon and started drawing his sword. Before he could pry the weapon out of its sheath, the back of an ax swung toward him and knocked him to the ground.

"Now," I said, running alongside the road, still hidden among shrubs and bushes. I could hear Aggabodhi's footsteps beside mine.

"I am Chief Jeevahatta," thundered a man as he climbed out of the cart. "You will be quartered into pieces for treason," he bellowed. His face contorted with fury while his silk dhoti fluttered against his legs.

Gray clouds blew into the sky above us, covering us in darkness. The wind whipped the fallen leaves, masking the sounds we made.

One of my men with bulging arms and fierce eyes stepped in front of the chief, twisting his dark mustache. "Tie him," he said in a calm voice that would have sent shivers down my spine if I did not know him. Another moved to comply with the command.

The charioteer on the ground moaned as we arrived close enough to hear it. One of my soldiers placed a foot on his head. "Lie still."

"Let the nobleman go," I said, emerging from the shadows with my sword drawn. Aggabodhi appeared beside me.

Chief Jeevahatta's face brightened, and then he squinted at us as though trying to guess who we were. Dressed in ordinary cotton, I held the sword awkwardly, not like it was an extension of my limb. The four Malla men who had arrived in Kashgar with me acted swiftly and pretended to attack us. I reacted sluggishly, letting their blows push me back.

The man with the bulging arms nicked the skin off my shoulder, and I dropped the sword dramatically. As it clanged to the ground, I saw him hesitate for the blink of an eye, his fist hovering in the air. He was part of my personal guards and had sworn to protect me with his life, so hurting me went against his oath. My eyes met his, giving him consent. His punch landed on my chin, causing my head to swing. I stumbled to the ground.

"Curse the gods," Chief Jeevahatta hissed.

"Tie them all up," came the order.

I spotted Aggabodhi flat on his back, clutching his left knee. A thin line of blood appeared near his eyebrow as he gazed at me and uttered a piercing cry of pain. I placed my palm across my mouth to hide the smile erupting on my face.

For a moment, I was a little boy, playing with my cousins in Akash, using the throne room as our playground. The three of us ruled the palace in our youth. Our laughter echoed in my mind as we enacted scenes from the great battles of Malla, with our wooden swords weaving in and out. The sun peaked out of the cloud, shattering my illusion and dropping me back to reality.

Malla men tied my arms loosely and led me to the carriage. I watched as Chief Jeevahatta and his charioteer were shoved into the back of the wagon with their arms and legs restrained tightly and a rag shoved into their mouths. Jeevahatta's guard was tied to a tree trunk, hidden from the road, his eyes blindfolded and mouth gagged. The head of the unconscious man dropped downward.

The carriage started rolling, and Chief Jeevahatta uttered a few grunts and then grew quiet. The charioteer whimpered occasionally. The sham kidnapping had gone according to our plan. The cart left the main road and went along a dirt path, causing the wagon to rattle.

In the darkened interior, my mind wandered back to Akash. I imagined Uncle Jay carrying my son to the throne room like he used to bring my cousin and me. Uncle Jay would point out the sculptures on the pillars and name each object. I wanted to be there to watch the world through the delighted eyes of my son, seeing everything for the first time. I wondered if my family missed me as much as I missed them.

The cart tossed us roughly and came to a halt, jolting me back to the current moment. We were dragged unceremoniously from the cart and dumped on the ground, some more gently than others.

My men hauled the charioteer onto his feet and tugged him along. I had instructed my men to isolate the chief. They followed that plan. The chief watched the two men pulling his charioteer by his shoulders deep into the forest, the dragged man's toes marking lines on the ground, while I regarded him surreptitiously.

A heart-wrenching cry erupted from the charioteer though all three men had vanished from our sight. Raw fear played on Jeevahatta's face for an instant, and then he rearranged it. I had told my men to spare the lives of these men, so I looked at the two men emerging from the trees to make sure they followed my intent. One met my eyes to indicate all went to plan. I wanted to avoid killing innocent lives that got caught in the web I spun.

My men hurled us back into the wagon, and we resumed our journey. It grew hotter in the wagon, and sweat trickled down my forehead. Though the guards had tied my hands loosely, it still took an effort to wipe the sweat away before it landed in my eyes. I imagined a cool wind rustling my long hair while I galloped across Malla's plains. I heard Aggabodhi fidgeting next to me.

The chariot stopped before either of us gave the game away.

"Can we discard these two idiots who disrupted our plan?" asked one, pointing at Aggabodhi and me. My men continued the charade that Aggabodhi and I were strangers. I sensed no suspicions from Jeevahatta about the elaborate drama we were enacting for his benefit.

"Let us keep them for a while. They may come in handy," answered another.

When I noticed my men pulling us to a spot with no shade, I subtly pointed to a large banyan tree with my chin. Thankfully, they understood my desire as they noticed my flushed face and ushered us under the tree.

They untied Jeevahatta's hands and mouth. "Write a letter to provide gold coins to the carrier of this message," said a Malla soldier, shoving a palm leaf toward him.

I noticed the chief's hand trembled as he wrote the simple message. "Will you let me go after?" he whispered, all traces of his earlier arrogance gone.

My men chuckled without answering. "Your ring," demanded one, stretching his palm.

Jeevahatta twisted and turned the ring to remove it.

My men tied the chief back, blindfolded all of us, and dispersed. In the quiet that followed, I could hear birds chirping in the large tree. Then Aggabodhi made weird noises while he chewed the cloth covering his mouth. Spitting it out, he exclaimed, "I will chew your knots, Brother."

I pulled my hands out of my knots while Aggabodhi pretended to bite the rope. I rubbed my wrists and untied the other two men.

Free of his bindings, Jeevahatta scanned the surroundings. "Do we wait till dark?"

"No," I whispered. "They will expect that. Let us escape now."

We crouched under the tree branches and made our way out. One of my men yelled, "Stop."

I feigned to hit him on the side of his head, and he collapsed in a striking manner, though I barely made contact. Hiding behind trees and shrubs, Aggabodhi and I scanned the surroundings and then signaled to Jeevahatta to move. Instead of striding out in a confident manner, he made little paddling steps as if he stepped on uncertain ground.

Pretending it was a great honor to help the chief, I held his elbow to support him. We walked silently for a few moments. After climbing a short hill, Jeevahatta gestured for us to stop. He glanced at us as he caught his breath. "Who are you?" he asked, letting out a deep breath from his mouth.

"We are brothers looking to join your army, my lord," I whispered humbly.

"I reward loyalty richly," he said, his voice regaining some of his vanity.

When dusk approached, the sky turned a reddish hue, and we heard the crunch of leaves. We ducked behind some tall grass. Chief Jeevahatta's guard, the one we had left on the roadside, approached us.

Chief Jeevahatta rose and faced him. "My lord," the man exclaimed. I noticed dried blood on his clothes.

With a twisted mouth, Jeevahatta ordered, "Kill him," with no hesitation in his voice.

Before I could react, Aggabodhi drew his short knife and plunged it into the heart of the man.

I watched in horror as the man collapsed to the ground. Bending down, Aggabodhi turned the man's head from side to side. "Dead," he said and wiped the blood off the knife on the man's clothes. Jeevahatta stepped on the man's chest and continued walking. Without a glance at me, Aggabodhi followed.

SUGANDHA

SPRING YEAR 1

Villagers gathered on the riverbanks to gape at the aftermath of the boat accident. A local healer arrived to help the injured, while a few others offered to search for missing family members to unite them.

As I stepped out of the river, I sensed someone calling my name in a singing voice. **"Sugandha**!" I looked around and found no one paid me any attention. I must be going mad. *Who even knew me this far from my home?*

I turned to a village elder who arrived at the shore. "Can you direct me to the swordsmith's house?"

He looked me up and down. "Are you his new apprentice?"

I nodded, realizing this was a close-knit community where news flowed like a river, leaving no secret safe from prying ears. "I am Selva."

"Follow this lane and turn left. It's the house with a burning furnace."

I thanked him and set out on foot. Trepidation filled my stomach with each step while a drizzle wet my skin. I did not even know the swordsmith's name, yet I planned to impersonate his dead cousin. My throat closed, and tears threatened to spill from my eyes. I wiped my eyes and nose with my forearm, failing to notice a man peering at me.

"Selva?" asked a man with broad shoulders.

Sniffling, I stared at him blankly, not registering the name for a moment. Then, recognition swept in like the waves that overturned our boat. "Are you my cousin?" I asked stupidly.

"Thank the moon, you are alive," he muttered, patting my head. Following tradition, I bent at my waist to touch his feet. When I rose, I emptied myself of all emotions.

"Did you lose your belongings?" he asked, looking at my empty hands.

That is when I realized my meager possessions drowned in the river. They were not the only things I had lost over the past three fortnights. I had left the lifeless body of my dear grandfather, who had raised me after my parent's death, and left the only home I knew and now sought shelter with complete strangers.

I walked beside him under a gray sky that hid the sun. He asked about Selva's family, and I replied with a safe answer. We arrived outside his modest house constructed of bricks weathered from the heat of the forge, and uncontrollable fear, like a rat chewing my insides, gripped me. I could not do this. A wave of nausea welled up in my throat, and I struggled to clamp it down. Facing the entrance guarded by an intricately carved wooden door, I took a deep breath, telling myself I had nothing else to lose in this world.

"Come," he said, "I will give you dry clothes to change into."

Stepping inside, he led me through his workshop, dominated by a colossal furnace burning dimly now. An array of tools, ranging from hammers to anvils and many more I could not name yet, were arranged meticulously on a long bench.

I noticed parchment scrolls depicting sketches and designs strewn on a table. Racks of gleaming blades adorned the walls.

A calmness settled over me as I inhaled the smell of heated metals and earthy oils.

I walked behind the swordsmith through a narrow hallway. A small room with a wooden door stood to my left, and a large open chamber to my right. Beyond that, I saw a kitchen. An older woman with stooped shoulders hummed a song as she leaned over a simmering pot. Steam wafted from the vessel as she stirred the stew.

"This is my mother," introduced the man. "Ma, this is Selva." The woman stood and glanced at me with gentle eyes. An image of my grandfather flooded my mind, reminding me of how much I missed him. I walked to her and touched her feet.

"Why are his clothes torn?" asked the grandmother as I rose.

"His boat overturned in the middle of the river. Only by a miracle he survived," my cousin replied. It was easier to think of him as my cousin than a stranger. My clothes were torn before the mishap, but I stayed silent.

"If you had drowned, Parimala's future would have become uncertain." Grandmother touched my head as if in blessing while squinting at me. "Poor boy. No one has cared for you since your mother died nearly a decade ago. Look at how skinny you are. Don't think of yourself as an orphan. This is your home now. Change into dry clothes. Food should be ready soon."

I sensed that she ruled this house, even though her son was the official head of the household. Selva's story mirrored mine in some ways. He was an orphan like me. My parents had perished due to an illness that swept through our village, a disease that spared me, a crawling child, and my grandfather.

My cousin led me to the chamber and opened an old wooden chest that bore the mark of time with dents, scratches, and nicks scattered across its surface. He pulled out a clean white dhoti and handed it to me.

"An upper garment?" I whispered. A sudden fear filled my

throat. *How do I pretend to be a boy if I lived with them day and night?* When I stayed with the drama troupe, the large number of men in the troupe provided me with some anonymity. We traveled from place to place and lived outdoors. While I dwelled under one roof with this family, a single slip can betray me.

"You are shy," chuckled my cousin and handed me a loose-fitting outfit. A musty aroma clung to the cloth like it had absorbed the essence of the trunk while it had stayed dormant inside. Grasping it, I scanned the house for a place to change.

Noticing my glance, my cousin pointed to a privacy screen made of multiple hinged panels standing in a corner. "You can change behind this screen. That room is where my mother and daughter sleep," he said, nodding toward the shut door leading to a small room across the way. "You and I will sleep here," he said, gesturing at the open chamber. I walked behind the screen tentatively, doubts creeping into my mind about my foolish idea.

Thankfully, my newly acquired cousin left me alone and walked to his workshop. Facing the wall, I quickly stripped my wet upper garment and pulled on the dry one. Hanging the damp cloth on the screen, I checked to ensure I was alone. I held the dry dhoti around my waist, covering my lower body, and then took off the wet one. My breathing returned to a normal rhythm only after I was fully clothed. I bundled the wet clothes and took them to the kitchen.

Grandmother said over her shoulder, "Put them in the bucket near the well. Parimala will wash them." She reached for a jar with one hand while pointing her index finger at the door leading outside with the other.

A large man would have to duck to cross the tiny doorway, but I had no such worries. The door was shut, not locked, so I pushed it open and stepped outside. The blazing sun blinded my eyes for a moment, so I shielded my eyes and gazed around for the well.

A small wooden shed in one corner housed two milking cows and a baby calf. I spotted some fruiting trees and a vegetable garden.

I sensed movement and turned my head. A girl hanging wet garments on a clothesline ducked behind a sari rustling in the wind. *Was that Parimala?*

"I have dirty clothes," I said, looking at the two feet I could see beneath the drying clothing.

"Over there," whispered the girl, and her hand came into view, pointing to the well hidden behind some banana trees.

I placed my bundle into an empty metal bucket while my mind frantically searched my memory for how a boy would act toward his soon-to-be betrothed. As soon as I conjured up those words, guilt rose in me for pretending to be Selva. Instead of looking for a new match for his daughter, the swordsmith would train and feed me, a girl who could not marry Parimala. I clamped down on the emotions swelling inside me. I would not stay long in this house.

"Parimala," called the grandmother, standing at the door, beckoning with one crook of her skinny finger. "Come and serve Selva his meal."

A thin girl wearing a cotton skirt and blouse walked toward the kitchen with her back to me. She had plaited her oiled hair into two braids. She looked like a ten-year-old child, definitely not old enough to marry anyone.

"Wash your hands and feet, Selva," said the grandmother, and I followed her words.

Once inside, I sat down on the floor, and Grandmother placed a two-foot-long banana leaf in front of me.

Using a thick cotton cloth to insulate her hands from the heat, the girl carried a still-warm brass pot. I worried the vessel would be heavy for her slender hands, but she held it steadily. She heaped one scoop of rice onto my plate and waited.

"Serve him more rice," instructed her grandmother.

"Grandmother, yesterday you told me to serve less rice," argued the girl.

"Silly child. That was for our worthless neighbor who would not miss a free meal. This is for your future husband."

The girl obliged by creating a small mound on my leaf, muttering under her breath. "More rice for a future husband. Less rice for a foolish neighbor."

My lips curled up at this conversation. I watched her feet move away, not daring to look at her face. I had little knowledge about the workings of a boy's mind. I wondered if Selva would be curious about her looks and sneak glances at her. It felt safer to avoid any contact that could result in entangling her emotions. She returned with a clay pot, still using the folded cotton cloth to grasp the hot container, and poured gourd stew on top of the rice.

I mixed the stew with the rice and ate with my fingers. I heard Grandmother mutter something to Parimala, and using the corner of my eyes, I watched them in silence. Parimala turned toward me, but her face remained in the dark because light from the window pooled behind her head. She approached me shyly with her eyes cast down, and I bent my head, not wishing to cause any offense.

"Can I serve you more rice?" she asked. I shook my head, still staring at the floor.

It took me a while to finish the generous helping of rice, and I felt stuffed with no room to breathe. I rose sluggishly and went to the backyard well. Parimala followed me and drew water from the well with swift movements that surprised me. She dipped a small pot into the bucket and handed it to me.

I noticed a thin bangle on her stretched hand as I grabbed the pot. After I washed my hands in the cold water, I turned, and she held out a dry towel. For an unknown reason, my eyes were drawn to hers, and I hardly dared to breathe. A shock reverberated in my stomach as I gazed at her as if she were death herself.

There was a finger-width opening between her mouth and her nose. The thud when the pot I held hit the ground echoed in my ears like my head had struck the mud. I had sunk to a new low by deceiving this girl with a disfigurement. Guilt pounded my chest. I had brought her ruin and despair.

ATUL

WINTER YEAR 2

Revulsion coiled in my throat, threatening to choke me. I glanced at Aggabodhi walking on the other side of Chief Jeevahatta. He kept his eyes firmly ahead. I had never killed a man in battle, let alone taken an innocent man's life. But Aggabodhi showed no hint of hesitation in carrying out the deed. He had plunged his blade into the guard, who was a victim of our stupid ploy to gain Jeevahatta's confidence. *Would Aggabodhi be a better king than I? Did I lack the cold ruthlessness to reign a kingdom?*

"There she is," muttered Chief Jeevahatta, intruding into my despondent thoughts. The dense forest had given way to farmlands intersected with canals and ditches.

My eyes followed the stream that ran beside us and landed on a mansion nestled alongside it, a seat of power for the House of Jalpaiguri. The building, constructed of sandstone, gleamed in the sun, mocking my fears. The three of us marched toward a robust wooden door adorned with iron studs that guarded the entry, Aggabodhi and I rearranging ourselves to follow a few steps behind the chief.

"Open the door," bellowed the chief, pointlessly loud and

ominous. As the door swung open, I glimpsed two modest towers rising above the main structure. A flag depicting a large eye fluttered in the light wind. A feeling of being watched swept over me, and I pressed my lips to stop my fanciful ideas.

As we walked across the inner courtyard, a man came running. "My lord."

"Take these two to the soldier's quarters and feed them," Jeevahatta ordered. Turning to us, he said, "I will not forget your help today. I will send for you later." With that, he climbed the palace steps and disappeared from our view. The small palace looming in front was no match for the mighty castles I grew up in.

Aggabodhi and I followed the servant. We passed maids carrying vegetable baskets to the kitchen and men holding yokes with milk buckets swinging from them. In Magadha, they would bow low to me, the Crown Prince. Here, I was invisible. Seldom did I get a chance to spend my days with the ones I would rule in Malla. This journey afforded Aggabodhi an opportunity to be among the ones he would command.

The servant took us to a large hall. Two men served rice from huge pots while four rows of men sat on the floor, breaking their morning fast. The smell of pepper, combined with the stench of people crowded into that small space, assaulted my senses.

"Get your food and eat with them," mumbled the servant and vanished. I longed to talk to Aggabodhi, to shake his shoulders for callously murdering the guard, whose only fault was being overpowered by my men. But I knew I had to wait till we were alone. So I suppressed that urge and went with him to the front.

After getting our food, Aggabodhi and I found two empty spots and sat down. Eating my food, I listened to the conversation floating around us. With the recent drought, these young men joined Chief Jeevahatta's army, leaving the women to work in the fields.

"I heard Chief Jeevahatta rescued Prince Aggabodhi," whispered one man. I sensed Aggabodhi lean toward the man to hear about this impostor.

"His father, King Rajasuriya, never cared for us, the people of this kingdom. Why do we have to fight to place his cub on the throne?" asked a young man, his voice rising in rage.

Several others hushed him. "These are matters beyond our understanding, and we should stay out of it."

"If I am going to spill my blood, it becomes my matter," answered the young man, heat coating his words.

"Maybe the chief has other intentions for the prince rather than crowning him," said a middle-aged man in a sagely voice. Having finished their meal, they rose and dispersed. Aggabodhi and I ate our rice in silence. I did not taste the morsel I shoved into my mouth while contemplating our next move.

In the training yard, an older warrior with stooped shoulders walked among the sparring partners, offering advice. A quick glance around the area confirmed what I suspected: these assorted men were not combat-ready.

"Many of my father's generals and commanders perished in the war," Aggabodhi whispered in my ear. That explained why we had not encountered many veteran warriors. The lads around me were too young to have fought during the rebellion. The few older men I saw were too old to fight then. Now, they mainly helped with training.

A man handed us rusted swords with blunt edges. "Bodhi, simple moves," I demanded urgently in a low whisper, making sure he heard the warning in my voice.

He nodded while walking a few feet away and turned to face me. We took turns attacking and defending. I blocked and deflected instinctively, so I let my eyes wander. Out of the corner of my eye, I observed Chief Jeevahatta enter the hall alongside another man taller than him.

Distracted, I failed to notice the thrust of Aggabodhi's sword toward my chest. Instinctively, I spun away from the blade and almost countered his move with a strike of my own. When I realized that the men around us stopped to stare, I clumsily hit Aggabodhi's sword.

Soon, others lost interest in our predictable moves, and my breathing returned to normal. Aggabodhi and I bowed to each other at the end of our training, and my eyes swept the hall. I could not find the chief and the man with him.

"Who was the man with the chief?" I asked the lad collecting the weapons.

The lad hesitated as if afraid. He cast a fearful look around us. Ensuring we were alone, he whispered, "That was Guru Ori, a renowned yogi." Ori! The man who had sent his warning message to Uncle Jay aboard a ship full of corpses.

The serpent of dread coiled in my stomach stirred to life. *Should I kill him right now while I had the chance?* No, even a king should hold court before dispensing any punishment. For all I knew, he could chant a *mantra* and turn me into a frog. It would be foolish to attack without knowing more about my opponent. *What can mere mortals do in front of sorcerers weaving magic?* Aggabodhi had a suggestion for overcoming this obstacle later that night.

After our evening meal, we swept the dining hall with brooms in our hands. In the airless room, the pleasant nutty smell of sesame lingered. I held the wooden handle of my dried grass broom and gathered the food particles littered on the stone floor.

"Did you catch a glimpse of Ori?" asked Aggabodhi tersely.

I nodded, making sure we were away from prying ears. "Does Ori really have magical powers? Or is he simply a scholar, a man of learning, who has studied the herbs and used them to poison the men on that ship? Deadly harm caused by unknown dark arts could strike terror in the hearts of even the bravest men. What if Ori had spread these rumors about himself to achieve that very purpose?"

"My father believed in sight and curses. He even drew up charts for the royal family. Our royal astrologer claimed he could foretell death and inheritance of the throne," whispered Aggabodhi reverently.

"Horoscopes? We have that in Magadha. Using star positions at the time of one's birth, our astrologers drew up birth charts. I have only heard vague predictions of danger from these charts. They have no practical value," I said in a hushed whisper as darkness fell around us. Uncle Jay never believed in these superstitions. I let Aggabodhi gather the dust and dirt while I went around the room, lighting the oil-wicker lamps. The glowing yellow light from them dispelled the darkness.

As we walked back to our sleeping quarters, Aggabodhi's brows knitted with worry. "Brother, I have seen the astrologers in Magadha. Those charlatans have no real learning. Magadha has forgotten the old ways, but not Kashgar. My ancestors have always provided a safe space for knowledge to flourish. This mastery has been passed down from one generation to another without disruption. In addition to astrology, our scholars are well-versed in *mantras* and charms that can produce a curse or a blessing. If Ori uses dark arts with malice, we must counter him. I remember my father mentioning a great yogi, Purohit Parivan."

I stopped and put a hand on his shoulder. He looked up at me. "We cannot indulge in any wicked plots, Bodhi. This is the realm of the unknown, and the rules are hidden from us. We have to use great caution. Even a well-trained archer can overshoot his arrow. A curse can go beyond our target and harm another." Though the night was warm, a shudder passed through me as I imagined untold evil released into the world.

"I seek great power, Brother. I understand the price for that is high," Aggabodhi said imperiously.

"Are you expecting innocents like the guard you killed to pay the price?" I asked grimly.

Aggabodhi flinched and said nothing for a while. "He failed his duty to protect his lord. I punished him for that. Don't your guards swear to protect you with their lives?" he asked steadily.

I clenched my hands into fists. His words shocked me into silence. He spoke the truth. My guards would take their own lives if they failed to protect me. As if attesting to that truth, two members of my guards walked toward me. I recognized Dayalu and Pusha.

With the briefest incline of their heads, they acknowledged me, letting me know of their presence, and continued to walk past me, disappearing down an alley leading to the stables. As we had planned earlier, two of them found a way into the castle. Their sole purpose here was to protect me.

We resumed our march toward our sleeping quarters. "King Jay would use all weapons under his command to keep his people safe," Aggabodhi pointed out dryly. "I am not going to hesitate to use yogic powers if that ensures the safety of Kashgar," he spoke with great conviction.

Aggabodhi seemed ablaze with determination, and standing next to him, I felt like a mere man of ash. This might be the difference between someone like Aggabodhi, groomed to rule a kingdom from birth, and me, an usurper with no birthright to sit on the throne. While Aggabodhi held firm beliefs, doubts filled my heart and mind as I pushed open a door and went inside.

The following day dawned with a loud call from a peacock seeking its mate. I sat up on my woven jute mat and rubbed my eyes, wishing I was waking up sprawled next to one of my wives rather than these unwashed men. I missed their warm lips more than I cared to admit.

A dozen others shared the sleeping quarters with me, our mats lying side by side. One of my guards, Dayalu, a young man about my age, glanced at me with alert eyes from his mat beside mine. He had accompanied me from Malla, one of the five guards sworn to protect the Heir to Malla.

I rose as the morning wind sighed through the window. The guard followed me as I went to the bathing spot along the river to wash. It was quiet that morning as I plunged into the flowing water, letting the cold water clear my head. In Malla, I would be swimming upstream in water considered unpolluted. Here, the section assigned to soldiers was downstream from the place used by the noblemen. The stream, a tributary of the Sunkosh River, appeared pristine to my eyes, and I saw no sign of any muck from the noble folks bathing upriver.

"**Protect her,**" the water whispered, swirling around my body.

Who? I asked in my head.

"**Sugandha,**" the answer filled the air like the fragrance of a flower. *Was someone casting this magic to cause me to lose my mind? Because it was working.*

The sun rose in the east as I dried myself briskly, driving the voice I heard out of my head. Instead, I thought about the rules we made to segregate people into different groups, not letting them mix. Those rules prevented my parents from marrying each other, though they were in love.

The brisk sun dazzled on the water uniformly, making no distinction, causing it to shimmer white and gold as the tide started coming in. I wished to reign like the sun, sharing my light and warmth with all alike.

After a quick meal of porridge, I entered the training yard with Dayalu, the guard who had accompanied me earlier. I chose him as my partner for hand-to-hand combat. While I pinned him down on the floor, he whispered an escape route to me. My men had scoured the area last night and planned a path to flee the castle in case of an attack.

"Can you find out about Purohit Parivan?" I muttered

quietly as he freed himself from my hold. I still hesitated about using magic, but Aggabodhi's remarks had merit in them. I wanted to track down this priest if only to find a way to safeguard ourselves from any dark magic.

A day later, the chief summoned us. Aggabodhi and I followed a few feet behind his servant as we strode toward the castle.

"Bodhi, I will be more open-minded about the gifts that Kashgar scholars carry," I said in a soft voice, putting to rest our earlier disagreement.

His face dissolved into a smile. "I would love to see you tolerate things that cannot be explained, things that cannot be understood."

"Tolerate, yes. But I will not stop questioning things that do not make much sense," I said, my lips curling up a tiny grain.

Aggabodhi leaned in closer. "Speaking of things we don't understand, why do you think the chief has summoned us now?" he whispered.

"Maybe he wants to reward us richly for saving his life?" I jested while my mind pondered the same question. Aggabodhi chuckled in response, and it gladdened my heart not to be annoyed with him.

Under the twilight sky, Aggabodhi and I made our way up the granite steps and strode inside the palace. The servant guided us to the great hall, and we walked through narrow hallways with light coming in through tiny windows in the thick stone walls.

The servant halted in front of a large door set in the wall and whispered to a sentry outside. I drew odd shapes on my hip with my index finger while pondering what waited on the other side. The sentry grabbed the iron ring placed on the door and pushed it open. I snatched a conversation before he announced us. "We need a man born to fight and win battles. Instead, we have this child, cold and damp, with no fire in his heart."

SUGANDHA

SPRING YEAR 1

"I guess no one told you," Parimala said, her thin shoulders sagging as if she carried the weight of the world on them.

I shook my head, hardly daring to deny my mortifying reaction to her disfigurement.

"Like others, you will think of me as the harbinger of evil," she said, her eyes dull and lifeless.

"I survived the storm while many perished. I would consider that a harbinger of fortune," I stated in an emotionless voice. I dared not say more lest I led Parimala astray with my words. She deserved a boy who loved her, not me, a girl on the run.

I went inside without waiting to offer her more comfort. I stepped into the stone-floored room of the workshop, and my nose prickled at something acidic and sharp. The smoke rising from the furnace stung my eyes. Gazing through the smoke, I saw my cousin stripped to his waist, working the bellows of a furnace. Its fiery glow illuminated the room.

Noticing me, my cousin wiped his hands and turned toward me. I shrank back, fearing he would expect me to remove my upper garment. He laughed at my pale face.

"Don't worry. You won't be working on the furnace yet. Put the leather apron on," he said, pointing to two cow skin aprons that hung on the wall. My beating heart took a while to settle while I put the smaller apron on.

My cousin guided me to little braziers set into the stone benches. "Grab some coal and start a fire in one of them."

I did as he instructed and then placed a bronze vessel on top. While I measured and added the ingredients, the oil inside bubbled. My cousin went back to shaping molten metal with precision. Sparks flew around him on each strike of the hammer as he forged a deadly weapon.

One day, a messenger delivered a palm leaf scroll.

"Leave it on the bench. I will read it when I finish here," Cousin said, polishing a rough blade on a grinding stone, particles of dust flying around him.

"I can read it for you," I answered.

"You can read?" he asked in a surprised tone. "I was planning to teach you myself."

I almost told him that my grandfather taught me to read and write in more than one language before remembering I pretended to be Selva, the boy who had drowned. Instead, I said, "I can read simple words."

Was it strange that my grandfather had taught a girl to read? I had never questioned all the times he had made me study the maps of Kashgar or narrated stories about the various Gods we worshiped. I had learned what crops grew in each region and what rivers flowed through them.

"I am surprised your father knew enough to teach you. I thought he was unread. Go on, read the message." My cousin paused burnishing the sword to hear me.

"The village elder has ordered a dozen daggers and short swords."

"And he will pay us in silver, unlike others. The turmoil in the kingdom has been good to us," he said while inspecting the luster on the sword he held.

Days passed swiftly. I cleaned the workshop at the start of the day and put all the tools and ingredients back in their places as the sun began its descent. Men who wanted to join Chief Vikramasinha's army exchanged their old farm tools for gleaming blades. I remembered that Chief Vikramasinha of Singalila was the dead king's brother-in-law.

I overheard two boys, barely older than me, discuss joining the army as they came to pick their weapons. "I heard Chief Jeevahatta is also mounting an army."

I crept closer to listen to them.

"I heard Guru Ori is offering a reward for anyone with information about his niece."

"Reward?" I blurted.

"Yes, fifty silver coins," the boy answered.

Before I could question him more, my cousin called for me.

"Boy, it does not matter who rules the kingdom," he muttered under his breath, "as long as they need weapons to keep it safe. Stay out of trouble." I retreated to my station awkwardly and worked on the task he set out for me.

Easy for him to say. Ori was not hunting him. *Why did Uncle Ori offer such a large reward for me?* He held no special love or regard for me. There must be another reason for him to look for me.

Though Parimala still served me my meals, boiled water for my bath, and washed my clothes—like a perfect little wife—I refrained from talking to her. I kept my gaze down as she heaped rice onto my banana leaf plate. Whenever I sensed the danger of being alone in her company, I fled the room. I knew this caused her anguish because she suspected her deformity kept me away. The truth was even worse. I wanted to leave but selfishly chose to stay because of the roof over my head and the food on my plate.

I kept myself busy in the workshop, under the gaze of her

father, from dawn to dusk. At night, I unrolled the jute mat in a corner and pretended to sleep while waiting for my cousin to fall asleep and his snores to settle to a steady, low roar and grunt. I could hear Grandmother and Parimala move around in the smaller room.

"Parimala, massage my ankle. I am getting too old to do all the work around this house."

"Grandmother, do your lips hurt from all the yelling, too?"

"Rude girl. If you obeyed me, I wouldn't have to shout so much."

I waited for their breathing to deepen and slow. Only then did I slide into my sleep.

"He is a diligent worker," I heard my cousin tell his mother one morning.

"He has been with us for over two months, and he avoids Parimala like she has the plague," Grandmother said with worry tinting her voice.

"Ma, he is only a child. He does not even have a mustache yet. He will wed her in time. And he will feed her and protect her. He will not defy my orders." There was a quiet menace in his tone, and I pictured his strong shoulders pounding the metal into shape. Most sane men would not dare disobey his commands. I was neither sane nor a man.

"She will never beget his children if he loathes her," Grandmother sighed. *She would never beget my children even if I cherished her.* "Let us take them to the temple of the divine couple, God Shiva and Goddess Parvati. Shiva gave half his body to Parvati to reside in him. Praying to them will kindle Selva's love for my granddaughter." My face reddened in shame as I considered my folly in continuing this charade.

That evening, under a rising moon, I tempered a blade my cousin had forged by quenching it in water. I kept the liquid at the right temperature to harden the steel without making it brittle. Working with water was one of my favorite activities in the workshop. When my fingers touched the clear liquid, a calmness entered my body. All my fears dissolved in the water, leaving my mind unclouded.

Absorbed in my work, I did not notice my cousin till he spoke. "You are a child of the moon and the water," he said, awe in his voice. I looked up to see him gaze at the gleaming weapon. "The water seems to obey your wishes."

I flushed at his praise. "Cousin, it is all your teaching," I said humbly.

He regarded me as if seeing me for the first time. "You work the best when the moon is ascendant." I had no reply to that.

In a few days, my cousin hired a cart to take us to the temple. Grandmother packed tamarind rice to eat at the river, and Parimala wore her good skirt and blouse for the occasion. I rode in the front with the cart driver while the two women sat inside the wagon, and my cousin sat in the back. Guilt ate my insides as the bull flicked his tail at my ankle.

At the temple, Grandmother placed Parimala and me side by side and whispered in the Priest's ear. He chanted a *mantra* while waving an oil wicker lamp in front of the idol of Shiva and Parvati sculpted into one form. The left side depicted Shiva with his matted hair, half a third eye on his forehead, and a snake coiled around his neck. The right side portrayed Parvati adorned with her jewelry and her right arm holding a lotus flower. This idol represented a perfect union of male and female energies and their harmonious coexistence. I wondered if there existed a man who complimented my nature, the sun to my moon.

The priest rang the bell, bringing me out of my reverie. Afterward, he took a flower from the feet of God and offered it to Parimala. She tucked it into her plaited braid with a blush spreading across her cheeks. I controlled my urge to flee the scene.

Parimala spread a blanket under a banyan tree and served us

rice in bowls made of dried lotus leaves. Birds chirped from the top of the dense, overgrown tree, a perfect place for nesting and feeding. Oil coated my fingers as I savored the tangy tamarind, highlighting the robust flavor of the spices. I noticed Parimala sat away from us to eat her food. With the opening in her mouth, it must be difficult for her to chew her food. I wished I could offer her some comfort, but that would only deepen her hurt when the truth became known to her.

My cousin belched with abandon while rubbing his stomach. "I am going to visit a local merchant," he said and departed.

"Take Parimala for a walk along the river, Selva. Don't wander too far," muttered Grandmother and stretched herself on the blanket.

We set out along the river in silence. Sweat erupted on my forehead from the heat, and I longed to swim in the water. Parimala gazed at me occasionally while I looked at the river flowing to my right. My mouth formed the words that I was not the boy she sought, but I uttered no sound. Her skirt fluttered against her legs in the breeze.

A haunting lament pierced the silence. "Did you hear that?" I asked, searching for the source of the sound. A smaller tributary joined the river a few yards away, and I ran toward it. My face contorted as fear invaded my senses.

Sounding out of breath, Parimala asked, "What is it?" Her voice came from a few feet behind me.

"A bird in distress," I said as a melodious cry echoed across the landscape. Soon, I came across the water brimming over the edge of some dark boulders in a smooth, gentle arc and dropping into a shimmering lake.

I stopped and broke an overhanging twig with my sharp movement. At last, I saw a young swan entangled in a fishing net, its feathers matted and tangled in the unforgiving threads. It strained its neck and arched its wings, but it remained ensnared.

I approached the bird with gentle steps, the water wetting my dhoti. It stopped quivering and regarded me. Cooing under my breath, I carefully released the net, liberating the bird. As the trap fell away, the young swan spread its wings, white feathers tinted with gold—an unusual color. As the wind from its feathers brushed my face, the swan lingered for a fleeting moment and then took flight.

I stood in knee-deep water, observing tiny waves ripple across the surface as I heard another cry. "Selva."

I turned to see Parimala standing between the roots of a giant tree, and something dark blended with shadows under her feet. Her body trembled in desperation, and with a heavy heart, I took a step toward her. The dark object lashed its tail, and I spotted twin orbs of molten gold shimmering in the light cascading through the leaves. Glistening waters concealed the scaly hide of a crocodile.

ATUL

WINTER YEAR 2

*A*ggabodhi and I entered the room, and silence fell around us.

"Leave and wait for my permission to enter," Chief Jeevahatta yelled at us, and we retreated quickly.

The sentry closed the door and shifted uneasily in front of it. I stood a few feet behind him, wondering who Jeevahatta proclaimed as the child with no fire in his heart. After a few moments passed, the sentry knocked timidly.

"Enter." Chief Jeevahatta's muffled voice reached us through the wooden door.

Once inside, I glanced at Aggabodhi and saw him bow his head. I followed his action and bent at my waist to dip my head.

"These are the two brothers I mentioned," said Chief Jeevahatta to another man. My eyes darted to this new man dressed in the saffron robes of a holy man. I recognized him as Guru Ori, the man who had sent a ship of corpses to Malla. Fear reverberated through my spine as I peeked at him from the corner of my eyes.

He was nearly my height, and his piercing eyes gazed at me

like he wanted to learn all my secrets. I lowered mine and adopted a humble demeanor.

"We can use them to escort the priests, Guru Ori," continued Chief Jeevahatta.

Ori looked through some scrolls on a table, seeming to have lost interest in us. After a long pause, Jeevahatta asked again in a deferential voice, "Do you have any objections, Guru?"

"I concur," Ori finally said, raising his head. "I will let you make the arrangements." As he left, Jeevahatta bowed stiffly to his retreating back. I knew who held the upper hand in this relationship. *What did Guru Ori want? Why did he threaten Magadha?*

"Do you lads know how to ride a horse?" Chief Jeevahatta asked.

Suppressing a smile, I nodded vigorously.

"Find Purohit Kashi and guide him back to my castle," he ordered, mentioning a village where we could find the priest. I noticed that Aggabodhi recognized the name of the place. "Depart at dawn tomorrow," he instructed, handing me a coin pouch. "The stable master will have two horses ready for your journey."

Early at dawn, I saddled a weary horse, showing signs of the passage of time. Its muted coat bore the mark of countless years gone by. I gently stroked its weathered mane and whispered in its ear.

In an instant, erasing all the distance between us, I traveled back home to Malla to my mare. With a shiny black coat, she had been a sight to behold, every line of her screaming her quality breeding. She would turn her knowing eye and wary ear toward any danger with almost a human quality. At any fork in the road, I would sense only curiosity from her, never any apprehension about unfamiliar roads. The tiniest touch from me, and she would relish the chance to stretch her muscles. Her hooves had made music on many a dark night, man and beast traveling as one. Astride her, a world of possibilities had unfurled before me. A longing for home and my trusted horse stirred in my stomach.

Pulling his mare along, Aggabodhi arrived next to me. "Did you hear the chief grumble about a cowardly child? I assume he was lamenting about the fake prince. I want to stay and find the impostor," he whispered. "Prove I have fire in my belly and am worthy of sworn loyalty. Instead of going on this silly journey to bring a priest."

"Patience, Bodhi." I smiled faintly. "Your time to shine will arrive soon. This errand will get us outside the castle, roaming the countryside. We can learn about the state of affairs along our route. Once we accomplish this simple task, the chief will entrust more demanding tasks to us."

We rode north along the meandering banks of a stream. I spotted migratory birds seeking shelter in Kashgar, escaping the harsh winter months in their homes far north of us.

"This is the best spot to cross the water," said Aggabodhi, pointing to a shallow area. With gentle encouragement, my horse ventured forth, cautiously stepping into the stream. With a keen sense of balance, it adapted to the shifting terrain beneath its hooves.

As we crossed the water, the droplets on my skin and its coat glistened like scattered diamonds. I seemed to have gained the animal's trust as we moved alongside fields of rice. The sky clouded ahead of us, and the air turned dense and heavy. It was the tail end of the rainy season here in Kashgar.

When we entered a forest, I felt a presence. I reined in my horse and signaled to Aggabodhi to do the same. A lone rider emerged from the brush soundlessly. I recognized him as one of the soldiers who had accompanied me to Kashgar.

"What news?" I asked, dismounting.

"Purohit Parivan died a year ago in a temple fire," replied the soldier.

"Dead?" echoed Aggabodhi. The soldier nodded. Aggabodhi glanced at me. "Nothing is going my way," he groaned, turning into a young child for a moment.

"We have just embarked on our mission, Bodhi," I said, turning around to face him. "And we have gained access to Chief Jeevahatta without revealing our identities. In our mission to seek Purohit Kashi, we may encounter another priest who can aid us."

A question bubbled up in my mind. *Did someone start the blaze to kill Purohit Parivan?* "Soldier, were there any suspicions around the fire?" I asked.

"None that I heard, my lord. I can ask around discreetly."

"Yes, do that. Any news of the King Rajasuriya's servant?" We sought him to confirm Aggabodhi's claim.

"We have not been able to trace him, my lord. But we heard Chief Vikramasinha has amassed a large troop in the North, larger than Chief Jeevahatta's. There are indications that he plans to battle the rebels holding Tipti and regain control of the capital," answered my man.

Vikramasinha was Aggabodhi's uncle by marriage and ruled the North. Aggabodhi grimaced on hearing the name. He held a grudge against his uncle for living while his father had perished. The rebels who killed the last king still ruled Tipti. Whoever was the next king would have to defeat them first.

Chief Jeevahatta of Jalpaiguri gathered his strength in the South and had an impostor faking a claim to the throne. Chief Vikramasinha's children with Princess Malathi, the sister of the former king, had their own claim to the throne.

Were either of them willing to pledge their loyalty to Aggabodhi? Should I ask my uncle to send more troops to capture Tipti and seat Aggabodhi on the throne? That would not be prudent at present. Kashgar people would see Aggabodhi as an invader rather than their genuine ruler. He needed to gain the support of one of the Kashgar chiefs before attempting to conquer Tipti.

"Find out who Vikramasinha is proclaiming as the heir to the throne. We are going to fetch a priest, Purohit Kashi," I said, providing him with the name of the village. "Stay away from us if he is in our company," I said, dismissing the man.

We mounted our rides and continued our journey north. A ribbon of lightning split the darkening sky, and the dull echo of thunder rumbled over the wall of trees. My stallion jerked his head and bared his teeth. I spoke in a quiet voice to calm his nerves.

"I should swap my horse for a donkey," muttered Aggabodhi, tugging the reins.

I laughed while scratching the itching insect bites on my neck. "I will remind you of that next time we come across one. The bugs are getting bloodthirsty with the approaching storm."

A strong wind whipped my hair, and tree branches lashed my face. Suddenly, the wind dropped, and a curtain of rain glided down. Initially, the leaves created a green roof over our heads, but soon, they drooped under the weight of the water, and the rain poured down intensely, drenching us. It grew dark, lightning providing the only light. Thunder followed with a roaring crash, and my horse skittered around. I was tired of being wet, of the mud on my path.

"Bodhi, let us find cover somewhere," I yelled, peering through the downpour as we rode. "I see a structure there," I said, pointing to a shelter. I rode toward it, and Aggabodhi followed. It was a simple, open formation with a roof supported by four pillars. I dismounted and guided my horse inside the dark space.

"Could the people who killed your father have targeted Purohit Parivan too?" I asked.

"I don't know. I only knew my father consulted him from time to time," said Aggabodhi. Then, he asked a question that troubled me. "If Ori is a skilled yogi, why does he need another priest?"

I thought about it. "In Malla, when we performed a yajna, a sacrificial fire ritual, more than one priest would chant the *mantra*. There is a belief that multiple priests would deepen the spiritual connection and improve the chances of the divine granting our wishes. Does a curse work the same way?"

"An army of priests unleashing horror," Aggabodhi uttered after a long pause. The thought caused me distress. *Was an army of priests any worse than an army of soldiers in inflicting harm?*

After some time, the rain eased off, and the thunder that deafened us earlier halted. A little brown bird alighted on a tree near us, shook the water off its back, and chirped.

We resumed our journey along roads that had turned into tiny creeks. That night, avoiding inns, we slept under the sky in an open meadow resounding with the croaking of frogs. My restless mind conjured up images of my wives. Stars glittering above my head reminded me of sparkling diamonds embedded in Rukmini's nose ring. The gentle breeze on my skin felt like the touch of Vibha's silk sari. I had been married for two years and rarely spent my nights alone.

The darkness churned a deep yearning in my heart. Aggabodhi, the boy prince for whom I made this journey, snoozed, curled up into a ball, his knees nearly touching his chin. While I preached patience to him during the day, nights tested mine. I sighed deeply, breathing in the air laden with moisture, and kept the first watch.

"Brother," Aggabodhi nudged me. "Dawn is upon us."

"Leave me alone," I whispered, keeping my eyes shut. It felt like barely any time had passed since my watch ended.

"You muttered about your wives and son in your sleep, Brother," said Aggabodhi.

I cursed and sat up, rubbing my eyes.

"I have not expressed my gratitude to you for forsaking your family and coming on this journey," said Aggabodhi.

"This is my fight too. Ori killed a ship full of Malla men. Thank me after I set the crown on your head," I answered.

We arrived at the village in the middle of the next day as the rains faded away. A weak sun reluctantly made an appearance. We passed modest houses, their exterior made of compact mud. Thatched roofs constructed of woven palm leaves arched over the walls. A few boys played with marbles and paused their game to stare at us. A donkey brayed from nearby. "There is the donkey for you to ride on," I teased Aggabodhi.

"My luck, it would be a donkey used to going around in circles to extract oil from nuts," said Aggabodhi. I chuckled lightly while my eyes scanned the surroundings.

Closer to the heart of the village stood a few brick houses. A small temple stood at the center, and four streets diverged from it in four directions. We halted near a man returning from the fields with a hoe slung over his shoulder.

"We are looking for Purohit Kashi," Aggabodhi said.

The man regarded us with curiosity and pointed us to a house next to the temple. We thanked him and set off. Dismounting at the entrance, Aggabodhi knocked on the door while I watched the area. No one answered the door. Aggabodhi went around the back.

"No one appears to be home," he said.

"Should we inquire at the temple?" I asked.

Aggabodhi nodded. Holding the reins of our horses, we approached the temple entrance. A woman strung flowers for the worshippers under a neem tree.

"Is Purohit Kashi here?"

"No, only the younger one," she answered without looking up.

"I will go ask him," muttered Aggabodhi while I waited outside. The sun reached overhead, and a stray dog ran to sniff our horses. I squatted and rubbed the dog behind its ears.

"He left the village yesterday," said Aggabodhi on his return.

I wondered if the priest knew of our errand to fetch him and decided to give us the slip.

I approached the flower woman. "I will buy some flowers for God," I said, handing her a copper coin.

She looked at me from head to toe. "Why are you looking for the priest?"

"Our master wants to perform a fire ritual to seek God's blessing for better rains," I said.

"We all need rain," she said, accepting the coin and putting it in her cloth pouch. She handed me a tightly woven jasmine garland. "His wife's parents are in the next village."

"Give the flowers to the next devotee," I said, mounting my ride.

The next village looked similar to the one we had passed. The evening sky glowed red and purple. "We are looking for Purohit Kashi's family," said Aggabodhi to a woman carrying a pot of water on her head.

"His father-in-law lives in the house by the temple," she said and strode away without spilling any water.

"Bodhi, I will keep an eye on the back while you knock on the door," I said, dismounting. I did not want to risk the priest giving us the slip a second time.

A tightly woven dried grass fence ran around the backyard. Looking inside the yard, I spotted a cluster of banana trees, a water well, and some Tulasi plants. I halted under the shade of a moringa tree that grew in the backyard.

Long, thin seed pods spilled over the fence within arm's reach. I heard a faint creak, and the back door opened. A louder knock sounded on the front door. A man hurried through the backyard and started climbing over the wall. Understanding his intention, I patted my horse to stay quiet and walked toward the fleeing man soundlessly.

As the man jumped over and adjusted his dhoti, I caught his upper arm. "Purohit Kashi?" He reeked of sandalwood.

The priest regarded me like a deer caught in a net, his eyes twitching nervously. "Who are you? What do you want?" he asked in a squeaky voice.

"We are messengers from Chief Jeevahatta. He asked us to escort you."

"I refuse to go with you," Purohit Kashi muttered while swiftly walking away from me.

A horse blocked his path. "We will take you willingly or unwillingly," threatened Aggabodhi, holding onto the reins with one hand and the hilt of his sword on the other.

"Your threat is of no use. Whatever you do, it can be no worse than Ori's plans for me. He intends to kill me," said Purohit Kashi in a quiet voice, trapped between us.

I stood rooted to the ground in shock.

SUGANDHA

SUMMER YEAR 1

Time seemed suspended as I assessed how to protect Parimala from the crocodile lurking three feet from her.

"Don't move, Parimala," I said calmly while a storm raged in my head. Both the girl and the beast stayed frozen in the water.

I scanned the surroundings and spotted a long fallen branch. I lunged toward it, keeping an eye on our formidable adversary. I grabbed the stick with both hands and swung it as hard as I could.

The water swirling around my feet appeared to lend me strength. My makeshift weapon caused a powerful splash as it cut through the water's surface. Startled, the crocodile shifted its head toward me. I pulled the branch out and held it over my head. Water dripped from the wet branch down my forehead, and each drop touching my skin energized me.

I eyed the beast as it contemplated if I was a genuine threat. Yelling loudly, I plunged the branch into the lake again, creating immense waves. I only had a moment to register surprise at my own strength.

The crocodile bared its teeth as a swell drenched it.

Suddenly, it moved toward me. Spasms of dread rose from my stomach as the protruding eyes regarded my skinny body. I exhaled with my mouth open to quell my fear.

"Parimala, back away slowly and reach dry land," I said, not taking my eyes off the reptile. My heart thudded violently against my ribs. With a sob, she took a step back, and then I heard her stumble.

To keep the beast's attention diverted from her, I threw the branch a few feet behind the crocodile, the rough bark scraping my palm. With a powerful flick of its tail, the predator swung around and snapped its sharp jaws at the branch as it fell.

I only had a few moments before the beast returned. I locked eyes with Parimala. "Look at me," I said in a reassuring voice, hiding all my fears. "Take one step back."

She wiped her nose with the back of her hand and retreated unsteadily, her gaze staying on me. Just before she reached land, she fell into the water and yelped loudly. The crocodile glided swiftly toward her.

After being her guest for many months, I could not let Parimala fall prey to the crocodile. Seeing no choice, I jumped high and landed with a tremendous force on the water, creating mighty waves. I had anticipated and worried the crocodile would move toward me, but the beast slithered back into the murky depth, vanishing like a ghost. I waited for a moment to see if the reptile would reappear. There was no sign of it.

Taking measured steps, I reached the girl and pulled her up. When we reached the dry shore, Parimala collapsed into my hands with a sigh. I felt the trembling softness of a frightened girl. If I had met her as Sugandha, we would have become friends. And I would have embraced her.

However, I was pretending to be Selva, so I patted her back awkwardly, whispering comforting words into her ear. "You are safe now." She smiled at me weakly in relief. Her face transformed, masking her disfigurement, and for a moment, my lips curled up in unison to share her happiness.

Parimala's elation deepened as her eyes gazed at me with adoration. Curse it. Horror rained on me at my blunder. I tensed up at this sign of fondness, wanting to flee. Clenching my fist to calm myself, I remained silent, not knowing what to say.

As her racing heart steadied, I hurriedly moved away from her.

With unshed tears in her eyes, Parimala whispered, "You saved my life. With no regard for yours."

Panic struck me as her gratitude washed over me. Unwittingly, I had forged a bond with her. *This could only lead to hurt for both of us.*

"Are you hurt?" Parimala asked with tender concern as we made our way back.

"No," I replied hastily, my mind elsewhere. After a long silence, I realized I should extend the same courtesy to her. "Did you suffer any injuries?" I asked, keeping my tone neutral.

Instead of answering, Parimala lifted her skirt to reveal a gash on one leg. A boy might have torn a piece of his cloth to cover his fiancé's wound. But I could not. Such a gesture would be unwise. "Grandmother can treat that." If she was disappointed by my lack of action, she hid it well.

"Selva protected me from a crocodile," Parimala gushed to her grandmother. The girl's eyes darted to my face, and the growing affection in them put me ill at ease. In her narration, I grew into a legend with mystical abilities.

Grandmother regarded me as I dropped my gaze to the ground, hoping it would swallow me whole. No such luck. "He only did his duty as your future husband." *I almost wished I had jumped into the mouth of the crocodile, ending my misery.* As soon as the thought bubbled up, shame followed. My grandfather died to protect me. I could not be indifferent about my life.

On the ride home, my cousin's praise unsettled me. That evening, Parimala smiled at me shyly as she drizzled extra ghee over the bed of rice on my plate. After I washed my hands by the well, her fingers touched mine as she handed me a cloth to dry them. As I gazed up, I saw her looking at the ground with a faint blush spreading across her cheeks. I decided to leave that night.

"Two boys are missing," said my cousin as he spread his mat on the floor.

"Missing?" I asked stupidly, my mind still plotting my escape.

"They had gone to the fair in our neighboring village. We suspect the men recruiting soldiers abducted them. Chief Jeevahatta and Chief Vikramasinha fear openly enlisting men. That will escalate into a battle. They are pretending to search for Prince Aggabodhi despite rumors that the prince is dead." He glanced at me. "I have heard other rumors about sorcerers gathering to commit dark deeds. Don't travel alone. I don't want you to get caught in one of their round-ups."

I had more to fear than a boy. If the soldiers found out I was a girl, I would be violated. My desire to flee vanished. I rested on the mat, sleep failing to claim me for a long while.

Sorcerers? I remembered the curse uttered by my grandfather on the night he perished. He cursed the men on that ship bound for Malla to die. *Was my Uncle Ori involved in this dark magic? Was he still looking for me?*

A change had come over Parimala. The shy girl, aware of the gaping hole in her face, vanished. Instead, a cheerful maid greeted me, who used every discreet opportunity to brush against me. While I celebrated her newfound confidence, I wished my deception was not the reason. I also worried she would notice my lack of reciprocation.

"Father, next time you go to the market, can I come? I want to buy yards of material to stitch some new clothes," she said as she served us food.

With my hand halfway to my mouth, I stopped to observe her. She took care of her appearance, braiding her oiled hair down to her waist. Kajal lined the eyelids beneath which her eyes peeked at me. Meeting my gaze, she dropped hers, color flooding her cheeks. I wondered what it would feel like to fall in love with a boy.

Her father regarded her. "Ma, is it time for her to drape a sari?" he asked his mother. Donning a sari would symbolize Parimala's transition from childhood to adulthood and highlight her readiness for marriage. A deep yearning to wear a silk sari and gold jewels surfaced in my heart. *Would I ever be able to dress as a girl and weave flowers in my hair?*

Grandmother stopped stirring a simmering pot and looked at Parimala and me. Her gaze rested on my face. "Let us wait till after the rains."

I let my breath out. That gave me another six months. I guessed grandmother expected my body to change then. Selva's would have had he survived. Mine had already transformed two years ago.

My cousin trusted me with tempering and quenching the weapons he shaped. I heated a blade rapidly in a coal-fired forge, watching the color of the sword to know when it reached the right temperature.

Then, I carefully immersed the entire blade in water to cool it. I enjoyed this part the most because water appeared to bend to my thoughts. I smiled at the absurdity of this belief as I watched my cousin test a newly polished sword's sharpness by slicing a cloth in half.

For a strange reason, my mind conjured up an image of the same weapon slashing someone's throat, and my heart quickened. I made weapons that, in the right hands, could be used for protecting the innocent. In the wrong hands, they would unleash terror.

Another notion simmered in my head. A blade was no

different from water. It could save lives by quenching our thirst, but just as easily, it could drown lives. I was unable to save Selva from the rage of the river. *Could I prevent the blades I crafted from falling into the wrong hands?*

"Selva," my cousin called my name, bringing me to the present. "Daydreaming?" he asked, raising his eyebrow. "I called your name twice."

"Just admiring the weapon in your hand," I mumbled.

"I want to craft a short sword for you," he said, beckoning me closer. A foot-long piece of iron rested on a wooden table. "Times are dangerous. It will come in handy if you fall into trouble. I will teach you to wield it."

Trouble sought me without any help. "Can you teach me to forge this into a blade?" I asked, touching the cold metal. My cousin nodded.

Over the next few days, I heated and hammered the metal to shape in the burning fire in the forge. Under my cousin's guidance, I polished the blade to a gleam and fitted it with a dark ebony wood hilt. My cousin taught me some simple defensive moves, and I practiced them against an imaginary foe in the backyard. Birds chirped as they returned to their nests under the twilight sky.

"You fought the crocodile bravely without a blade," Parimala whispered. I paused my training and turned in the direction of the sound. She stood under a tree with a smile that extended from ear to ear. My stomach twisted into knots at her cheer.

As darkness draped over us, she approached me shyly. "Can you tie my blouse?" she asked while turning her back to me. She pulled her braid to the front. Without a thought, I retied the knot. With a burst of movement, she kissed my cheek as lightly as a breeze and ran into the kitchen.

It was then I realized Selva would have acted differently. Very differently. I felt like I climbed a giant ladder whose rungs shattered with each step I took. Guilt at my deception struggled against my will to survive. As I remembered the long months spent alone with no roof over my head and no food in my stomach, I convinced myself I should not be ashamed of bringing temporary joy to Parimala's otherwise empty life.

Still, I hid from her. When I heard her approaching footsteps, I walked the opposite way. Once, I climbed a tree as she prowled the yard looking for me. A few days later, I worked alone in the workshop. "Selva," hissed Parimala. She had never sought me here before. Worry pooled in my stomach. If she came looking for me here, I had nowhere to go. Reluctantly, I looked up from the weapon I was grinding. Instead of her usual pleasant face, dark clouds hung over her head. She strode toward me and shoved my dhoti in my face. I squinted at the white cotton fabric.

"For the third day in a row, there is blood on the fabric," she said while her eyes scanned me head to toe. I swallowed the panic rising in my throat. I was very careful about cleaning my soiled clothes. *How did I miss this?*

Her hand felt around the middle of my back until it found the cloth I had wrapped around my chest. She dropped her hand as if burned. With fire in her eyes, she spat, "I understand your indifference now. Take off your shirt."

I looked her in the eye and shook my head. My secret was out.

"You are a girl," Parimala accused me, her eyes breathing fire.

ATUL

WINTER YEAR 2

With Aggabodhi and I blocking his escape path, Purohit Kashi looked like a fish out of water. I was still trying to digest the priest's words. *Why did Ori go to all the trouble to fetch Kashi if he intended to kill him?* It would have been simpler to send an assassin.

"We mean you no harm," I said, hoping I spoke the truth.

"Son, it is not you I'm worried about. Anyway, if you move out of my way, I will not have to turn you into donkeys."

Before I said something witty, Aggabodhi clasped his hands together into one giant fist and hit the priest. Thud, the knock sounded as it made contact with the skull. His head swung to the left, and the priest collapsed to the ground.

I rushed to his side and checked his breathing. Still alive. With my hands on my hips, I stared at the young prince. "How do we transport an unconscious man?"

Aggabodhi shrugged. "It will be easier than transporting donkeys."

Despite myself, I smiled. "You wanted to turn your horse into a donkey. He would have fulfilled your desire in a twisted way."

He laughed. "By making me a donkey instead?"

"Curses are fickle. Who knows what Purohit Kashi was capable of." Using his shawl, I bound the priest's hands to his waist. "Help me lift him." We hoisted him onto my horse, and I climbed behind him. "Let us leave before we attract attention." The night descended around us, giving us cover. We rode swiftly past the villages.

"Why is a priest capable of turning men into animals afraid of Ori?" asked Aggabodhi.

I pondered the same question. "Jeevahatta does have soldiers like us at his command," I muttered. "But Purohit Kashi's worries centered around Ori's intent. What does Ori want from Kashi? Ori sent a cursed ship filled with rotting corpses to Malla. Who cast the curse? What happened to those priests if Ori is recruiting new ones?" One question after another tumbled out of me.

Aggabodhi turned in his saddle to stare at me. "I have heard that curses and blessings come with a toll."

"A penalty makes sense. Otherwise, kings would employ priests to dispense curses like grains," I said. "When Purohit Kashi regains his senses, let us probe him delicately."

"Delicately? That is your expertise. I will let you take the lead. If you want me to shatter something, I will be ready." Aggabodhi grinned.

I snorted. "Since when have you waited for my approval?" His grin widened, and his face changed into that of a young boy. The visage of another boy about the same age with curly hair floated into my vision. I had failed my cousin, who was more than a brother to me. I prayed that I would not let Aggabodhi down.

The priest stirred. "I have no interest in hurting you," I muttered in his ear. The man nearly jumped off the horse in fright.

Aggabodhi sniggered. "Unless you try to turn us into

donkeys or other farm animals."

I stared at the impudent prince pointedly. Understanding the displeasure on my face, he rearranged his face quickly. "Forgive my brother. He forgets the respect due to a person of your stature," I stated.

"If you respect me, let me go. I am a father of two children. I wish to see them grow up before I pass on," pleaded the priest.

"We cannot disobey our master's order to escort you. However, we may be able to protect you if you share your fears with us."

"The only way you can protect me is to allow me to return to my village. I will go into hiding, and you can tell your master, that puppet Jeevahatta, that you could not find me." Contempt oozed from his tone, along with fear.

A sound caught my attention before I could answer him. Horse hooves came from some distance away. *Who was traveling at night?* I did not want to encounter strangers while we were abducting a priest.

"We will have company soon. Bodhi, let us head into the forest," I said. I pulled the reins and shifted my stallion toward the looming trees. Lighted by stars, the dark offered us cover, but a neigh from our animal or a shout from our captive would reveal us. I jumped off. "Bodhi, hide here and see who they are. I will lead the horses further in."

Aggabodhi dismounted and handed me the reins. I watched him climb a tree. After ensuring he remained hidden from view, I guided the horses further away from the road.

"Chief Vikramasinha has been sending scouts along these roads to gauge Chief Jeevahatta's preparedness. If these are his men, they have gotten more brazen to travel on the main thoroughfare," said Purohit Kashi.

I looked up at him. Faint light filtering through the trees highlighted his silhouette as he sat on the horse. I pretended to be Chief Jeevahatta's man but uttered no words to defend my master. I led the two horses deeper into the forest. A gentle wind rustled the leaves, and a bat flew overhead.

"A war is coming. Whoever wins will only be a weakened ruler," he continued.

The horses could see better than me, and I let them go in front. "Do you know Purohit Parivan?" I asked.

"Purohit Parivan? He was much older than me. My guru had mentioned his name as one of the greatest sages of his times. Purohit Parivan was a regular at the court of the old king, King Jayadheer, the grandfather of our last ruler, King Rajasuriya. After the old king died, Purohit Parivan retired to his hometown. He had disappeared from public view. Then, last year, I heard rumors that he died in a fire," he whispered. I could tell he held something back, but I was unsure what he kept to himself. "Who are you, lad? You don't sound like a brute farm boy who has joined Jeevahatta thinking it will be fun to wield a sword." I could sense he had turned his face to gaze at me.

"My mother is high born, but I am her base-born son," I said, speaking the truth while hiding my identity.

"If you sought the Kashgar throne, you would not be alone. Chief Jeevahatta and Chief Vikramasinha have lined up boys to stake their claims," he said.

"I have no desire for the Kashgar throne," I said as I pulled the reins to bring the horses to a halt. Being the heir to one throne I had no birthright to was plenty. Crickets chirped monotonously around us.

"How deftly you answer my questions without revealing anything of importance," he said, chuckling lightly.

I heard footsteps and stood alert. A shape in the form of Aggabodhi approached between the tree trunks. I walked toward him, out of Purohit Kashi's earshot. "Royal messengers, based on their insignia. I guess they are bearing a message for Jeevahatta."

"They could be from Vikramasinha inviting Jeevahatta to a

royal council," I answered.

"Brother, we should attend the gathering to present my claim," he said in earnest, touching my arm.

"We will, Bodhi," I assured him. "Let us rest here tonight. I don't want to risk encountering any others."

I helped Purohit Kashi down and found him a spot among fallen leaves to rest.

"I will keep the first watch," said Aggabodhi.

I shut my eyes while my mind raced a hundred miles. If neither chief supported Aggabodhi, I would use Malla's might to place him on the throne.

As light crept along the horizon, I hunched over my knees and watched the priest snore with his mouth open. As the first rays of the sun hit the trees, the birds tweeted incessantly in welcome. The priest stirred slowly and yawned. He tried to rub his eyes, but his bound hands restricted his movements. Wearing a scowl, he scanned the surroundings. Then his eyes landed on me, and his shoulders sagged. "It was not a nightmare then," he uttered.

I helped him sit. "What are you afraid of, Purohit Kashi?"

"Ori recruited a few other priests before me. All of them have disappeared. The rumor is they are dead," he said in a resigned tone.

"Dead? What is Ori seeking?" *Was he after Amrut, the nectar that bestowed immortality? Maybe divine weapons that tilted the battle in your favor?*

"He is searching for his niece," answered the priest.

"His niece? Why would that cause your death?" asked Aggabodhi, rising.

Purohit Kashi shrugged his shoulders.

Something rustled in my memory. "Do you know her name, the name of his niece?" I asked.

"Sugandha," replied the priest, stunning me. It was the name I heard in my head.

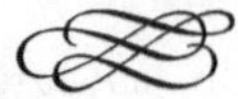

"You are a girl," hissed Parimala, her face reddening in anger. Before she yelled again, I covered her mouth with my hand.

I looked at Parimala. "I will explain everything if you give me a chance." My eyes darted around the workshop. My cousin had left to see a merchant and would return only in the evening. Grandmother was visiting a new mother and her baby. But a customer could walk in anytime through the door.

I uncovered her mouth, praying she would stay silent. She stamped her foot on mine, causing me to gasp in pain, but stayed quiet. Limping slightly, I tugged her into a tiny space beside the forge.

After ensuring our privacy, I let go of her hand. "I am an orphan," I started. She crossed her arms across her chest, glaring at me. "To be safe from predators, I disguised myself as a boy. I traveled on the same boat as Selva, and he told me about you."

Her lips trembled on her thin face. "Where is Selva?" she asked.

I hesitated to reveal the truth that would wound her. "Did

you kill Selva to take his place?" she accused, taking a step forward.

"No," I stammered. I dug deep to find my courage. "He drowned in the storm that overturned our boat," I whispered.

She staggered back, uttering a gut-wrenching sound. I drew a shuddering breath as I felt her pain in my bones. *Was I any better than the boys I hid from? I wrecked an innocent girl's life.* Not entirely, answered a part of my mind still capable of thinking. Selva's death ruined her life. I gave her a glimpse of a future, even if it was a mirage. I extended my hand to support her, but she swatted it away and leaned against the wall. "What will become of me now?" she cried. My heart broke into a thousand tiny pieces at her grief. I wanted to comfort her but stood still.

Suddenly, she wiped her tears and turned toward me. There was a moment's silence, then the yelling started, combined with disbelief and fury. "You betrayed me. While enjoying our hospitality, you deceived us." Her slender body shook with rage.

"I am guilty of that," I said.

Her fists pounded my chest as sobs rocked her. "You stole my chance at happiness." Then she collapsed onto me, and I lost my balance, both of us almost falling. I reached out to the wall for support and steadied us.

"Parimala, I will leave immediately. Your father can find another boy—"

"Who will marry a girl with a hideous face?" she asked, looking up with tears streaming down her cheeks. "The villagers suspect I am barren. That is why my father fetched Selva from far away. If word gets out he perished in the river, they would add ill luck to my fatal flaws."

I had no answer for her, so I stood like a dumb goat, my arms falling uselessly at my sides. I was a girl about her age and on the run. My fate was worse than hers, but I did not state that. My fate was not an excuse for my deception.

"You have nowhere to go. Stay here and continue the

charade. We can marry as planned. If we have no offspring, villagers will blame my sickness," she said, determination creeping into her voice.

"I am pretending to be a beardless boy. That will work for a year or two. What about after?" I pricked at her scheme instinctively. I also had to worry about Uncle Ori finding me. I had stayed in one place for too long.

"We will figure something out. You can wear a disguise," Parimala suggested, carried away by her ideas.

"Parimala, you deserve better. I will pack my bags and leave now. I will write a letter saying I am returning to my brother."

"Where will you go?" she asked with narrowed eyes.

I shrugged my shoulders. I could find work as a swordsmith apprentice, but I did not share that with her.

"You will find another innocent life to corrupt," she poked my chest with her finger.

"I—" Parimala was right. I would continue my disguise.

"I cannot let that happen," she vowed, fisting her hands.

"What will you do?" I whispered, staring at her flushed face.

"I will curse you," she muttered feverishly.

"Don't," I urged, remembering my grandfather's fate. He spent his life force on that deadly curse.

"Why? Are you afraid of what will befall you?"

"No, I fear for you. Curses are fickle and harm the caster as much as the intended recipient."

"Harm me? More than the injury you caused?" She planted her feet firmly on the floor. "You will fall in love with a boy with endearing qualities. He will break your heart by abandoning you. You are doomed to a solitary life. When you are lonely, I will haunt your sleepless nights," she said as if in a trance. The wind swept over me, carrying her words. She slumped to the floor.

ATUL

WINTER YEAR 2

"Sugandha," I said the name. The voice that whispered in my head asked me to find and protect a Sugandha. *Was it the same Sugandha as Ori's niece?* I could not dismiss it as a coincidence. There could not be many Sugandhas in Kashgar that needed my protection.

"Well, no harm in uniting families," said Aggabodhi as he saddled the horses. The smell of fresh blooming flowers swirled around me as the tree branches swung toward the sun.

"You don't understand. Ori has been searching for his niece for nearly a year. The priests he had employed would have detected her unless she was under a protective spell. Ori is trying to break that protection, but he kills the priests instead," said Purohit Kashi. Deep lines creased his forehead.

"To put his niece under a protective spell, someone must have suspected Ori would harm her," I said, thinking furiously. "Whoever cast it must be a powerful priest."

His earlier reticence gone, Purohit Kashi answered eagerly. "Only two priests I know are capable of such magic. Purohit Parivan and Ori's father."

"Guru Ori's father?" *His own father did not trust him, I thought.*

Purohit Kashi echoed my thoughts. "Ori's father raised the child after her parents died. For some reason, he did not want his son to find his granddaughter. Rumors are floating around that Ori killed his father. Luckily, the girl fled before her uncle captured her."

I drew a circle on my shoulder. "Why does Guru Ori need the girl?" *Why did a voice whisper in my head to protect her?*

Purohit Kashi shrugged his shoulders. "He promised his sister that he would marry her daughter." A brother marrying his sister's daughter was allowed in some cultures, but that did not explain the protective spell.

Aggabodhi chimed in. "Why would Ori's father thwart his son's efforts to fulfill a promise made to his daughter?"

Using my sharp knife, I cut the cloth binding Purohit Kashi's hands and helped him to his feet. We led the horses to a stream nearby.

"Rumors swirl around Sugandha's mother. Some claim Ori's father fostered her and is not her birth father. Her lineage is a mystery, but I suspect she hails from a royal family."

"Royal family?" Aggabodhi halted. His eyebrows nearly reached his hairline.

"It is only rumors," said Purohit Kashi. "I should not spread them." I sensed his reluctance to part with this piece of news. I waded into the water to wash my face.

"**Find Sugandha**," a voice reverberated in my head.

I looked at Kashi and Aggabodhi to see if they, too, had heard the voice. Facing the sun, Kashi chanted his morning prayers while Aggabodhi cupped his fingers to drink the water. No sign either of them caught what I did. I thought back to the previous times I heard the voice. I had stood in the water each time. Throwing caution to the wind, I dove into the stream.

"**Protect the girl**," the waves said.

"Why should I protect a stranger?" I asked in my head. A

school of fish swam into my view, and their silver bodies glittered against the light filtering in.

"**A curse to break**," replied the voice. *Curse?* I surfaced and took in a deep breath with my mouth open. The mystery around this girl deepened each time I learned something new. I felt like a boat in the middle of an ocean with no land in sight.

"My brother has an unusual kinship with staying clean," Aggabodhi teased, a grin sprouting on his face.

I stood and squeezed the water out of my dhoti. "You do know the layer of dirt offers no protection in a fight?" I jested. *How would I find a girl hiding from Ori?* The water sparkled like molten silver, reflecting my pensive face.

Purohit Kashi put up no resistance as I helped him mount the horse. I sat behind him and tugged the reins. We rode in silence, each immersed in our thoughts.

"How do you find someone using *mantra*?" I asked the priest. The horse knew the way back home, needing very little of my attention.

"If it is a person I have a connection with, I can reach them through their dreams," said Purohit Kashi.

"Dreams?"

"Yes, I can send a message to my wife in her dreams."

I chuckled. "Did you contact her last night?"

"I did not want her to worry," he said with no guilt. I would have done the same in his place.

"That is why you presume there is a protective spell. Otherwise, Guru Ori would have reached his niece through her dreams."

He nodded. "A powerful yogi could send hidden messages through dreams and even ask the dreamer to come to a certain place at a certain time. I suspect this spell is acting as a shield and blocking Guru Ori from contacting his niece."

"But any priest seeking the girl on Guru Ori's behalf would likely encounter the same barriers."

He dipped his head again. *Would I be able to reach her through her dreams?* I decided against it. She had stayed hidden from Ori for a year. I could protect her best by thwarting Ori's efforts to find her.

"Any ideas on how you can stay alive while carrying out Guru Ori's orders?" My mind pondered the ways to achieve this.

He shook his head slowly. "He knows the *mantra*, so I cannot trick him there."

"Tell him it is futile to break the spell," I said.

"Do you want me to die sooner?" Purohit Kashi asked, looking over his shoulder.

I did not say anything for a moment while I followed the web of threads in my head. "Guru Ori has failed repeatedly in this quest. Tell him to circumvent the spell."

"Circumvent?" Aggabodhi asked, following along with our conversation.

"I don't know how," I said, turning toward him. "But it will allow Purohit Kashi to live while he and Ori concoct ways to overcome their obstacles." And give me time to learn more about Sugandha.

As the sun disappeared for the day, we arrived at Chief Jeevahatta's castle. The palace bustled with activity. Usually, invisible servants ran around on errands. Guards patrolled the surroundings in greater numbers. At the entrance to the stables, I leaped off and helped Purohit Kashi dismount.

"What is going on?" I asked a stable boy as I handed him the reins.

"Messengers arrived from Chief Vikramasinha this morning," answered the boy while rubbing the mane of the gentle horse.

As I pondered whether I should find sleeping quarters for the priest or seek an audience with Ori, one of the chief's close advisors hailed me. "Is that Purohit Kashi?"

"Yes, Master," I said humbly.

"Purohit Kashi, let me take you to Guru Ori. He has been eagerly awaiting you."

"Can we come along, Master?" I asked with an exaggerated bow. "Guru Ori might reward us," I said with a sheepish smile.

"The two brothers took good care of me on the road," Purohit Kashi chimed in.

"Yes, join us. Guru Ori may have questions for you," waved the advisor and strode inside. Aggabodhi and I followed them a few feet behind.

As we approached Guru Ori's chamber in an isolated corner of the castle, Chief Jeevahatta marched toward us. When he neared us, his eyes swept the priest up and down. Instead of a jubilant welcome, his face reddened, and his nostrils flared.

"Ruin upon us," he cursed angrily and stormed past us without a greeting. Before I could understand the reason behind this fury, we arrived in a dimly lit corridor and stopped in front of two massive wooden doors.

The advisor whispered to a guard outside, who opened the door. However, the guard entered the room alone and shut the door behind him. Soon, the same man threw open the doors, and Ori arrived to greet us with a smile.

"Purohit Kashi, I welcome you to my humble abode." Guru Ori bowed to the priest with his palms touching. Standing only a few feet from Ori, I felt disconcerted to view him face to face. I disguised our similarity in height by stooping my shoulders low and hunching my back. Dressed in simple saffron-colored robes, he radiated a quiet strength.

"You sent two persuasive boys to fetch me," said Purohit Kashi, mirroring Ori's gesture.

Ori glanced at us. "Hope the journey was pleasant," he said, leading Kashi to a simple wooden chair. Then, Guru Ori placed Kashi's feet on a silver plate and washed them reverently with water from a small clay pot. Surprised at this gesture of hospitality, I watched the proceedings intently.

Kashi's eyes widened at this sign of humility. "May the divine mother bless you with the wisdom you seek," he said.

Ori guided Kashi to a tiger skin mat on the floor. Both men sat cross-legged on it. The two men appeared to have forgotten about us. Light from hanging wicker lamps cast a golden glow on them.

A servant set a plate of fruits and a jug of milk in front of Kashi. While Kashi ate, Ori fanned him with a peacock feather fan. Aggabodhi and I hovered in the shadows, exchanging furtive glances. I was not expecting to see this mild side of Ori.

Once the servant removed the plate, Kashi cleared his throat. "Guru Ori, I am honored by your kindness. Please tell me what I can do for you."

Ori pressed his palms together. "I should be helping Jeevahatta achieve peace in this beloved kingdom of mine. Instead, worries for my niece Sugandha, daughter of my dear departed sister, plague my mind. If I can be assured of her safety, my mind will be at ease."

Kashi gazed at the man. "Guru Ori, I have heard others before me have tried to find her in vain."

Ori's brows furrowed. "An enemy of mine has hidden her from me with a curse. But I will not rest until my niece is safely under my protection."

Kashi rubbed his beard. "If there is a curse, let me check the boundaries of it."

"How?" asked Ori, leaning in.

"Let me find out if she is alive. Please fetch me clothing or jewelry worn by the child."

Kashi sat in front of a lit silver lamp. With his eyes closed, he held a cotton skirt in his hand while muttering a *mantra*. Sweat broke out on his forehead and dripped down his cheek. His body shook, and blood oozed out of his nose. Aggabodhi took a step forward, but I held up my hand to halt him.

"Sugandha is alive," gasped Kashi, opening his eyes. Then he clutched his throat and wheezed, "But in danger." His face reddened, and his neck swung from side to side. He croaked something unrecognizable and collapsed.

SUGANDHA

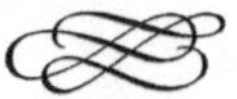

SUMMER YEAR 1

I nearly laughed at hearing Parimala's curse. *How will I ever fall in love with a boy if I run from place to place like a wind-blown leaf?* With my uncle chasing me, I would never set roots in one place. A profound sadness coated my skin. Getting my heart broken sounded like a blessing. It would reveal I had a heart like a normal girl.

Parimala slumped to the floor, and fear gripped me. "Please, God, spare the innocent girl's life," I prayed, rushing to her side. I placed my finger under her nose. Warm breath tingled my skin. I sighed in relief. I fetched water from a clay pot and sprinkled it on her face. Her eyes fluttered open. *Give her strength*, I thought, while offering her a sip of water. I carried Parimala to her room and placed her on the floor. She sat up, staring at me wordlessly.

"Parimala, I am sorry for the pain I caused you. You are a beautiful girl, and I pray you find a boy that is worthy of you." A lone tear slid down her cheek.

I knew there was nothing I could do to make amends. I noticed the hair around Parimala's temples turning gray. I thought one had to be a gifted yogi to cast blessings and curses.

My grandfather had nearly died when he had cursed the Malla ship. I had assumed her words, spoken in distress, were harmless. But the curse seemed to be aging her. *Did that mean her words were potent?* The curse echoed in my head—doomed to a lonely life. I swallowed the swell of emotions threatening to choke me.

As I gathered my meager belongings, I found the short sword I had crafted. My fingers caressed the ebony wood. I left the blade behind and snuck out, tears streaming down my face. I stumbled along, nearly blind, walking away from the place that had offered me shelter and protection.

Thud. I collided with someone. "Boy, watch where you are going," said a voice I recognized. A middle-aged man who came to the shop occasionally adjusted his dhoti with his eyes cast down. I wiped my eyes with the back of my hand.

"Apologies. I was in a hurry," I said, running around him. I wanted to escape before he could look at me and ask questions. Once he disappeared from my view, I slowed down. I could not afford to meet anyone else who knew Selva.

I hid in the shadows as I marched toward the forest at the end of the village. Like a simmering pot, rage bubbled up in me. Anger at my grandfather for dying and leaving me alone and at my uncle for killing his father rose in my stomach like steam from boiling water. Frightened by my emotions, the sun vanished into the night. Even stars concealed themselves under cloud cover.

When I reached the towering trees, I plowed deeper into the forest. Something slithered near my foot, and I stopped. Whatever beast it was, it disappeared into the woods. Standing in the darkness, with tears flowing down my chin, I screamed.

Birds fluttered into the sky. With frustration, I punched a tree with my fist and winced. My helplessness and loneliness cloaked me. I sank to the ground and hugged my knees. Sobs rocked my chest.

This was no life to lead. I wanted a normal life. I wanted to fall in love with a boy, curse or not. I desired to fill my heart with warmth, not this cold fear. I wanted to return home. *Where was home if I had no family?* I found it impossible to get up, even as the night deepened. I curled up on the ground, pulling my knees to my chin.

I couldn't sleep. All I could see was Parimala's wide-staring eyes, accusing me of ruining her life. I groaned, feeling as if stones pinned down my limbs. There was only one way to fix this. I needed to confront Uncle Ori. Instead of running away from him, I would go to him and tell him to leave me alone. A calmness filled me as I made this decision. I would find Uncle Ori.

I climbed up a tree and tied myself to the trunk. Staring at the sky, I pondered how to find my uncle. My grandfather had blessed me to stay hidden from my uncle. *Would that spell break if I sought him?*

I slipped into a troubled sleep chased by hunters and magicians. I woke up to the sound of loud chirping. A mother pigeon circled above my head. I suspected her babies were nearby from the loud ruckus that emanated above my head.

"I am leaving," I muttered as I slid down the tree. My dhoti got caught in a branch and tore. Cursing loudly, I tied the torn pieces together. Beyond not sleeping well, my heart raced at the slightest sound.

I needed to move far from here. Using the sun as my guide, I marched west. At the edge of the forest, I scanned the surroundings. The Sunkosh River flowed several yards away, but I saw many villagers around the area.

Among the crowd, I spotted my *cousin* talking to a boatman. Sweat erupted on my forehead, and I trembled. I did not know what he would do if he found me, especially if Parimala had revealed I was a girl. I could not breathe. *How could I go on like this?*

The wind carried my name—Sugandha. I gazed at the water as if pulled by a string, and it seemed to lend me strength. My pounding heart slowed down. I breathed slowly, in and out, through my nose. I would carry on for my grandfather's sake.

I stayed among the trees and walked further south. Finding an isolated area, I strode to the river, crossing a sandy beach. The water glistened invitingly. The sunshine felt good on my skin. I waded in and washed my face.

A movement caught my eye, and my first instinct was to hide. Then, a swan glided into my view. I recognized the golden-tipped feathers. I smiled as the bird cocked its head to look at me. Tentatively, I held my hand out. The bird swam close to me.

"Do you remember me?" I asked, gently stroking its neck. The anger pooled in my stomach slowly dissipated. The bird arched its long neck to gaze at me. "I am glad you are doing well," I whispered as the bird flowed with the river. I watched it glide away like a boat.

My thoughts returned to Uncle Ori. I last saw him with Chief Jeevahatta. He lived on the other side of the river. I would have to cross the river to reach his castle. I cupped my hands and drank the water. It quenched my thirst and cleared my mind.

"**Don't seek Ori**," echoed a voice.

"Why not," I argued in my head.

"**Because that was your grandfather's dying wish**," it reasoned.

The desire to find Ori vanished like a deer at the sight of a tiger. First, I had to move away from my *cousin*. Then, I could decide what to do next. With that goal, I entered the forest again. I picked berries here and there to quench my hunger, and I stayed away from people for most of the day.

In the evening, I climbed a tree and scanned the surroundings. I spotted a temple tower a mile away and decided to take shelter there for the night. I crossed a meadow of tall grass that reached my waist. I let my fingers touch the grass as four cows grazed in the twilight, looking content. Nearby, two calves tumbled, jumped, and skittered back to their mothers, who placidly ignored them and chewed their food. Watching them, a strange yearning filled my heart.

I missed my pretend family. I remembered Grandmother admonishing me if my hair was still wet after drying it with a cloth, my cousin observing me with pride as I shaped a weapon, and Parimala heaping extra servings of lentil fritters onto my plate.

With a heavy heart, I approached the temple. The main sanctum housed an idol of the Sun God driving a chariot drawn by seven horses. I gazed at the intricately carved stone wheels and the lifelike horses.

I remembered my cousin calling me a child of the moon. I knew my heart craved the safety and comfort of the home I fled. But that life no longer belonged to me. With a fervent mind, I asked the Sun to guide me. After saying my prayers, I accepted a banana from the priest and struck up a conversation with him.

"Have you heard any news of Guru Ori?" I asked. My heart thudded erratically at the mention of my uncle's name. I knew I could not hide from him forever. My grandfather had assumed Purohit Parivan would help me. But he died, too. Surely, my grandfather, who had cherished me, would not want me to spend my life in dread. I had to put an end to this. I wanted to live in a house where I could raise my own family. I did not want to be a nomad.

"Why do you ask?" questioned the priest with his hands on his hips. He appeared neither young nor old and had a large mole on his cheek.

"I heard he was looking for his niece. I might have some information for him," I said, my back stooped. I knew this put my life at risk, but I was tired of hiding and staying in disguise.

"Boy," the priest with the large mole said with a stern expression. "Priests older and wiser than you have died trying to find that girl. If you think you can earn a quick coin with your lies, you are mistaken. Stay away from Ori." With that, he stormed away.

I took the banana to the steps leading to the temple ponds. *What did he mean by priests dying trying to find me?* I peeled the fruit and bit into it. My mind raced furiously. My grandfather cast a blessing on me to protect me from Uncle Ori. *Did my uncle suspect that?* He probably did. It explained why he was using other priests to find me. *But what caused those priests to die?* No answer came to me.

When the priest with the large mole started closing the temple, I concealed myself behind a pillar, waiting for him to leave. I had already chosen a dark corner to spend the night. I heard a loud creak as he pulled the main doors shut. I let my shoulders slump in relief. Humming, I walked to my sleeping spot.

Footsteps? Was the priest with the large mole back? Before I could react, a hand clamped my mouth shut and dragged me. I elbowed and kicked to no avail. Whoever held me tugged me toward the temple pond. The water glittered in the moonlight.

Another man stepped in front of me, his face hidden in the shadows. "Listen carefully. If you reveal what you know about Guru Ori's niece, we will leave you alone. If not, we will drown you in that pond."

ATUL

WINTER YEAR 2

"Why is Guru Ori wasting time trying to find his niece?" asked Aggabodhi as we walked to our quarters. We left Priest Kashi under the care of a healer. In the stillness of the night, I could hear the soft crunch of our feet on the ground.

"She is his niece," I said feebly. After a year, even parents would wind down their search. *Did a voice whisper in Ori's head to seek and protect Sugandha? Like it did in mine?*

"But she has been missing for a year," said Aggabodhi, interrupting my thoughts. "No wonder Chief Jeevahatta looked murderous." The chief did have reasons to be unhappy with his guru if Ori spent time and money seeking his niece rather than aiding him in conquering the kingdom.

"Chief Jeevahatta is likely running low on funds. I heard the soldiers grumble about receiving no coins for the past moon month. No one has offered to pay us either," I stated. I contemplated whether I should tell Aggabodhi about hearing a voice and seek his advice on what I should do.

"All the more reason for the chief to be annoyed. In his place, I would be mad, too. His guru has failed several times to find his niece and has killed many priests along the way. It would be like you stopping to help me win my throne and embarking on a distraction," ranted Aggabodhi. In his words, Sugandha would be a distraction. I decided not to bring her up.

"Guru Ori being distracted will help us, though," I said. "We have time to learn where everyone's loyalties lie. Let me see if my men have any news about the royal messenger."

I walked past the stables and watched the stars bursting to life over my head. The darkness embraced me like a cloak. I heard a shuffle of feet and peeked behind my shoulders, and my guard, Dayalu, inclined his head. I slowed down away from curious eyes and ears.

"A messenger arrived from Chief Vikramasinha today. He has called for a gathering on the shores of the Sunkosh River. Chief Vikramasinha wants the council to pick the next ruler at this event, which is set to take place in a month. He has no sons with Princess Malathi, but he plans to claim the throne on behalf of his pregnant daughter. Whoever they choose as their next king, he wants others to pledge their men to battle the rebels in control of Tipti. The news has made Chief Jeevahatta unhappy," Dayalu said as he walked a foot behind me.

If the fake prince was not ready for an audience, I could understand Jeevahatta's disappointment. There were three contenders for the throne: Aggabodhi, fake Aggabodhi fielded by Chief Jeevahatta of Jalpaiguri, and this cousin of Aggabodhi fielded by her father, Chief Vikramasinha of Singalila.

Aggabodhi had the strongest claim of all if we could prove his identity beyond a doubt. I realized this situation in Kashgar mirrored what had happened in Malla. Aggabodhi's father, King Rajasuriya, and his aunt, Princess Malathi, were brother and sister, like Uncle Jay and my mother.

My claim to the throne was through my mother. If my cousin Vikram, son of Uncle Jay, were still alive, he would have a stronger claim to the Malla throne. I would have never accepted being crowned heir to the throne if Vikram still breathed.

I still felt like an usurper and struggled to crush that feeling. My cousin died two years ago. I was a poor substitute, but I could no more abandon Malla than I could abandon my mother. I brought my focus back to Kashgar with difficulty. These other contenders put Aggabodhi's life at risk. We needed to be careful about revealing his identity.

"Is the fake prince fostered by Chief Jeevahatta here in the castle?" We had seen no sign of him.

"No, my l—" Dayalu stopped himself in time before addressing me as lord. "No, he is not here. But the chief dispatched half a dozen men today. I suspect it is to fetch the prince." I imagined the chief wanted to keep the boy safe. With many pretenders vying for the throne, it would be difficult to know who to trust.

"Did we find the old king's servant?" If Chief Vikramasinha wanted to rule through his daughter, he would not support Aggabodhi's claim unless we could prove he was the old king's son.

His signet ring, bearing their royal crest—a banyan tree— would help, but questions would still linger. With the might of the Malla army, I could seat him on the throne, but the people of Kashgar might scorn Aggabodhi as a conqueror rather than the birthright ruler.

"There is no trace of the servant," said Dayalu.

He could have died along with his master, King Rajasuriya. "Check the prisons in Tipti before we abandon the search."

I laid on my mat, sleep eluding me, listening to the chorus of snoring men and the occasional rustle of bodies adjusting in slumber. The fresh fragrance of the night barely covered the odor of bodies around me.

At the first sign of dawn, I rose and went to Priest Kashi's room. I bent my head to enter through the small door. The priest rested on a simple wooden cot. A faint scent of sandalwood and herbs emanated from the salve applied to his skin. A young healer's apprentice tended to him.

"How is he?" I asked as I approached them.

"He is paralyzed on the right side of his body," the man said, feeding him some liquid.

"Paralyzed?" I asked in agony. Priest Kashi's eyes found mine, and I sensed despair in them. I felt guilty about bringing him here.

Before I could say more, I heard voices outside. I slid to a corner and made myself smaller.

Guru Ori nearly hit his head on the door frame. "Why are your doors designed for midgets?" he asked as he stooped in. Chief Jeevahatta, almost a foot shorter than his guru, made no reply as he followed.

"What's his condition?" asked Guru Ori as he reached the bed.

The healer rose and bowed. "He is paralyzed on the right side. My master doubts he will regain his functionality."

Guru Ori frowned as he observed Priest Kashi. "Can he speak?"

"No, Guru Ori. His other faculties could be impacted as well," the healer answered.

"Shame. Take care of him, Jeevahatta," said the guru and left the room. I saw no sign of the guru who had humbly welcomed the priest yesterday.

Jeevahatta hovered near the door, pinching his lips into a thin line. I separated from the shadows and came forward.

"I fetched Priest Kashi, my lord. Give me your orders. I will take care of it," I said, bowing deeply from my waist.

The chief beckoned me closer. I hunched my shoulders so I did not tower over him. "Kill him. Leave no trace. We don't want rumors spreading," he whispered in my ear.

I wanted to strangle his throat. Instead, with difficulty, I managed to nod. Chief Jeevahatta disappeared, and I went back to the priest. His eyes widened in fear as he gazed at me. "Can you make him ready for travel?" I asked the young healer.

"Travel? I would not recommend it."

"Chief's order. Make him ready," I said curtly and went to find Aggabodhi. I pulled him to a quiet corner. "Bodhi, Priest Kashi is paralyzed. Chief wants me to kill him discreetly."

I did not intend to fulfill his orders, but I left that out. If Jeevahatta found that I had disobeyed him, my disguise would fall apart. *Was I being foolish in taking this risk? If saving one life jeopardized the crown, was it worth it?* But the priest was not a soldier pledging to die for his kingdom. I did not want to be a ruler that could not protect innocent lives.

"What a waste of time," said Aggabodhi. "I can come with you," he offered, unaware of the turmoil brewing in my head.

"No, stay here and keep your eyes and ears open. I will return this evening."

By midday, I set out on a horse-driven cart. One of my men drove while I sat beside the priest in the covered carriage. The straw strewn on the bottom scratched my legs while I tried to find a comfortable position to sit.

Priest Kashi touched my arm with his useful hand, and I stopped fidgeting. "Priest Kashi, my orders were to kill you," I said gravely. "I am going to hide you instead." I removed the gold chain around his neck and looked for anything else that would identify him. "I will keep the chain safe and return to you when the time is right."

The priest traced something on my arm. He could not speak. *Was he writing instead?* "Are you writing me a message?"

He blinked his eyes. I took that as a yes. He traced each letter on my arm. I had studied the Kashgar language. However, it took a long time for me to decipher the message due to my lack of proficiency and the priest's shaking handwriting. "Su . . .

gandha . . . is power . . . ful." I let that sink in. "Powerful, how?" I asked.

He gestured with his unaffected hand. He did not know.

"Did you sense her power when you sought her?"

He nodded gently and shut his eyes. The exercise of writing those simple words had worn him. Her power, in whatever form, had kept Sugandha safe until now. I hoped it would continue to protect her till I found her.

I had sent a message ahead to my commander to find a healer. We met in an isolated area that evening. "I found an elderly woman willing to care for him," he said. After exchanging other news, we transferred the priest to his bullock cart.

"Priest Kashi, I hope to unite you with your wife and family. Until then, stay hidden and get well," I said. A lone tear flowed down his left eye.

I returned to the castle as the moon rose. "Brother, the chief is looking for us," Aggabodhi greeted me as I sat down to eat. I ate quickly and went with him.

We found the chief in a medium-sized room with a round rosewood table. I noticed a few other men seated at the table. A young man about Aggabodhi's age eyed me shyly. I registered his rich clothes.

"Did you take care of it?" asked the chief.

I dipped my head, not betraying my anger at him.

"Good, get some rest. I have more work for you tomorrow."

I bowed and turned to go, but Aggabodhi stood rooted to the spot, his eyes on the young man. I glanced at the boy dressed in silk clothes again. I had never seen him before. Draping my arm over Aggabodhi's shoulder, I dragged the shocked prince outside.

"Bodhi, what happened?"

"That was my father's bastard. That is who they are parading as me," said Aggabodhi.

SUGANDHA

SUMMER YEAR 1

I struggled against the man holding me tightly across the shoulders. His fingernails dug into my skin as he pulled me closer. His unpleasant body odor nearly caused me to retch. I had mentioned Uncle Ori once in my conversation with the priest. *How did these men find me?*

"What do you know about Guru Ori's niece?" asked the other man in the shadows.

I had lied so many times in the past few months that I did not think twice about lying again. "Someone I knew saw her in Tipti." The man holding me tightened his grip.

"Who saw her there? When did they see her?" asked the other man in the shadows.

"I worked as a swordsmith's apprentice. One of the men who came to our workshop to repair his weapon mentioned seeing the girl." I worried the man holding me would hear my treacherous heartbeat and know I lied.

"You are lying. Drown him."

"No," I screamed. I glanced at the water in fear. The image of Selva drowning in the river, the boy I had pretended to be, flashed in my head. Something strange happened then.

"You will be safe with me," the water whispered.

"What do you know about Guru Ori's niece?" asked the man in the shadows, taking a step forward.

"I don't know anything else," I said, still eyeing the water. *Was I going mad?*

"Come to me," it whispered. I was going crazy.

The man in the shadows approached me and punched my face. My head swung to the side while the other man held me in an iron grip. Curse them. *Did he break my nose?* Blood oozed out of my nostrils, and I could not even raise my hand to wipe it.

"She is in Tipti," I screamed while I tried to kick the man in front. He jumped aside to avoid me.

"Drown him," he repeated ominously.

The man with the unpleasant body odor pulled my arm, dragging me down the stairs. I sunk my teeth into his fleshy arms. He yelped and slapped me hard. My ears rang.

Yelling, the second man came to his aid. Both men tugged me along, my feet scraping the ground. I pondered how they found me. Then it came to me. It must be the priest with the large mole. I spoke to the priest about my uncle. He sent these men.

I was tired of hiding. Tired of not living. I would let them drown me. I stopped fighting. I allowed them to pull me into chest-high water. One of the men dunked my head into the water and held it there.

"What do you know about Sugandha?" he shouted.

I forgot to breathe, preparing to die. Water rocked me. An image of a woman rocking a child drifted into my mind. *Mother?* Warmth and comfort spread in my stomach. **"You are strong,"** a voice whispered in my head. I would not surrender. I straightened up with water dripping down my body and pushed my elbows away to break free of his arm shackle. I lifted my arms, and the water swirled around their feet. I watched the confusion in their eyes.

"Who sent you to me?" I demanded.

Both men tried to climb the stairs, but I tugged them deeper into the pond like I was pulling a rope attached to them. I did not know how I did it. Their confusion turned to panic. "I can drown you with a flick of my fingers." I flicked my finger, and water rose to their necks. It felt heady to have this kind of power over two grown men. I need not fear them anymore. "Don't test my patience."

"The priest," one of them stuttered.

"Why?" I asked. I let the water reach his chin.

The man eyed my fingers with trepidation. "We came to fetch the priest on Guru Ori's orders and were waiting for him outside. He said a boy hiding inside the temple knew where we could find Guru Ori's niece."

The first time I uttered my uncle's name in over six months to a stranger, he betrayed me. I could trust no one. My loneliness threatened to choke me. Water climbed up and covered their mouths. I could kill them both. They tilted their heads up and screamed for mercy. I clenched my fist. *I was not a murderer.* I took a deep breath to calm myself. "Stay in the water till I leave. If you try to follow me, I will drown you."

I did not know if I could control the water once I stepped on land, but neither man attempted to follow me. I climbed a tree next to the courtyard wall, scrambled down its trunk, and vaulted over the wall. Then I went to find the priest with the large mole who set these men upon me.

I had no difficulty finding him because he stood outside his door watching the temple. When his eyes fell on me, my wet clothes clinging to my body, he stood rooted to the ground in shock.

"You sent assassins after me," I hissed.

"I tried to save my own life," he mumbled.

I furrowed my brows in confusion. "Why was your life in danger?"

The priest sighed. "Guru Ori has been recruiting priests to find his niece. These priests have disappeared, including one from the neighboring village. His wife has not heard from him in over two months. We suspect he is dead."

"My un—" I stopped in time before I revealed Ori was my uncle. I swallowed and tried again. "Guru Ori is killing priests as a sacrifice?"

The priest shuffled his feet. "In a way, he is. His niece must be under a protective spell. My guess is he is recruiting priests to break the spell. And the priests are dying in that process. Those two men showed up on my doorstep to escort me to Guru Ori. More skilled priests than I have failed in locating his niece. I did not want to die trying. When I heard you mention Guru Ori, I told Ori's men about you. I apologize for putting your life in danger, but somehow, you have managed to escape their clutches. I might not be so lucky. They will return to capture me, so I am going into hiding." He ran inside his house, and I followed him.

"Do you know why Guru Ori is looking for his niece?"

He tossed clothes and other essentials into a sack. "An uncle searching for his missing niece is normal. I have heard rumors about Ori's sister, but I don't want to repeat any falsehoods."

Ori's sister? My mother? "What rumors?" I asked.

He paused in his action. "Why are you interested in this?" His eyes widened slightly. "Are you—? No, don't tell me. I heard Ori's sister was adopted by his father; her true parentage remains a mystery and must tie in with the reason he is looking for his niece."

Adopted? My head spun. I had no recollection of my parents. My grandfather had cared for me like I was his own. No, this rumor could not be true.

"Don't hover here. Leave," the priest said. I stood rooted inside his house, unable to move. I felt like I was losing my grandfather again. The priest reached the door and then turned to look at me. "Come, child. Let us get to safety before Ori's men come looking for us."

With a heavy heart, I followed him. I did not trust this priest with the large mole who had sent killers after me. But I wanted to learn more about my family. We blended into the dark. A light rain misted my already wet skin. We walked across a field with waist-high plants I did not recognize, mud squelching under our feet. I could hear frogs croak, welcoming the rain.

"How did you escape the clutches of those two men? They were seasoned warriors," said the priest.

"I pushed them into the temple pond," I said, shrugging my shoulders.

"Pushed? How could you push two grown men?" He eyed my wet clothes.

I shrugged again. I still did not understand what had happened. *Did the water aid me? Was that what it was?* I had drawn some kind of power from the pond.

"How did you do it?" the priest persisted in his questioning.

"It felt like the water wanted to help me," I said tentatively. I sounded like a village idiot telling tall tales.

"A Sunkosh river tributary feeds the temple pond," he whispered with awe. *Why did that matter?* "Are you a child of the river?" he asked. *Child of what?*

As I contemplated my connection with water, I heard the thundering of feet. Before I could react, someone threw a jute sack over my head, and my hands were bound roughly.

"Obey our orders, and I will spare your life," a hoarse voice ordered.

ATUL

WINTER YEAR 2

"Your father's bastard?" I asked. Revulsion flashed across Aggabodhi's face as he nodded. I was a baseborn son, too, and I was not worthy of being the Heir to Malla. *Would Aggabodhi be repulsed if he knew my story?* Just thinking these thoughts seemed like a dishonor to my mother. Except for the momentary weakness that resulted in my birth, my mother had led a blemish-free life. The moon shone brightly with no regard for the state of my mind.

"He has grown in the last two years, but I recognized him. My father kept a concubine, a dancer of renowned beauty. My mother tolerated the relationship on the condition that my father did not marry the dancer. The dancer bore him a son. While my father never acknowledged him, he resembled my father in looks, so there was no denying his paternity. My mother hated that boy while she lived. She would pray that I grew to look less like her and more like my father. Much to her chagrin, my likeness to her increased."

I resembled my mother as well. In my case, that was a blessing because it hid my parentage. "If fake Aggabodhi is your

127

half-brother and resembles your father, that makes our quest harder."

"I resemble the last queen of Kashgar. Those who knew my mother would recognize me," said Aggabodhi. For his sake, I hoped his mother was a beloved queen like mine.

I drew a circle on my palm as I collected my thoughts. "Two years have passed since you fled Kashgar. With the passage of time, memories become faulty. And resembling the last king is more potent than resembling the queen," I said. "However, you still are the oldest son of the dead king, so your claim to the crown takes precedence over his. Chief Jeevahatta would contest that claim. He would want to install your half-brother on the throne and rule the kingdom through him. Chief Vikramasinha wants his grandson on the throne and would not be inclined to support your claim. But there is a path for us. When the council gathers, and these two chiefs stake their claims, their differences will split the royal men into two camps. You can then emerge as the real heir to the throne, the eldest trueborn son of King Rajasuriya. We can peel support from both camps."

A strange smile twisted Aggabodhi's face. "Or I can kill that bastard for thinking himself worthy of the crown." Every word of his stabbed my heart. In my nightmares, I had imagined these words uttered behind my back. Hearing someone close to me say them in front of me tore my spirit to shreds. Others may react similarly if they find out about my birth father. *Why did I agree to be crowned as king in waiting?*

Calling his brother a bastard was not the worst of his offenses. I hid my turmoil and drew myself to my full height, towering over Aggabodhi. "He is your brother," I admonished him. "I cannot condone kin slaying."

Color crept up his neck. "Do you want me to crown him myself?"

"Why don't we find out what the poor boy wants? Maybe he has no interest in ruling and will support your claim."

"My mother should have killed him before he rose to contest me," Aggabodhi said scornfully and started walking away.

I tugged his arm to pull him back. "Enough. I won't hear of you turning into a murderer. If you face him on a battlefield, fight like a warrior. Outside of that, he is your kin."

Aggabodhi stared at me, and I met his gaze. He lowered his eyes first. "How does a younger brother apologize to his older brother?"

I let go of Aggabodhi. My mind traveled to my older brother, Nala. He had ruled as King of Padi for most of my life, and I had worshiped him. While Uncle Jay radiated power like the sun, Nala emanated a gentle strength like a warm blanket on a cold night. A gentleness that led people to underestimate his vigor and sharp intellect. His friends felt an urge to protect him while his foes thought him vulnerable. Nala used this to his advantage to rule wisely, ensuring all his subjects prospered under him.

Unfortunately, my brother died in front of me, and I failed to protect him. The agony from that memory twisted my stomach, so I snatched a happier one. "How do you apologize? By taking a beating on the training ground. I was much younger than my older brother. Once, when I was being obnoxious, he offered to train with me. Every punch of his that landed taught me a valuable lesson I have not forgotten. I have not held a sword properly in ages. Are you up for some sparring?"

Aggabodhi grinned. "I won't be easy to beat. I was trained by a skilled warrior. You."

"I still have some secrets I have not revealed."

With Dayalu and Pusha keeping watch, we found a secluded place to train. "Locals consider this place haunted, so we won't be bothered," said Aggabodhi.

Instead of replying, I lunged at him. Our swords, gleaming like silver threads in the moonlight, met in a symphony of clashing metal. The night breeze carried a hint of jasmine, mingling with the scent of dew-kissed earth.

At first, we fought like two baby elephants learning to walk. Our movements were uncoordinated. But as time went on, my body and weapon moved as one. My eyes, focused and unwavering, locked onto Aggabodhi, analyzing every move, every shift in stance.

His attacks grew swift and daring, a reflection of his youthful vigor and eagerness to prove himself. He parried with a boldness that kept me on my toes. My cousin had a similar recklessness in him.

For a blink of an eye, I traveled back to Malla, training with my cousin under my uncle's watchful eyes. Aggabodhi's laughter filled the air as he struck my sword, bringing me back to the present.

I forgot my worries and let my training take over. My body moved like a river, keeping Aggabodhi guessing my direction. I watched him like a predator, willing him to make a mistake. He gave me no ground, but I was patient. As I sensed his restlessness, I slowed down slightly. Aggabodhi sensed an opportunity and leaped at me. I was waiting for it, so I sidestepped deftly and disarmed him. As his sword clattered to the ground, I draped my arm around his shoulders.

"You fight like a beast, with such precision, making no mistakes," said Aggabodhi, his eyes lighting up.

"You matched me every step of the way," I said, wiping the sweat on my forehead.

He picked up his sword, and we returned to our quarters.

"Bodhi, if you intend to be a king, you are the king of all your people. Don't forget that. You decide when to protect and when to punish. Wielding such power can corrupt one's mind. I want you to be on guard."

"If I am ever king. The curse must be real," Aggabodhi sighed.

"What curse?" I asked, my mind still on our fight.

"Whenever something went wrong, my father would lament

a curse cast by his step-grandmother. I don't know if there is any truth to it."

"We know of a girl under an unbreakable protective spell. A curse would not surprise me," I said. I wanted to face my foes on a battlefield. I was not trained to fight enemies casting spells. It would be impossible to win against someone wielding mystical powers. "Why would this grandmother curse your father?" I asked.

"She might have cursed my family. I never knew the complete story. When my grandfather's half-brother died, his heartbroken mother blamed her stepson for the death and cursed him. Killing half-brothers runs in the family," jested Aggabodhi.

"You have been calling me brother. Should I be worried?"

"Sleep with a dagger, Brother," he said with a smile.

"If you come armed with curses, little help will the dagger be," I said, giving him a friendly shove.

"Fortunately for you, I was trained in Malla by folks completely oblivious to magic."

I laughed, releasing the tight knot in my stomach. Then, a more serious concern occurred to me. "Bodhi, would this half-brother of yours recognize you?

Aggabodhi gaped at me with his mouth open. I took that as an affirmative. "Let us hope he ignores servants like most noblemen. Still, it is better to be cautious. Stay away from him. If you come in his presence, blend into the shadows."

The next morning, Chief Jeevahatta sent for me. I dressed hastily and went with his servant. When I arrived, the chief paced the room, and I dipped my head. I was growing tired of all the bowing to undeserving men.

Noblemen in Malla inspired respect by virtue of their noble character. Uncle Jay, King of Malla, would command the attention of every man when he walked into a room. I had seen grown men talk about my uncle in reverence and describe his prowess on a battlefield with awe. None of the Kashgar nobles I had met so far had risen to that.

"I want you and your brother to be sparring partners for Prince Aggabodhi. I only have a handful of boys his age in my army, and they could not tell the pointy end of a sword if it stabbed them in their stomach," said Chief Jeevahatta.

I knew Aggabodhi could not spar with his brother, so I lied. "My brother was taken ill last night, my lord. But I will be honored to train with the prince."

The chief gestured for me to come closer. "The prince needs his confidence built up. Go easy on him."

I nodded my understanding, making a mental note of this weakness. I hurried back to my quarters and found Aggabodhi lying on his blanket. "Bodhi, since you are ill, don't work too hard," I said.

He stared at me blankly for a moment. Then he curled up. "My body aches everywhere. I will stay here for some more time."

"I am training with the prince," I whispered and left.

Yesterday, I had briefly glanced at the fake Aggabodhi while he sat beside others. Today, a child stood before me in the training yard, holding his sword like he wished it would vanish. *How old was this boy? Twelve or thirteen? Why would anyone think he is sixteen?* Ordinary folks might not remember their birthdays. But princes were a different story. Their birth was recorded and celebrated.

The fake prince stared at me, and I realized I had not greeted him properly. I bowed from my waist. "It is an honor to train with you, my lord."

"You are very tall," he replied.

I almost stated that I took after my father in height. The father who had claimed me and gave me his name, King Atul, was of medium size. I inherited my stature from my birth father, Rish Vindhya. But revealing that would be disclosing that I was born out of wedlock. So, I simply bowed again.

"Shall we start?" he asked as if I led him to slaughter. I noticed he had a tooth missing. *Did he still have his milk teeth?*

"I will start with simple attacks. Show me what you can do, my lord," I said and began with a simple forward thrust with slow footwork. Instead of blocking my attack, the fake prince shut his eyes and squealed. The master in training came over to check what was going on.

"Boy, if you hurt the prince, I will skin you alive," he threatened me while gripping the hilt of his sword tightly.

"Master, I will ensure no harm comes to the prince," I said meekly.

"Continue," he said, hovering nearby. The prince trembled in his presence.

I made a quick decision. "My lord, let us drop our weapons and do some footwork."

"Footwork?"

"Yes, please move with me. Forward and backward. Left and right. Forward and backward." I made it into a game, and after some tentativeness, the boy eagerly jumped side to side.

"Slowly, my lord," I said with a grin. I found some wooden swords for us to train with. "When you step forward, strike. When you retreat, block."

"I like you," he said with a child's simplicity.

"I am blessed," I said more sincerely than I intended, taking a liking to him as well.

"I want you to be my guard."

"Guard?"

He came closer and whispered. "I think my present guard will run away if someone attacks me. You seem different. Will you swear to protect me with your life?"

SUGANDHA

SUMMER YEAR 1

Something tiny crawled on my neck. *Was it a spider that made its home in the musty jute bag?* I inhaled small grain particles, remnants of the rice once stored in the bag covering my head.

"Our orders were to bring the priest. What do we do with the boy?" someone asked. By boy, I assumed he meant me. The voice did not sound like the men I had nearly drowned in the temple pond. How many men did my uncle send to recruit priests?

Before I could find a suitable reply, the priest with the large mole responded. "She—he is my nephew. Please bring him along." Exactly what I needed in my life. Another man who claimed to be my uncle. He had thrown me to the wolves once to save his own life. I knew he would do the same again. I did not know if my grandfather's blessings would still protect me. I needed to find a way to escape these men before they took me to my other uncle.

"Start walking," a voice ordered while shoving me in the back. After stumbling along for a few feet, I managed to put one foot in front of the other.

The misty rain continued to descend from the sky, reminding me of Parimala's tears when she learned my true identity. I had pretended to be her fiancé and shattered the poor girl's heart for my selfish reasons. *How could I blame the priest with the large mole for acting in his own interest?*

A light breeze ruffled the moisture-laden leaves, and the raindrops falling from them echoed the rain. I heard the soft tinkle of bells and a sound like the creak of a wooden door. *Were we near a village?* The plodding of hooves on the damp earth changed my mind. A cart was approaching us.

I peered through the thick sack. With the darkness and rain, I could not see anything. *Should I scream for help? Would they come to the rescue of strangers?* Before I could decide, the rattling of the wheels slowed down. I sensed no panic from the men who had captured us. *Did they know the people arriving in the cart?*

"Who are you? Where are you taking us?" asked the priest with the large mole while our captors pulled us to a stop.

"Get in," said one of them as he shoved me into the cart. I crawled in with my tied arms. I stopped next to a pile of bags filled with supplies. Before I could straighten to a seated position, the priest tumbled onto my back, causing me to land on my stomach. The heavier man struggled to sit up. I could barely breathe, with his weight crushing my lungs. Slowly, I pushed him away and rolled onto my side. I thought one of the guards would climb in after us, but no one did. They must consider us too weak to escape.

The cart started moving again. "Who are these men? Where are they taking us?" I repeated the questions he had asked earlier.

"I don't know," came his muffled reply. After a long pause, he added, "I don't think these are Ori's men." *Not Ori's men? Who else captured priests? What should I do?* I did not trust this priest. I suspected he had guessed my secret. What would he do with this knowledge? If it kept him safe, he would reveal it.

Would my grandfather's blessing still protect me from my uncle?

The priest with the large mole had hinted at a rumor surrounding my mother. I remembered my dream of Purohit Parivan and a man who looked remarkably like a younger version of my grandfather.

In my vision, Purohit Parivan had handed a baby to my grandfather. *Was that baby me or my mother?* Based on my grandfather's appearance, I would guess that vision had occurred when he was in his third decade of life. That had been decades before I was born. *Did someone ask my grandfather to foster my mother?*

My grandfather had told me my parents had perished in an illness. *Was that even true? How did my parents die?* All these questions with no answers frustrated me. And since when had I gained this mysterious connection with the river? *Why did my grandfather not share his knowledge with me while he lived?* With Purohit Parivan also dead, I might never learn the answers unless I confronted Uncle Ori. I did not cherish that prospect.

The rocking motion of the cart lulled me to sleep.

∼

"She does not know her own powers," said a male voice.

"Why haven't you sought her?" asked another.

"I am on the run. She is safer where she is. When the time is ripe, I will seek her."

"Don't wait too long. We may miss the window to set right the wrongs of the past."

∼

I bumped my head against the wall of the cart and woke up. A dull throbbing pain thudded in my skull. Some vague conversations from my dreams stirred in my head. Before I could make sense of it, the cart came to a stop. A man drew the curtain covering the opening.

"Get down. There is a pond a few yards from here for you to wash. We have a long journey ahead today."

I could hear the priest sliding through the opening as someone tugged his arm. Thud. Did he fall? Before I could react, an arm held my elbow and dragged me out. I managed to land on my feet. A man yanked the sack over my head, and I blinked my eyes. I noticed three men of varying ages. All bore scars on their faces, necks, or arms. One of them untied my arms and shoved me in the direction of the pond.

"Take your uncle along. Don't think about escaping. Our arrows will find your hearts."

That was when I heard the loud moan. The priest lay on the ground with one leg extended out.

"Uncle, are you hurt?" I said and squatted down beside him.

"I have twisted my leg," he said with a grimace.

I moved his dhoti and observed his swollen ankle. Gently, my fingers traced the contours of his ankle. His breath caught as I navigated his pain spots. I did not sense any broken bones, but I could make him a makeshift compress to alleviate his suffering.

"I need to gather some herbs for his leg," I said.

"No, we don't have time to linger. You only have time to get a drink of water," came the answer.

"Please, my uncle is in agony and might not endure the long journey," I pleaded.

"Do it quickly. We cannot wait here for long," the man relented.

My grandfather had taken me with him to gather medicinal plants, so I strolled around the wild shrubs, looking for leaves to reduce his swelling. I smashed the leaves I found and tied them around the priest's ankle with a cloth I tore from my dhoti. I helped him up slowly.

The priest leaned on me with his face contorted in agony as I guided us to the small pond. One of the men followed us with two horses. The cart driver was already at the pond watering his oxen. That meant four men made up our escort, including the cart driver.

At the edge of the pond, I held the priest's hand as he moved close to the water. His pain momentarily forgotten, he offered me a soft smile. "You remind me of your grandfather," he muttered.

"My grandfather?" A sudden fear threatened to choke me. I suspected that he had guessed my identity. But to hear him state it twisted my stomach.

"Don't worry. Your secret is safe with me. I won't forget this kindness," he whispered with warmth. I asked him no questions about my grandfather to avoid confirming his belief about me.

I helped him squat by the shore. Using both his hands as a cup, he drank greedily and washed his face. After ensuring he was in no danger of falling, I waded into the water. I stood, waiting for energy from the water to course through my body like it had at the temple pond. Nothing happened. Curse the gods. *Did this power come and go as it pleased?*

I rinsed my face and neck and drank the water. The guard, a man with long hair, chatted with the cart driver while the animals drank deeply. With all these men around, I could not head to a bush to relieve myself. I moved to a corner of the pond, untied the dhoti tied around my waist, and took care of my duty. I moved away from that spot to scrub my legs clean and draped the cloth back.

"Time to go," yelled the guard with the long hair.

Could I push him into the water and run? I scanned the surroundings and noticed the archer beside the cart with a bow strung over his shoulder. The trees around me would offer no protection against an arrow. And for a strange reason, I felt reluctant to leave the hurt priest behind.

Why did I feel compassion for a man who had betrayed me once—who might betray me again? What would my grandfather do in my situation? The answer came to me clearly. He would aid the priest. Setting aside my escape plans, I assisted the priest back to the shore. Our guards gave us a banana each. I peeled the bruised fruit and ate it hungrily. My stomach growled for more food. They tied our hands. I helped the priest climb in and heaved myself up after him.

"If they were taking us to Ori, we would have crossed the river. Instead, they are taking us north," whispered the priest. The sun's rays reached me through the tiny gaps in the thatched walls on the right side of the cart.

"North? Are they taking us to Tipti?" I asked. The rebels still held the fort there.

"If we keep following the river north, they might take us to Chief Vikramasinha." He was the other powerful chief who ruled Kashgar. After the rebels took over Tipti, he went into hiding with his family.

What did he want with the priest? What would he do with me? My grandfather's blessings only protected me from my uncle. If the priest revealed me as Ori's niece, would the chief trade me to Ori? I could not imagine he had any use for me, whether he knew my identity or not.

Along with the sun, the heat inside the cart also rose. Though we no longer had a sack covering our faces to suffocate our breath, sweat still trickled down my neck. The coarse wooden bed, worn down by countless journeys, offered no respite from the vibrations that shot through my body. The jagged edges of the wooden planks pressed harshly against my skin.

I was sure the priest felt each jolt of the carriage in his bones. I tried to help him find the most comfortable position against the battering. He curled up on the long side and shut his eyes against the pain. I worried about him as if he were my child who needed rest. I puzzled over this feeling toward a man who had given me up to assassins.

I caught glimpses of the river through the gaps in the planks. That meant they were taking us north. I could hear the hooves of the horses trotting alongside our cart. I peeked through the planks again. The man with the long hair and the archer rode on either side of the carriage. The other guard sat beside the cart driver. These men would catch me if I tried to escape now.

At night, I could attempt to roll off the cart. They might not notice me in the dark. Like a leaf tossed in the wind, my mind oscillated between staying with the priest and escaping. After living with Parimala's family for months, I realized I detested being alone. The known danger of the priest seemed better than roaming the country on my own.

When the sun disappeared, the cart halted again. I stayed alert. The men dragged me out and then reached out to pull the priest.

"My uncle is hurt. Please allow me to help him down," I protested.

"I am a temple priest. You are treating me like a common criminal," chimed in the priest.

"Purohit, you are more dangerous than a thief. I don't have to worry about a robber cursing me," answered one of the men.

"Casting a curse exacts a toll on me. Why would I waste it on you?" retorted the priest.

"Be thankful we are not gagging you," the man with the long hair answered. Still, he allowed me to help the priest down. They untied our hands and gave us some old rice to eat. I ate the stale and dry food, leaving not a single morsel.

The men tied us to the same tree trunk. "If you try to escape, I will break every bone in your legs." Laughing at their twisted humor, they laid down to rest for the night, taking turns to watch.

The priest with the large mole sat propped against the gnarled trunk, all energy drained out of him. "Uncle, how is your leg?"

He sighed in response.

"What does Chief Vikramasinha want with you?"

He made no response for a while. I thought he fell asleep. I moved around as ants crawled up my leg. It would be a long night. "He will want to know what Guru Ori's secret is."

While my grandfather rarely used his mystical powers, I knew there were *mantras* that would give one access to another's dreams, plant a vision, or communicate with them. Purohit Parivan had used it to reach me. *What spells could the priest with the large mole cast?*

The night grew quiet. The man keeping the first watch snored softly. "I had a vision last night," murmured the priest. My mind wandered to a warm bed and a roof over my head. "A vision about you," the priest continued. I hauled up my head. "Death follows you."

ATUL

WINTER YEAR 2

"You did what?" screamed Aggabodhi.

"Quiet, Bodhi," I said sternly, drawing him aside to a secluded spot on the grounds.

"You swore an oath to protect that bastard?" spit Aggabodhi, color flooding his face.

"Yes," I said forcefully, tired of Aggabodhi addressing his brother as a baseborn. I knew my own birth clouded my mind, but the fake prince and I had no choice in the matter. We were both victims of our parents' whims.

"Did you also swear to seat him on the throne?" hissed Aggabodhi, his index finger digging into my chest.

"Careful, Bodhi. You are forgetting I am older than you."

He huffed and crossed his arms.

"The prince asked me to join his guard. I could not refuse him," I said, forcing myself to be calm. Aggabodhi shifted away from me. "I think this is to our advantage. Whenever Chief Jeevahatta visits the royal council, he will bring the fake prince with him. Now, I will be part of the entourage. And I will make sure you can come along too, as long as you can stay concealed from your brother."

"You swore an oath to protect the fake prince with your life," repeated Aggabodhi.

"I did. Why does this bother you? I forbade you from killing your brother. He is still a child. I can crown you without us resorting to kin slaying."

"I am starting to doubt your loyalty—"

"My loyalty?" I asked, heat coating my words. "I left my wives and son to travel with you. I am pretending to be a foot soldier and sleeping on the ground, all for the sake of restoring you to your rightful place on the throne. You doubt my loyalty?"

My wife, Vibha, had not wanted me to leave. Childless, she had wanted me to stay until she got pregnant. We had tried for many months at all times—night and midmorning—but nothing had happened.

Sometimes, I could not even face her while we did the deed, so we would turn away from each other. The exhausting act had killed any romance. I had felt guilty boarding that ship and setting sail to Kashgar, knowing Vibha desperately wanted a child. I drew to my full height, towering over Aggabodhi. I resisted the urge to punch his face as he stared at me with trembling lips.

He lowered his head, rubbing his forehead. "I apologize, Brother. Since seeing that baseborn son of my father, my worries have intensified. My aunt, Princess Malathi, who would have recognized me, is dead. We cannot find my father's servant. How will we prove I am the legitimate prince to win the support of the chiefs?"

I touched his shoulder. "Bodhi, I will befriend your half-brother and find out more details from him. Is his mother alive?"

"His mother? The dancer? She was still alive when I fled Kashgar," he said, turning toward me.

"Let me ask my men to find her. In the coming days, I will spend more time with the prince and sleep in his castle. During my absence, maintain the pretense of being a simple soldier and keep your patience."

Aggabodhi grunted his affirmation.

As if summoned by magic, Dayalu, one of my guards, appeared by my side as I made my way back to the fake Aggabodhi. "I heard you have become a sworn guard for the prince," he said with a smile.

"Yes. Matters took a turn this morning. As a veteran in protecting princes, do you have any advice for me?"

His grin broadened. "If your prince is anything like mine, you have your hands full. You cannot sleep a wink because he would insist on putting himself in danger."

I laughed. "My prince is still a child. I doubt he will lead us into war or go on clandestine missions."

"In that case, keeping your eyes and ears open would be sufficient," he answered.

I had a task for him. "King Rajasuriya kept a concubine, a dancer, who begot him a son. Find out what happened to the mother and child."

I returned to the fake Aggabodhi. While I walked along a dark hallway to his chamber, a hand grabbed my shoulder. "Guard, what is your name?" asked a stern voice.

I spun to face the commander of Chief Jeevahatta's small army. The man before me was no Kapil Biha, the beloved Malla Chief Guard. While Chief Guard Kapil looked like he could move mountains, the man who stopped me looked like he would have trouble climbing stairs.

I gave him the name Aggabodhi had picked for me. "My mother named me after my king," I said. Not a lie. My mother had named me after King Atul, though I hoped the man assumed I was named after King Rajasuriya. The commander stared at me with a frown. "You can call me Suriya," I added.

He dropped his hand from my shoulder and frowned. "I cannot call you by that name. That would be disrespectful to our last king. What name should I use for you?" He paused while I waited. "I will come up with something," he said, giving up shortly. I silently applauded Aggabodhi for choosing this name. No one wanted to use it, sparing me the effort to answer to it. "I heard you joined the prince's guard."

I dipped my head but said nothing.

"If any harm befalls the prince on your watch, I will behead you publicly," he threatened while twisting his mustache. The gesture would have looked menacing on a warrior. On him, with his large belly heaving with each breath, it reminded me that I could outrun him.

Still, I did not want to make him my enemy. "I will safeguard the prince with my life," I said with a bow.

His face glistened with sweat as he stared at me intensely. I assumed a humble posture. "You are on guard duty till midnight," he ordered.

I inclined my head in acknowledgment and went to find the prince.

"Guard, come join me for my midday meal. I have too much food," greeted the prince. He sat at a large rosewood table, his legs swinging front to back.

A rich tapestry of vegetables, succulent seafood, and fragrant rice dishes adorned the surface. "Freshly caught fish from the Sunkosh River," he said as he saw me regarding the food. The spread was smaller than what I ate in Malla but better than the fare they served the soldiers here.

"I will be honored," I said. We were in a fortified castle, so I would not be negligent in my guard duty if I ate with him. A servant handed me a plate, and I thanked him and accepted it. Seated on the ground, I relished eating the pepper-crusted fish and the sweet and spicy mango relish on the side.

"You never told me your name," said the prince as he nibbled his food.

"My mother named me after the king," I repeated my story.

"You can call me Suriya."

"That is my father's name. I cannot address you by that," he said, chewing loudly. "What is your favorite weapon?"

Puzzled by his question, I said, "Sword."

"I will call you *Sword* then," he said, grinning ear to ear.

I chuckled. "That is a clever name. Though, if we are in the weapons room, your servants might rush to hand you a blade."

"As long as you answer to that name, I don't care," the boy replied callously. If he were in real trouble, yelling *sword* would not be the wisest choice. I decided to worry about this later.

The fake Aggabodhi's training progressed slowly. After a few minutes of practice, he lost interest and wanted to do something else. Without mastering the basics, he was not ready for the more advanced moves, so that limited what I could teach him. Aggabodhi, at fourteen, had a lot more discipline than this prince at twelve or thirteen. Placed side by side, I hoped the nobles would choose Aggabodhi over this untrained child.

That night, I stood guard by the door, bored of standing still. Light from a lone brass lamp flickered in the room. "Are your parents alive?" asked the boy from under his bed sheets.

My parents—my father, King Atul, who claimed me and after whom I was named, died before my birth—my mother, Queen Meera, and my birth father, Rish Vindhya, lived in Magadha.

I had resented my mother, not always, but for long periods of my childhood. Growing up in Malla with my uncle, I had felt loved and safe. My mother had visited often. When she had, she would pull me onto her lap and teach me songs from her childhood.

Then, the year I turned eight, I had realized that my older brothers and sister lived with my mother, and I only saw her for brief visits. When she had arrived in Malla that year, I had clung to her, never letting her out of my sight.

On the day of her departure, I had buried my face in her

stomach, sobbing, begging her to stay with me. With tears in her eyes, she had freed herself from my clasp, promising to return. I had fallen on the floor, thrashing and screaming. My mother had still left me, and I had started hating myself.

A mother's love is supposed to be unconditional. If my mother did not love me enough to stay, I felt unlovable, like a monster. The next time my mother visited, I had not let her pull me onto her lap. I had remained distant, wanting her to prove how much she loved me. I had needed that demonstration of her affection so much that it had terrified me. So I had pushed her away. In my young eyes, it had felt like she had never tried enough.

A few years later, she had broken my heart again by confessing the secret about my birth. She had shattered my world by revealing I was not the son of King Atul, my namesake. I was the son of her guard, Rish Vindhya.

I had understood why she had sent me away. I reminded her of her infidelity. I knew that was not the only reason. She had worried I would resemble my birth father and had decided I was safer in Malla with my uncle. What my head had understood, my heart had not. I had struggled to forgive her and my birth father, Rish Vindhya, though I had known they both loved me in their own ways.

My mother had traveled to Malla to send me off on this journey. I remembered the last conversation I had with her. "You are a reflection of your uncle in action," she had said.

"I am a poor imitation," I had answered. She had smiled then in amusement. "What is funny, Mother?"

"I remember my brother as a nineteen-year-old boy. He was no different from you with even rougher edges," she had replied.

While all my other discussions had been about seating Aggabodhi on the Kashgar throne, my mother had offered a different view. "Atul, do what is best for the people of Kashgar."

That was what set her apart from others. She put the people of Magadha over everything. While I struggled with the right thing to do, her instincts never led her astray. She could navigate royal relations with an ease that rivaled a skilled ship captain steering a ship through a rocky shore.

I wished I could talk to her about the doubts plaguing me. Not all of them. It would be hurtful to bring up my birth with her. In all other matters of the crown, her insight would be invaluable. Generally, a king who can unite the kingdom and rule wisely would be in the interests of the people. Aggabodhi, given time and surrounded by good advisors, could be that king.

I realized my mind had wandered into the past. Fake Aggabodhi gazed at me, waiting for my answer.

I had almost forgotten his question in my meandering. He had asked about my parents. I replied, "My mother is alive."

He sighed and turned away from me. I felt sorry for the boy. He was a pawn in royal chess, and no one looked out for his interest.

Sensing a chance to probe him about his mother, I asked, "I know King Rajasuriya perished in the fight against the rebels. How about your mother?"

A sob escaped him. "My lord?" I approached him. He looked tiny among the silk sheets. A strange urge to protect this child flooded my mind. I knew Aggabodhi would hurl more insults at me if he found out. He would be right to criticize me. I could not let this boy jeopardize our mission.

"My mother," he paused with a hiccup. Aggabodhi had lost his mother as a child. But the fake prince's mother likely still lived. Would he reveal that truth? "A woman took care of me since I was a baby. She is alive, but I have not seen her for two years. Will you bring her to me?" I saw tears streaming down his cheek.

SUGANDHA

SUMMER YEAR 1

"Two horses and two oxen. This is our lucky day," whispered a voice in the dark.

Hearing it, I opened my eyes a slit. Silhouetted against the dark sky, I found my captors asleep on the ground in front of me. I heard faint footsteps from behind me. I guessed the newcomers did not see me or the priest tied to the trees. Since the death of King Rajasuriya, robbers roamed the land freely. *What should I do? Allow them to steal or alert my captors?*

"Kill the sleeping men and snatch their possessions," said another voice closer to me.

That made my decision. I uttered an unearthly scream, mimicking a wolf howling in pain. My captors sat up in confusion. The footsteps behind me halted. The guard with the long hair scanned the surroundings. When his eyes swept past me, I signaled to him with my eyebrows. He did not seem to notice my gesture. Curse it. The intruders likely stopped a few feet behind me. If I gave my location away by talking, they would fall upon me in no time.

The man with the long hair peered past me, and I mouthed thieves. Finally, as if drawn by my will, he met my gaze. With a slight tilt of my head, I pointed behind me. He seemed to understand.

He jumped and drew his sword, signaling to the others. The archer grabbed his bow and slung his quiver over his shoulder. Breathing in heaving gasps, one of the intruders burst through the thick underbrush and emerged into the clearing.

Noting the path he took, I stretched my right leg, concealed beneath fallen leaves, waiting for my prey. Crunching dry leaves and brittle bark, a second man followed him. Tripping over my extended leg, the man sped to meet the ground in a flurry of motion. Using his startled curse as a guide, I aimed a kick in the direction of his face. The impact resonated in my foot. Before the second intruder could gain his footing, one of the guards rushed to pin him down.

The man with the long hair fought with the first intruder. "There is a man behind me," said the priest, speaking for the first time. The archer notched his arrow, alert for any movement. With a loud rustle, I heard the vanishing steps of the third intruder running away.

The cart driver attempted to go after the third intruder. "No point chasing him through the jungle. Let him go," said the man with the long hair, disarming the first intruder. My captors stripped the two intruders of their weapons and tied them together. I glanced at them in the dim light. Their youthful faces shocked me. Why did they turn to stealing?

"I am grateful for your warning," the man with the long hair said, untying my hands. His face hovered inches from mine, and I noticed the smooth skin on his forehead. I realized he was only a few years older than me.

He stretched his hand to help me stand. I grasped it, noticing how my palm disappeared in his. With a strong grip, he pulled me up, and I grinned at him sheepishly. A moment later, I remembered I pretended to be a boy. With a grimace, I rubbed my wrists together to get the blood flowing.

Despite the priest's premonition about death following me, no one died that night. However, we got on our way while the sky still slept with only stars for company. Before I climbed into the cart, I scanned my surroundings. To the east, I saw fields burned to the ground, a sign that the fighting that had claimed our king's life still raged.

The priest with the large mole followed the direction of my gaze. "Along the way to Tipti, you will see our kingdom laid to waste and ruin. The fighting has slowed, but robbers and thieves rule the land." That must be why we have three soldiers accompanying us on this journey. Living west of the river, I was unaware of most of the skirmishes and battles.

As I helped him onto the carriage, I noticed the priest's sallow skin. His eyes seemed coated with pain. "You are hurting."

"Injured but not slain," he said, managing a smile. I nestled him among the bags, making sure he was comfortable.

When I was sick, my grandfather had nursed me back to health. He would putter around the kitchen, coaxing the fire to life, while I had watched from my bed, too sick to help. He would place his hand on my forehead, recounting his day.

With care, he would wipe my head with a damp cloth, gently push back my hair, and feed me warm gruel. Sitting beside me, he would scratch his nose and hold my hand softly, telling stories until I had fallen asleep. I would have given up everything for one more moment in my house to talk to my grandfather.

The cart rolled along the dusty road. Through the gaps in the planks, I could see men out fishing, their canoes gliding on the flat black water. As we passed villages, silver-blue columns of smoke rose from cooking fires.

I slid to the edge of the cart and peeked through the curtain that hung over the opening. Because the monsoon had not arrived, the road appeared to be a hard crust. I saw some children behind the houses. I could hear their giggling as they sought a place to hide. For a moment, I experienced an urge to join in their play.

As we passed, I heard a collective scream as the seeker caught someone. I sighed at what I had lost, for I would never be a child again. I let the curtain fall back to cover my view.

Time stretched like a frayed rope pulled taut. The inside of the cart glowed golden from the sun. What awaited us at the end of this journey? The priest muttered in his sleep, and I quickly turned to him. He felt warm to my touch.

"You are ill," I muttered. He shuddered in response. I looked through the bags and found a fan made of palm leaves. I fanned him until my joints ached. *Should I ask the guards to find a healer?*

"Help," I shouted.

The cart stopped, and I heard a thud as the horse riders dismounted. I waited for the man with the long hair to open the curtain. "My uncle is unwell. He needs a healer," I said.

"What is wrong with him," he grumbled.

"My uncle has a fever," I said.

Another man joined him as they muttered to each other. I could sense the sickness frightened them.

"Can I fetch him water?" I asked.

They waved me away, still in conversation. It was hard to get the priest to drink. I lifted his head and placed it in the crook of my elbow. Then I wedged the makeshift cup I had fashioned using leaves between his lips and tilted the cup. Most of it dribbled down his chin. His breath turned my stomach, and I resisted the urge to vomit. I wet a cloth with the remaining water and placed it on his forehead.

"We will get him a healer when we get to our destination," said the man with the long hair.

I sensed the cart move again. The priest looked flushed. Suddenly, he writhed like a snake with his mouth open. I knelt beside him, trying my best to keep him from flailing around while balancing in the shifting vehicle. "Uncle," I whispered. He groaned and then stiffened. I felt relieved when he finally slept.

Only then did my exhaustion and hunger hit me. The sun was overhead, and the heat wrapped its fingers around me. I placed my head by the opening and let the swaying of the cart lull me to sleep.

Fire from a dying torch cast a feeble light around the room. Pillars with elaborate carvings lined the hall. With stooped shoulders, a man with a top knot moved among the pillars as if he sought something on the sculptures.

"Beware the—." His words dispersed into the wings of bats that took flight and did not reach my ears. "She knows your secret."

"Who knows my secrets? What secrets? Who are you?" I yelled.

I hit my head on a plank and opened my eyes. A dull pain rattled inside my skull.

"What happened?" asked the man with the long hair. I realized I had screamed in my dream, and the cart had stopped. Was it really a dream or another one of my visions? *Why did I not know any of these secrets?* I felt rising anger against my grandfather for keeping me in the dark.

The curtain opened, and I sat up, rubbing my throbbing head. The priest mumbled from the corner.

"Is he okay?" asked our captors. They assumed the screams

came from the priest. Ashamed of my dreams, I did not correct them.

"He is alive. But I am not sure I can keep him that way. When will we go to the healer?"

"Soon, if we don't stop the cart every few yards," came the swift reply. We were on our way again. I tended to the priest while praying to the gods to cure his illness.

I heard noises and peeked outside. Horse-drawn carts carrying people and oxen pulling ones overflowing with sacks passed us on the other side of the road. A man pushed a cart filled with vegetables. I sensed we neared the castle.

A few vendors hawked their wares, but the atmosphere appeared subdued. The sarees and wares on display seemed simpler than what I had imagined from my grandfather's stories of the great cities of Kashgar. Only a handful of people stopped at the shops. The cart slowed down, and I craned my neck to see through the gap in the curtain. A mighty fort made of sandstone loomed ahead of us.

The priest shifted and turned on his side. "We are here," I said animatedly. The priest merely grunted in reply.

I drew aside the curtain to get a better view. Against the twilight sky, the castle shone like a precious stone. A giant flag depicting a lion's head, the symbol of the House of Singalila, fluttered in the wind atop a tower. It almost appeared like the wind rustled the lion's mane.

Amidst the grandeur, I also saw bruising. Sections of the wall exhibited signs of battering from the battles during the rebellion. Portions of the parapet had collapsed, leaving vulnerable gaps. Still, it did not dampen my excitement. I had never been to a large city before. The man with the long hair spoke to the guards at the enormous gate and showed them a palm leaf. They waved the cart in.

Inside the fort, the cart stopped in front of the stables. I jumped down and gaped at my surroundings with my mouth hanging open. I saw wooden scaffolding against the walls where masons repaired the damages; their chisels and hammers chipped away broken stones, replacing them with freshly quarried ones. A cloud of dust lingered over them.

Ropes and pulleys lifted the heavy stones, and sweat-drenched laborers fitted them in place. The noise brought back memories of the time I spent in the workshop crafting new swords. I wondered if I could find work here as a swordsmith's apprentice.

In all the anticipation of seeing a new city, I had momentarily forgotten the sick priest. I climbed back in to help him down. "Are we there?" he asked.

"Yes," I said. I let him lean on my shoulder as he stepped down.

Once on firm ground, the priest swatted my arm away. "I am well," he said. Then he fell to the ground like a chopped banana tree.

ATUL

WINTER YEAR 2

The fake Aggabodhi gazed at me with eyes brimming with tears. I did seek his mother, not to reunite mother and child like he wanted, but to find out the truth about him. "My lord, uniting you with the woman who cared for you is something beyond me," I said. "Maybe you can bring it up with the chief," I suggested.

"No," he said, wiping his eyes. "The chief already thinks I am weak."

My heart tugged for the boy, his grief so raw and painful. "You are young, my lord. Not weak. I know you lost your mother as a young child. There is nothing wrong with you missing her." I gave him a path to grieve for the mother they separated him from.

He looked at me mournfully as if he would disintegrate at the slightest touch. "I doubt someone strong like you would miss your mother."

I chuckled lightly. "I do miss my mother, especially when difficult problems arrive at my door." I realized it was not a lie. Becoming a father had made me forgiving. I understood my mother's struggles more. It must have pained her to part with her newborn son.

"How? What do you do?" he asked.

I understood his question. "My mother is too far away for me to visit. So I think of her and act in a way she would be proud of." He sniffed, pulling his covers up to his chin, his fingers wrapped tightly around the cloth. "Your mother would be proud of how you treat me with kindness," I said sincerely. His eyes brightened. Slowly, he drifted off to sleep while I paced the floor.

A guard relieved me closer to dawn, muffling a yawn, rather than at midnight. Looking at his tired face, I swallowed my anger. Chief Jeevahatta had only a few men capable of fighting. I had heard his soldiers grumbling about the meager coins he paid them, so I doubted he could recruit more men to his cause. That meant long hours for the ones who remained.

Aggabodhi stirred when I plonked beside him. Without greeting him, I shut my eyes tightly. No sooner had I slipped into a disturbed slumber than the world around me awakened. Shuffling feet, loud talk, coughing, and an elbow into my ribs, all in rapid succession, proved destined to wake me. I tugged my thin blanket over my ears and curled up on one side.

"Your prince is looking for you," said Aggabodhi, shaking my arms. He sounded faint and muted, as if he spoke from inside a well.

I muttered a curse and rolled away from him, my eyes still closed.

"Brother, he is outside," he said more loudly.

To my annoyance, this time, I heard him clearly. I sat up, rubbing my sleep-crusted eyes. Bright light filtered in, nearly blinding me. "Who is outside? This is no time to jest," I snapped.

"The king is in a foul temper," he smirked.

"Not now, Bodhi," I admonished him. I felt a dry patch at the back of my throat. I needed a drink of water.

"You look terrible," he said, staring at my face.

"I have barely slept a wink," I grumbled, attempting to lie down again.

He shook me and whispered in my ear. "The prince you are guarding is outside."

"I am tired of Kashgar princes. Both of you," I muttered. My head felt heavy, and I held it in my palms for a moment. I could hear Aggabodhi tapping the floor with his nails. I would get no peace in here. I combed my hair with my fingers and went outside.

"Sword, I need you to accompany me to my morning meal with the chief," said the fake prince.

"My lord, allow me to wash my face," I pleaded. *I should pay my guards more coins, I thought, for putting up with the demands of a prince.*

"Hurry. I cannot be late."

Soon, feeling barely like myself, I accompanied the fake prince into the castle. If I had been alert, I would have asked the question earlier. My sleep-addled brain took time to wake up. "Why do you need me by your side, my lord?"

"Chief Jeevahatta's daughter will be there," he answered.

"His daughter?" I wondered why that made him nervous.

"Yes. The chief wants me to wed her," he said, twisting the gold chain around his neck.

The chief's motives became clearer. With his daughter as the queen, his grandson would become king one day. An idea started to form in my head—a way to gain Chief Jeevahatta's support for Aggabodhi.

As we approached the chief's chamber, my steps faltered. Guards typically waited outside. It would be unseemly for me to enter without permission. The fake prince solved my dilemma.

"Come inside and praise my fighting skills," he said, clutching my elbow tightly. Sweat gleamed on his forehead. He opened and shut his mouth like a goat chewing grass. I had no need for my mother's intuition to recognize his nervousness.

I followed him, and the rich furniture in the room dripping with gold, silver, silk, and ivory assaulted my vision. In my sleep-deprived state, I could not tolerate what looked like all their possessions crammed into one space. Pretending to be a humble guard, I tried to blend into the shadows.

"My guard can tell you about my progress in the training yard," said the fake prince, sounding like he wanted to rip his eyes out. That made two of us. Pulling myself together, I glanced at the table.

Chief Jeevahatta sat at the head of the table, glaring at the fake prince. His wife, dressed in a rich silk sari with gold threads, whispered something to the servant serving them. I could only see the back of the chief's daughter, her thick braided hair tapering down her neck. The fake prince took the chair next to her. Sitting on the edge of his seat, he leaned away from her.

The chief cleared his throat, and the fake prince jumped as if the chief just stabbed him with a spear. I decided to rescue the poor boy.

"The prince is progressing well in his training, my lord," I said calmly. That was true. He no longer yelped as frequently or loudly when I attacked him with a blunt wooden blade.

The chief's daughter swiveled her head to gaze at me. For a moment, she appeared like a goddess emerging from a lotus flower. I definitely needed my sleep. I blinked, and she turned into a normal girl about fifteen or sixteen years old, with eyes too large for her face and a small mole above her lips. Some would call her beautiful.

She scanned my face as if she wanted to paint my portrait in the future. My stomach contracted as a sensation I had not felt in a long while coursed through me. Before I could decipher my emotion, I realized that I was staring at the chief's daughter, which was not a fitting behavior for a guard, and lowered my eyes.

"I will reward you richly if the prince can swing his sword without hurting himself," the chief said, regarding the boy he had crafted into a prince. The fake prince squirmed on his chair.

I dipped my head and blended into the shadows. Since the chief had not dismissed me, I decided to stay in the room to learn more about his plans. The presence of the girl had nothing to do with my decision. Not wholly.

The servants served jackfruit dipped in honey, sesame cakes, coconut rice, and a pumpkin stew. The peppery aroma of the stew drifted into my nostrils, and my stomach growled. My last meal was yesterday at midday with the prince. Except for the chief, everyone else nibbled at their food while I felt ravenous enough to eat all of it.

"What did Vikramasinha want?" asked the chief's wife.

"He wants to claim the throne for his unborn grandson, though his message does not say that. He wants to discuss plans to muster troops to fight the rebels and regain control of Tipti. Once Tipti is safely in his hands, he will make his move. I am not going to let that happen." While I heard every word he uttered, my eyes stayed firmly on the food on the chief's plate.

"Are you going to meet him?" asked the lady, showing little interest in the rice on her plate.

"Yes, it is vital to see him face to face. I need a fortnight to get ready. Sunkosh River is also brimming with water from the rains. Better to cross her when the water levels have subsided," answered the chief, ripping a piece of the jackfruit and stuffing it in his mouth.

I tore my eyes away from the food. A plan began to take shape in my head. I should get my men to cross the river before me so they could position themselves around the meeting spot. At the right time, I could reveal myself and throw my support behind Aggabodhi.

"Father, please allow me to go horse riding with the prince," the girl asked sweetly.

"Gowri, no horse riding before your wedding. I don't want you to fall and break your bones," answered her mother.

"Your mother is right," said the chief, his eyes softening as he gazed at his daughter. "Take your cousin along, and the three of you can float down the stream."

"My guard can row the boat," blurted the fake prince, sounding rattled. Now, I wanted to strangle him after I ate a hearty meal.

SUGANDHA

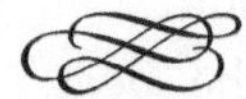

SUMMER YEAR 1

I woke to falling rain on the roof, a rhythmic drumming noise. I lay on the floor, listening to the sound that brought me peace. A light wind stirred the trees. With a gurgling noise, a steady deluge flowed down. I breathed in the earthy fragrance as the parched ground welcomed the rainwater. I closed my eyes, not wanting to get up just yet. I would be lazy one morning. No one would care. I slept poorly last night. Twice, I woke up with my muscles clenched, some vague dreams disrupting my sleep.

"Burning," the priest muttered from a wooden cot. I pushed aside my thin blanket and stood, seeing blackness at the edges of my vision. It passed as I steadied myself with a deep breath.

I glanced through the small window. A gray sky greeted me, and I could not tell if it was dawn yet. The priest moaned again, and I rushed to his side and knelt down. Last night, when he fainted outside, it took two men to carry him inside. A healer arrived soon after and made the priest a potion of bitter herb mixture. I had sat by his side, placing a damp cloth on his forehead to bring his fever down. The priest tossed and turned for a long while and finally fell asleep when I could barely keep my eyes open.

Grabbing a blanket, I had slept on the bare floor beside his cot. Now, I touched his forehead—still warm to the touch.

"I can fetch the healer," I said and stood up.

"I am on fire," the priest wailed like a man possessed by a ghost. His body convulsed with uncontrollable tremors. Each spasm twisted my heart. *How would I tame this sickness?* I placed my hands on his shoulders to hold him down. Beads of sweat glistened on his furrowed forehead, and he clenched his fists tightly. The skin around his large mole had turned red. Then the screams turned into cries. "Help me," he sobbed like a child.

I rushed to the window and found no one in the rain. Opening the wooden door to our small room, I looked on either side of the narrow, dark hallway—empty. I wondered why no guards were placed outside our door. With the priest's ill health, they likely decided we would not attempt to leave.

I shut the door and approached the cot. *Should I leave him alone to seek aid?* I heard voices outside and approaching footsteps. Men! Before I could cry for help, a knock sounded on our door. I ran to it. As I reached the door, it swung open, sweeping in a blast of humid air. Three men stood outside—a man about Uncle Ori's age in the center wore a silk dhoti and gold jewelry —a younger man in similar clothes to his left—the healer from yesterday in simple cotton attire to his right. Moisture from the rain clung to their hair and skin.

When I saw the healer, I grabbed his hand and pulled him in. "My uncle is thrashing around like he is in pain. I don't know what to do."

The healer hurried to the cot and pulled the priest's eyelids open to check his eyes. I hovered beside him. The other two men halted in the center of the room.

The healer handed me a pouch. "Mix this in water and feed him." I poured water from a clay pot into a cup and emptied the mixture into it. I blended the ingredients with my finger and attempted to feed the priest. I could feel the priest's labored breathing as I trickled the potion down his throat.

"I have treated a few people with this fever. It takes a few days to cure, my lord," the healer said, addressing the older of the two men. I guessed he must be Chief Vikramasinha.

"Check on him frequently," the chief replied. "When the priest is well, I need his help to find Ori's niece," he continued to his younger companion.

His words crushed me like a boulder. I could no longer move. The spell that protected me from Ori might not protect me from Chief Vikramasinha. I felt like I would pass out at any moment. My hands holding the cup shook, and I set it down. Fear collected in my stomach, and a primal scream gathered inside me. I clamped my lips shut.

Could I trust the priest not to betray me? Faced with choosing between his own life or mine, he would choose his own. I could no longer hide. I needed to find out the secrets buried in my past. *Why did these men seek me?*

Deep in my thoughts, I did not realize the others had departed, leaving me alone. The priest succumbed to a restless sleep, and I decided to venture into the city.

A faint drizzle misted from the sky, not fully light, the air warm and soft. A memory came so fast. I was four, my grandfather carrying me out to the backyard, and the sound of the rain against the ground, a gentle breeze, beautiful hues in the sky. Watching the rain touch my skin, I stood still for a moment, savoring the memory of my beloved grandfather. I worried that my memories of my grandfather would fade like my footprints in the rain and disappear like everything else I had possessed.

I saw him again—the young man who had come with the chief. He held the reins of a horse, talking to a girl wearing a silk sari with lotus embroidered in silver thread. I remembered Chief Vikramasinha had a daughter. *Was that her?* She said something to him, and the man, likely her husband, shook his head. I imagined the scene differently in my head. I saw her smile shyly at her husband.

Something broke in me. Grief swept over me, for she had all I lacked—a home, a family, a husband. I looked down at my clothes, shapeless and ugly. I pictured her grin broadening across her face while I grimaced. Her life was just beginning, while mine had already ended. No, I should not give up so easily. I could change the course of my life. Fill it with love, children, and warmth. An idea took shape in my head.

I walked along the narrow alleys with towering castle walls on either side. I strode away from the center of the city and soon entered neighborhoods occupied by ordinary folks. I stood on my toes and looked into one backyard. Clothes dried on ropes hung between two trees. I spotted a cotton sari among them. I quickly scanned the yard to ensure it was empty and jumped the fence. I grabbed the sari and ran.

Foolishly, I kicked a metal pot that rolled on the ground with a rattle. Curse my ill luck. I ducked behind a shrub, holding my breath. I counted to ten, and no one came looking for a thief. Sighing, I left the yard in a hurry.

Thick green grass stretched down to the stream's edge. I washed myself clean and draped the new sari. I felt like a snake casting off old skin to emerge gleaming and new. After having masked my identity in male clothes, I felt bare in my sari. I gazed at my reflection in the stream.

My cheeks had filled out while I had pretended to be Selva. I braided my long hair. My grandfather would recognize me now. Fear clutched my throat again. My uncle Ori would recognize me as well. I had to take this risk if I wanted to live.

With determination, I concealed my old clothes under a rock. I entered a temple and found some vermillion to apply to my forehead. I tucked a jasmine flower at the top of my braid and prayed to the presiding deity to keep me safe. Then, I set out to find the chief's daughter.

I sought the largest castle in the city and snuck into its garden. And I waited by the lily pond. As the day progressed, my confidence leaked out of me. I grew stiff from crouching in one place. I pondered whether I should abandon my plan and return to the priest. An insect crawled up my leg, and I brushed my skin.

I heard the rustle of a sari first. Then came the sweet scent of flowers as a woman approached the pond. I parted the branches to view her. No sign of the young girl I saw earlier. Instead, an older woman who resembled her stared at a lily bud.

"What did you find out?"

That is when I noticed a slight woman beside her. "Princess Malathi, the priest is here, but he is ill. It will be a few days before he recovers enough to recite any hymns."

Princess Malathi, wife of Chief Vikramasinha, traces of youthful beauty still clinging to her, continued to stare straight ahead. "Come to me as soon as he recovers. I don't need to find the girl. I need to kill her," she said in a quiet voice.

ATUL

SPRING YEAR 2

I convinced the fake prince that the midday sun was not conducive to a boat ride, especially with a girl betrothed to him. I did not know if a formal betrothal had taken place, but when a powerful father decides to wed his girl to you, it usually happens. After forming a new plan to take the lady out in the gentle evening sun, we returned to his room.

"My lord, I have not slept since yesterday," I said, suppressing a yawn.

The fake prince looked at me in alarm. "Here, lie in my bed," he said, pulling back the cover. Though tempted, I realized the folly of this. Princes, as a rule, did not like their guards to sleep in their beds. I should know this, having been a prince all my life.

I thanked him and returned to my quarters. I grabbed a blanket and lay down in a dark corner. I knew I had to talk to Aggabodhi about my plan, but I could no longer keep my eyes open. I passed out immediately.

It seemed but moments later that a loud grumble in my stomach nudged me awake. Hunger and tiredness battled it out, and hunger won. I rose, shaking the blanket. I noticed a plate covered with a banana leaf beside me. Aggabodhi must have left it for me.

His thoughtful gesture touched me. While he tried my patience at times, I was grateful for his friendship. I had too many noble companions. I must call each one a friend and favor none of them, lest I slight the father of one. Aggabodhi had become my one true friend.

Rice cooked with lentils and slightly bitter greens seasoned with coconut and peppers awaited me. I ate like this was my last meal: initially gulping my food down and, once satiated, savoring each bite. The rice lacked the generous helping of ghee that would coat one's fingers, but it filled my stomach.

Rested and full, I went to find Aggabodhi, training in the yard with other young men. I stood to one side and watched the prince of Kashgar. Though he held back his full strength, I could see what a long way he had come since I met him two years ago.

His attacks landed precisely. He moved with lightning speed while defending himself. When he saw me from the corner of his eyes, he grinned. "Want to move those tired muscles of yours, Brother? I will go gentle on you."

"I can beat you with one arm tied behind my back," I countered. "Bring your spear. We can train by the water." Understanding that I wanted to talk to him away from prying ears, Aggabodhi marched with me.

"Chief Jeevahatta intends to wed his daughter Gowri to your half-brother," I said.

He grunted in response, wiping his sweaty forehead with the back of his hand.

We reached a clearing and circled each other. "I am going to take them on a boat ride this evening. That gives you a great opportunity to meet the girl and win her heart," I said, plunging my weapon into the air beside his left shoulder.

He rotated away from me, his brows furrowed. "How?"

He stepped toward me, attacking my thigh. I blocked him.

"The same strategy we used for her father. I will capsize the boat. You come and rescue the girl from the river. Gratitude is a powerful emotion that you can turn to more with your charm." A tiny tremor ran through my back as I thought about toppling the boat, a vision of my cousin drowning in the ocean drifting in. I pushed aside that memory.

"How does she look?" he asked, his eyes narrowed.

"Like a girl. Why do her looks matter? She is Chief Jeevahatta's unmarried daughter," I admonished him.

"If she has a beard sprouting on her chin—"

"You will still marry her," I said sternly. I could have set his mind at ease by describing Gowri as a pretty girl, but I wanted Aggabodhi to understand that wearing the crown required sacrifices.

I had married two girls from the most powerful houses in Malla. I walked on a tightrope, treating them both equally, not seen to favor one over the other, to keep their fathers firmly on my side.

Since Rukmini had become pregnant nearly two years ago, I had had to refrain from our marriage bed, though I had longed for her warm smiles. I had done this not because of any health concerns for Rukmini but to retain the loyalty of Vibha's noble house. The house with a royal child gained the upper hand, so I had spent my time with Vibha to ensure she bore an heir as well.

Every month, euphoria had swept me when her flow was late, replaced by despair when it had come. I had hidden my disappointment to comfort her. I had held her when she had sobbed. Then, after she had slept, her energy spent, I had walked around the castle grounds, unable to sleep, a tight knot in my stomach. In the last few months, I had become desperate for it to work. Being a prince required patience. When I had reached the end of my rope, I had to dig deeper to find more within myself to withstand another day of the storm.

Aggabodhi saw my face and sighed in resignation. We devised a plan, and I returned to my duties guarding the fake prince.

As the day progressed, the boy started chewing his fingernails. I attributed this to his nervousness about seeing Gowri. One of the easiest things about being a prince was girls were disposed to like you, at least girls not married to you. With little effort and kindness, you could win them over. I wondered if I should pass this wisdom to him. I decided against it. He had time to learn this on his own.

When the sun began its descent across the sky, we headed out to the river. I checked the boat and the oars. And then we waited. The fake prince paced along the shore while I leaned against a tree. I knew my guards, Dayalu and Pusha, kept an eye on me, so I felt safe to drift into sleep.

"They are coming," the boy squealed and shook my shoulder. Reluctantly, I returned to the world. I stood and stretched my hands overhead. Then, I went into the water to wash sleep off my face.

"Prince Aggabodhi," greeted Gowri while her gaze darted toward me. I bent my head and pulled the boat into the water.

"My lord, the boat is ready," I said. The boy tried to jump in first, forgetting all my advice from earlier. I whispered in his ear. "Help Gowri first." An older cousin had accompanied her. I held the boat while the cousin lifted her sari nearly to her knees and climbed in.

The boy scratched his chest while Gowri approached the craft. She lifted her sari an inch and waded into the water. As she put a foot inside, she slipped and fell back. I waited for the blink of an eye for the fake prince to catch her, but he stood frozen. I leaned forward and grasped her waist to halt her. She collapsed against me. I placed my hand on her back and steadied her. "Careful, my lady."

She glanced up, her thick lashes framing her large eyes. "Are you hurt, Gowri?" asked her cousin, and she shook her head.

I released her, and she climbed in, sitting beside her cousin. We got underway. The girls faced me, and Aggabodhi sat between us with his back to me. I rowed along the river that glittered like gold in the sunlight. The night-blooming flowers slowly opened their petals and spread their sweet fragrances around us. Birds sang as they returned to their nests. A light breeze stirred my hair.

Then I glanced at the fake prince, slouched on his seat. I suppressed the urge to poke his back with my oar. Good posture was essential on the battlefield or on a boat. My eyes swept past him and landed on the girl. She sat straight, her gaze on the water.

My mind traveled to Malla and my boat rides with Rukmini, the only time I could still spend alone with my wife. While I rowed, she would talk about the palace happenings—who married whom, who had given birth, which siblings fought—gossip on the surface but valuable insight for a prince learning to govern. I would look at her lovely face with kind eyes and say, "Kiss me." She would smile shyly and lean forward to kiss me deeply, passionately.

A smile lingered on my face as I stared ahead vacantly. Slowly, reality crept in, and I realized I was staring at Gowri. The girl peeked at me from the corner of her eye. Prince Atul would have met her eyes. I pretended to be a guard now, so I lowered mine.

We neared an outcropping of rocks that created a mild rapid, water frothing around the obstacles in its path. A sensible boatman would navigate around it, but I had different intentions. I let the current pull me toward the rocks. Unaware of my plan, the occupants of the boat enjoyed the beautiful landscape around them. Waves crashed against the side of the craft and sprayed us with mist.

I let the vessel teeter precariously on the edge, pretending to steer us clear of the rocks. "Sword?" I sensed panic in the fake prince's voice. The boat shuddered, and water flooded in. I let the boat spin, and screams erupted around me. With force, I upended the boat, sending everyone into the embrace of the river.

"**Find Sugandha**," a voice stirred to life in my head. My heart gave a little lurch. I shut my eyes for an instant, hoping to suppress the call. "**Cross the river**," it persisted. A riddle to solve. An unknown girl to find. Other thoughts had crowded her out of my mind.

"Another time," I answered. I dragged myself back to the present.

I surfaced immediately and took note of everyone's position. Chaos reigned as bodies tumbled, their shouts lost in the turmoil. The boat, now capsized and at the mercy of the river, bobbed like a fallen warrior, defeated but not yet surrendered.

The cousin was closest to the shore, clutching a floating branch. I prioritized rescuing her last. The fake prince surfaced, screamed, and then submerged again. Gowri was the farthest from the shore.

I heard a splash and saw Aggabodhi jump in, according to plan. I started swimming to the fake prince. I planned to pull him out first while Aggabodhi rescued Gowri. I stopped mid-stroke, confused at seeing Aggabodhi head toward his brother. Had he forgotten our plan? If he rescued his brother, he would not have time for Gowri. In a moment, I changed direction and swam toward the girl, cursing the foolish Kashgar princes.

The girl gulped the river water, her eyes wide with terror. I swam behind her and held her waist. She trembled and tried to clasp my neck. I stayed out of her reach. "You are safe, my lady," I whispered in her ear. Then, with powerful strokes, I swam to the shore.

On my way, a shocking sight caused me to halt my movement. Aggabodhi appeared to be pushing his half-brother into the river. *Had he hit his head on a rock and taken complete leave of his senses?*

Frantically, I searched the shore and found my guards hiding behind bushes. They had been masquerading as members of Chief Jeevahatta's army for the past few days, so their presence here would not surprise Gowri or the fake prince. "Save them," I yelled. Both my guards jumped in and swam toward the brothers.

When I reached waist-level water, I stood and scooped up Gowri in my arms. She buried her face in my chest, her body quivering. I laid her gently on the shore. Kneeling beside her, I rolled her to the side. The press of my palms on her back pushed the water clogging her chest up into her mouth. She spat out water, gasping for breath.

"Stay here. I will rescue your cousin," I said. She flung her arms around my neck, sobs rocking her body. I felt her warm skin against mine. A delicate flowery scent rose from her hair. Temptation coursed through me to wrap my arms around her. Reluctantly, I patted her head. "You will be alright, my lady," I said softly.

What a nightmare if I became entangled with her. It would destroy my friendship with Aggabodhi, even though the fault lay with him for ignoring her and going after his brother. And I had to worry about my mother. She, who put her kingdom ahead of everything, would be unhappy if her son forgot himself. She had good reason. For a monarch, marriage cemented alliances with wavering lords. And a bond out of wedlock would bring shame. I knew all about it because my own birth still stung.

My guards dragged the two brothers to the shore. "Save the lady's cousin," I shouted. Leaving the fake prince coughing on the ground, my guard, Dayalu, dived into the river again. Aggabodhi glanced at me. If looks could kill, mine would have set him on fire.

When the cousin recovered enough, I handed Gowri to her care and pulled Aggabodhi aside. "Why didn't you rescue the girl?" I asked, resisting the urge to slap some sense into him.

"I will never deceive you, Brother. When I saw him, something snapped in me. All I wanted to do was kill the pretender," said Aggabodhi, staring at me fervently. I sensed the boy in him who still believed mistakes would not be fatal. He was utterly wrong, and I had no will to break his belief.

SUGANDHA

SUMMER YEAR 1

*P*rincess Malathi's words still reverberated in my head. *Kill me. Why did she want to assassinate me?* I sat frozen in panic, feeling my earlier strength seeping out of me. A sense of foreboding prickled me. When I finally calmed my racing heart, I realized the princess had left the area.

I abandoned my plan to seek the chief's daughter and returned to the rock where I hid my clothes. I donned my old outfit as a boy and concealed my sari in the same place. I changed my braid to a top knot and stared at my reflection in the water.

A light breeze blew over the surface, creating tiny ripples. My face appeared distorted, matching the turmoil in my mind. I stretched, rolling my tight shoulders and letting the wind blow away my headache.

I looked at my hands held out before me. They were not a girl's hands, tough and callused, stained dark by the sun. My disguise bristled me, and I wanted to break out of this mask and become Sugandha again. Not as I had been but as I might have been if my uncle did not chase me.

With heavy legs, I returned to the priest with a large mole. A healer's apprentice tended to him as I entered our shared room. The priest dozed on the cot. "I gave him some herbs mixed with warm milk and honey. He will likely sleep through the night," said the young apprentice before he left.

I looked around for chores to do. The floor appeared clean. I had no clothes to wash. Then, my stomach grumbled loudly, and I realized I had not eaten since yesterday. I walked the streets looking for the communal kitchen.

Light from oil lamps flickered from the castles and buildings. At an open courtyard, folks began to gather to watch a play. I paused to watch a scene from the Mahabharatha epic, where the elder brother gambled away his wealth, kingdom, and even his brothers.

The audience cried in horror when the king lost everything. The drama rekindled my memories from nearly six months ago. My brief stay with the drama troupe brought me companionship and purpose.

Something gnawed at me, and my peace shattered. I could not have stayed with them, even if I wanted to. I would have been at the mercy of that boy who had learned my secret, sharing his mat, betrayed by him, feeling horrible about myself. Feeling distressed and upset, I left the courtyard and wandered the streets.

I came across the dust and noise of a crowded market, with vendors hawking spices and herbs, yarns of cotton, jute rugs, and more. From the goods, I guessed this was more a market for the common folk than the noblemen. No silks or silverware here.

An older man, his hair completely gray, with stooped shoulders, stopped me. "Girl," he started, and I startled. He stepped closer, peering up at my clothes, and I realized his eyesight was not keen. "Forgive me, you are dressed as a boy," he said.

Without his vision, he had used his other senses and perceived me correctly. I hastened away from him, afraid of him revealing more. I wondered how long I would have to hide from my uncle before he stopped looking for me.

A trail of smoke rose from a large hall. A man stirred a large pot cooking over a wooden fire. Steam rose from it and covered him in a haze.

I hesitated outside, wondering if they would welcome me. The man with the long hair spotted me and beckoned me inside.

"How is your uncle?"

"The worst seems to be over," I muttered, following him to stand in the food line.

A kitchen maid dumped a bowl of rice onto a leaf plate, made a hole in the center of the rice, poured some stew into it, and handed me the plate. I plonked down beside the man who had kidnapped the priest and me and brought us here.

He started eating his food in silence, and I followed him, mixing the rice with pumpkin stew and chewing a mouthful. The sour tamarind, sweet pumpkin, and spicy peppers danced on my tongue.

The man with the long hair was in high spirits, conversing in a friendly manner. I listened, nodding my head from time to time, my heart racing like that of a girl who found him pleasing, which I did. My heart had not learned any lessons from my time with the drama troupe.

"I saw the chief's daughter outside," I whispered, pausing with food near my mouth.

"She has been married for a year, and the chief is anxious for a grandchild," he answered.

Many people, anxious for a child or a grandchild, would approach my grandfather for charms. Several charlatans were peddling lucky amulets to the gullible. My grandfather was not one of them. He had only accepted certain wishes, such as protecting their harvest, securing a good marriage match for their daughters, or ensuring fertility.

He would use dried rudraksha seeds to create the beads and string them. To bless each good-luck amulet, he had prayed to the respective deity for a few days, eating nothing but fruits. Once, to save a young child from an illness, he had meditated in a headstand posture all night long. He could barely stand straight the next morning. Still, he had insisted on walking to the child's house and had tied the amulet with a wooden bead around her hand. Her fever had broken the following day.

He had told me his heartfelt prayers invited the divine to bless the amulet. When he had blessed me, he had had no divine blessing from a deity. He had used his own life force and had died in the process. Guilt washed through me for the death I caused. *Was I worth saving?* Suddenly, I did not want to know the answer.

I went from that discordant thought to another. For a man who had cared so deeply for me, I had wondered why he had never taught me any magic or mantra. Once, after he had read the palms of a man embarking on a ship journey, I had asked him to teach me. He had ordered me to turn my hands over, and I had, eager to learn.

He had held my palm and taught me not to foretell the future but to decipher the past. He had shown me how a hand that wielded a sword differed from the one that held a hoe. That day, I learned all about the calluses on one's palms. Then, he had told me to read his palms. I had noticed the callus between his thumb and index fingers from holding a feather. He had written down all the births and deaths in our villages. He had scribed the history of our village and drawn horoscopes for the rich who could afford his services. I had felt the bumps on him from chopping down wood with the axe.

After this lesson, I had insisted he teach me to read the

future as well. He had replied, "The past cannot be changed, so the truth lies there."

Nevertheless, I knew enough of my grandfather's ways to pretend to be a palm reader and a *tantrika*—someone who practices rituals and ceremonies for mystical purposes. Pretending was all I did these days.

I returned my attention to the man with the long hair. "My cousin lives in a village around here, and she is well-versed in spells and incantations for producing healthy babies."

"Your cousin?"

"She moved here after her marriage to a priest from one of the local temples." I decided that a married woman would be safer from unwanted attention and could help me control my errant feelings for the man beside me.

As a girl, his kind face might tempt me to lavish him with attention, and he might return it. It was better to take charge of my destiny than to let something happen to me. "If the chief's daughter wants, my cousin can make her a charm."

"The chief's daughter will visit the river temple tomorrow. If your cousin comes there, I can introduce them," answered the man with the long hair.

I nodded my head.

"What is her name?" the man asked.

After a brief hesitation, I answered, "Selvi." I played as Selva once. Pretending to be Selvi would not be harder.

Night caught me as I departed, but a moon hung low in the sky, lighting my path. A cooling wind brought relief from the day's heat. The chirping of insects filled the air. Oil lamps flickered behind windows. The moisture in the air awoke all the scents—the sweat of the human bodies passing me, the earthy aroma of the soil from the rain, the fragrance of the flowers adorning the women's hair, and the pungency of turmeric and pepper wafting from the evening meals. I drew in a deep breath, sensing the city more fully. I let go of my worries, becoming one with the night splendor.

Evening temple bells rang, and I walked toward the sound. Houses and shops squatted on either side of the narrow streets. I wended my way slowly, looking for one that sold beads. I found a small workshop with tools on one side and assorted beads and simple jewelry on the other. In the fading light, the shop owner packed up for the night. I decided to return tomorrow, in daylight.

I made my way to the temple courtyard and joined the small crowd entering the temple. I climbed the five stairs to the raised platform. The Sunkosh river, personified as a goddess, gleamed from the inner sanctum. Gazing at her serene face, I felt like a leaf floating on the river's current, flowing in one direction to join the ocean.

Gentle music broke through me. "**I know you**," it sang. The voice seemed to emanate from the idol. It was a pure connection of joining myself to the world. My heart yearned for it like a child yearned for a mother's hug. "Please, please," I pleaded, wanting to be swept away, and something shoved me back to wakefulness.

Disoriented, I blinked my misty eyes. The priest said his closing prayers and offered the devotees holy water. I cupped my trembling hands while he poured a spoonful. I drank a sip and sprinkled the rest on my head.

Somehow, it restored me to my senses. Then I sat down with my legs crossed and meditated, an aura of stillness clinging to me. I kept my purpose in the forefront of my mind. Princess Malathi wanted to kill me. My uncle, Ori, wanted to marry me. Priest Parivan handed a baby to my grandfather decades ago. What was the connection between these disparate events?

A thread ran through these, but I could not track it. Princess Malathi was the sister of the last ruler of Kashgar. *Why did she want to destroy a stranger?* The secret must lie with the royal family. I needed to learn more about them.

I opened my eyes and sensed the priest closing the door to the sanctum. I rose to my feet and prostrated before the goddess, my stomach touching the ground. A woman would bow with her knees and head touching the floor but not her stomach. Since I wore a man's disguise, I prayed like one. "Guide me on the right path," I beseeched.

When I stepped outside the temple, I stood still for a moment, letting my eyes adjust to the darkness. In no hurry, I returned to the room I shared with the priest and found him still sleeping, his chest rising and falling under the blanket. I touched his forehead. While warm, it no longer burned like before. He appeared to be on the mend. I spread a mat on the floor and sank instantly into a bottomless sleep.

When next I woke, it was because the priest was gently shaking me. I sat bolt upright, flung from sleep.

"My nephew, I thought you would have left me by now," he said. I gazed at him. Sweat sheathed his pale face, and his mouth appeared dry as dust.

"Uncle, how are you feeling?"

"My head is cracking like a coconut shell," he said piteously.

"Lie back, Uncle," I said and returned with a damp cloth in my hand. I placed the cold fabric on his brow. He took short, panting breaths.

"I will fetch the healer," I said.

"I am in no hurry to get well," he whispered.

"Why?" I asked.

"Use your common sense. Once I am well, the chief will order me to seek Guru Ori's niece. They will use me as a weapon against you." He paused and gazed at me. Some emotion I could not decipher flickered in his eyes. "Better be ill for now," he added gruffly.

I did not trust the priest completely, though I sensed a

thawing from him. Many had betrayed me in the last six months. Fear mingled with the tension that sprouted in my neck. He was right. The chief would command him to seek me, but his wife would instruct him to kill me. Anxiety tumbled me in a wave. I needed to learn the reason behind Princess Malathi's hatred before she found me. *What if I failed?*

"Flee from here, where I cannot reach you," the priest muttered as if reassuring me. Instead, his words rattled me.

ATUL

SPRING YEAR 2

That evening, I arrived with the fake prince for his meal with the chief. Gowri was watching the door. The moment I entered behind the fake prince, she gleamed like a lantern in the darkness. The fake prince, for all his youth and naivety, noticed this transformation. He went very still and cold. Dismay clutched at my throat. I wanted no part of this.

I acknowledged the girl like a humble servant, my eyes downcast, hoping she had the sense to know a servant beneath her. I stood like a statue behind the fake prince's chair, only my eyes moving.

When the chief praised my swift action in rescuing his daughter and handed me a bag of coins, I bowed my head to my waist and accepted this reward. I knew Gowri glanced at me throughout the meal, but I never met her eyes.

The chief gave me a small room in the castle as befitting the prince's guard. Holding a lantern in one hand, I flung open the door with my other and peered inside the small room. I could see the stars in the night sky through a tiny window. I spotted a narrow wooden cot and a trunk for my belongings.

Even my bed from my princely chambers in Akash would

not have fit in the room. At least in the quarters I shared with other soldiers, I had their company to keep me occupied. I steeled myself to endure this life for Aggabodhi's sake.

The next day, while working in the stables filling grains into the horses' feed bin, Gowri approached me to saddle her mount. As I obliged, the girl leaned forward, giggling nervously, and started talking to me.

The animal sensed my agitation and pranced restlessly. I took a breath, gathering control over myself, and stroked the mare's sleek neck. I brushed her coat until it shone while listening silently to Gowri. As I handed Gowri the reins, her fingers hovered near mine, and I delicately moved them away. With a blush, she asked, "Would you help me get on the horse?"

Aggabodhi chose that moment to enter the stables. He watched me help the girl—I tried awkwardly to avoid touching her longer than I had to while she clung to me with her arms around my neck like her life depended on it. Aggabodhi muttered a curse and stalked away.

Like a flower leaning toward the sun, Gowri sought me. The gray clouds I cast did not deter her. I knew what she felt. The freshest years of her womanhood would be spent waiting for the fake prince to grow into manhood.

No one sought her happiness in a marriage. Her preferences had no bearing on the situation. I understood her very well. Though I was a royal bastard, I was also the heir to the throne. I could not be free with my words, deeds, or love. My wives had been chosen for me. I never knew the sweetness of a stolen kiss, the elation and suspense of wondering if a girl would stay with me a moment longer, or her sweet rebuke of my entreaties.

My heart ached for what I had missed. But I knew I should not seek what I never had. Not with Gowri. I had to build a wall around my feelings. Lock them in a rusty trunk and lose the key.

Later that day, I scratched my chin and felt the long beard. I decided to shave before my guard duties, glad that my uncle had forced me to learn basic tasks for my survival. Under his insistence, I learned to sew, cook, and care for myself. While I trusted my servant in Malla with a knife at my throat, I preferred to do the act myself away from home. I had scarcely begun my task when a knock sounded on my door. "Come in," I said, and the fake prince walked in.

For a moment, I forgot my role and continued my work. The fake prince lingered in the vicinity. Soon, I became aware of his scrutiny. When I nicked myself in the poor light, he leaned closer. Suppressing a curse, I demanded, "Have you never seen a man grooming himself before?"

He reddened slightly. "No," he said and looked away. "I have been in the company of other men and, of course, trained with boys my age. But..." He trailed off silently.

Curse the boy. His mother likely raised him alone. I let him watch while I finished. "Did that hurt?" he asked with curiosity.

"Some. When I hurry and cut myself."

The boy glanced out the window quietly. "What can I do for you, my prince?"

"Gowri likes you," he said sourly. I sensed his fear that he had made a fool of himself. He would close himself off to me, and I would lose his trust if I did not act.

"My lord, she likes the idea of a man my age. An illusion. Not me. I am a nobody. Nothing compared to you." My gaze did not leave the prince's face. "I am here to serve you, my lord. If you will still have me," I offered humbly.

I could sense his relief that I would not snatch his girl. But something else lingered in the air between us. "Is that why you came to see me, my lord?"

"I am eating my midday meal with the chief and his guru," he said, chewing his nails.

"Guru Ori?" I wondered if he had brought any new priests to seek his niece. *Why did the river bid me to find her?* I was no closer to solving that mystery. It would be useful to attend the meal with him.

"I can accompany you as your guard if that will bring you comfort."

He brightened immediately like a child given a new toy. We arrived before the others. Light poured in through the large windows, illuminating dust clouds. The fake prince paced the room while I stood stoically in the shadows. The chief barely noticed me as he entered. He took a chair, facing the window. The trees swayed in the light wind. I could hear the birds singing to each other.

"Sit down. You are making me anxious," barked the chief at the boy.

Before the fake prince acted, Guru Ori paused at the entrance, his eyes sweeping the room. I felt my skin prickle as he passed me. The chief jumped from his chair and bowed. He beckoned the guru to the head of the table. Ignoring this, Guru Ori sat on the floor, his legs crossed. The chief tugged the fake prince by his elbow, and they both sank down across from the guru. A faint smell of sandalwood wafted in the air.

A servant placed a large banana leaf in front of each one and served their meal on top of it. Slices of banana garnished with powdered jaggery and shredded coconut, tamarind rice, and sautéed long beans formed their first course.

"Instead of finding my niece, you are running to conspire with Vikramasinha," accused Guru Ori.

The chief squirmed like an insect caught in a spider web. "I will never abandon your mission. I have heard rumors that the girl has crossed the river. Our chances of catching her. . ." The chief faltered under a withering gaze from Guru Ori.

"All lies," bellowed Guru Ori. The boy reacted like a cub cowed by a wolf, his fingers trembling as he pushed his food around.

Guru Ori lowered his voice, forcing us to listen carefully. "I can find no future where the boy sits on the throne without my niece. If she dies, so does he." My spine tingled while my mind raced furiously. *What connected Sugandha to the throne?*

"It will be the end of Kashgar," added Guru Ori. His face went sallow. Every hair on my body stood up in horror. *What did he mean by that remark?* Suddenly, his eyes found me. "Is that the lad who fetched the priest?" he asked, looking at me.

I gazed at the ground, playing my role as the servant. "Yes, he is. He has assumed guard duties for the prince. However, his brother is available for missions," replied the chief.

"Magic has failed me. Time to use spies to find my niece," said Guru Ori. Insidious waves of fear gushed at me. *Did the protective spell block the spies from finding her?* Why I agonized over an unknown girl when many of my men had come prepared to die, I could not tell. I kept my grim thoughts to myself and made sure my face remained a mask.

"Yes, we can use spies," agreed the chief eagerly.

The fake prince made no response to any of this. He appeared to be in a trance. Ignoring him, I forced order onto my thoughts. I must find Sugandha before Guru Ori finds her. Along with the voice in my head urging me to protect her, I now knew she was linked to the throne. I should warn Aggabodhi ahead of time and make sure he was part of the team searching for her.

After my guard duties that night, I went to find Aggabodhi. The crisp air cleared my mind. I found him caught in a sleep of exhaustion. With guilt, I nudged his shoulder. "Bodhi." He sat up abruptly and stared at me. I motioned him to follow me outside.

I halted in a quiet spot under a big banyan tree with many roots sprouting from its branches. When Aggabodhi joined me, he asked callously, "Thinking of your girl?"

I swiveled toward him, startled. "She would not be my girl if you had followed our plan," I spat savagely.

It had the desired effect. Aggabodhi looked remorseful. "Why do you want to see me?"

"Bodhi, the chief is sending spies to rout out Sugandha. I want you to join that expedition. Make sure one of my guards is also part of the team."

Aggabodhi looked confused. "Brother, is it wise for us to go on this wild goose chase for Guru Ori's niece? It takes our attention away from the throne."

I recalled all that I had heard from Guru Ori earlier that day. While I had nothing concrete to tell Aggabodhi, I still decided to share some of my vague suspicions with him. "Bodhi, Sugandha seems to be tied to the throne and our quest. I don't understand how, but I think it is important to find her before Guru Ori does."

A slight flicker in Aggabodhi's eyes told me of his doubts. "Is this your plot to get me away so you can have Gowri all to yourself?"

"Gowri? If I wanted the girl, I would not resort to such cowardly acts. Next time you insult me, your bloodline will not protect you," I warned him. I wanted to give him a violent shake, but I suppressed my temper. "I have taken two wives. Why would I seek a third one? Especially without my mother's consent? I gain nothing from the alliance. Neither does she. I told you to rescue Gowri in the water. Instead, you tried to drown your kin. If you had succeeded, you would have exposed us all."

"So what are we going to do about Gowri?" He sounded annoyed, as if it were all my fault.

"Nothing at present. You are not stupid, so stop acting like it. Seek Ori's niece. Don't do anything foolish."

"And your guard will spy on me," he muttered. I made no reply to that. Of course, my men would keep me informed. He knew it as well as I did.

Aggabodhi gave me a piercing look, one with much mistrust

in it. I saw his shoulders heave with the breath he took. "You like that bastard better than me." His voice rose on the words.

If I had kept my senses, I would have recognized the jealousy that coated his words. My temper got the better of me. I shoved him violently, and he staggered back, nearly losing his footing. "Don't ever call him that. A prince should be mindful of what accusations he flings at others. Especially at one who holds his fortune in his hands," I warned him.

SUGANDHA

SUMMER YEAR 1

I left the priest in the care of the healer and departed. Birds in the trees overhead welcomed the day, and their carefree music filled me with sadness. The priest's words still rang in my head.

He had advised me to flee—a sensible suggestion because trouble pursued me like bees desiring nectar. Peril came from all corners—from my uncle, who wished to marry me, to a princess who sought my death. I longed to be as free as a bird, able to fly away from danger. All I could do was mask and camouflage.

I neared the stream, and the sun bounced off the water's surface. I collected the sari from under the rock and found a quiet spot behind a cluster of trees. Fallen leaves crunched under my feet as I discarded my old clothes and draped the sari.

I braided my hair with a parting in the middle. I applied the vermilion I had saved from my temple visit yesterday on my forehead, where my hair parted. With that, I assumed the identity of Selvi, a married woman.

I stood still to check my reflection in the water. A bird glided in and landed gracefully on the stream. Swan! The white feather tipped with gold shone in the light. I held out my hand. The bird swam to me.

When it arrived at arm's distance from me, it cocked its head. *Do you recognize me?* I stroked its neck with no hesitation. For an instant, I felt like I shared a skin with it. It had followed me. Suddenly, I no longer felt alone in the world.

I smiled broadly as I strolled to the temple. The streets bustled with activity from vendors hawking vegetables and traders spreading their wares on mats. I looked for the man selling beads. I found him arranging them in neat piles. The man left me alone without any friendly patter of talk, and that suited me.

I picked some *rudraksha* beads and paid him a copper coin for them. Near the temple, a middle-aged woman strung fragrant flower garlands, and a small crowd gathered around her to purchase them.

I entered the main sanctum and stared at the river Goddess idol. Two eyes, shaped like fish, seemed to gaze at me tenderly, with a mother's affection. Several flower garlands hung around her stone neck, filling the hall with a sweet scent. Her serene face brought me peace. Shutting my eyes, I prayed for strength to do what was right. Afterward, I circled the sanctum, attempting to bring order to my chaotic thoughts.

Ahead, in an area decorated with rangoli patterns on the floor, a devotee held a coconut firmly in his hand. Uttering sacred *mantras*, in one swift motion, he brought it down onto the designated stone covered with turmeric. The coconut shell split open, and the water spilled onto a small idol placed underneath.

As I approached, the man turned around. Spotting me, he handed me half the shell. "I am celebrating the birth of my grandson," he said, smiling. His kind, crinkled eyes reminded me of my grandfather.

A terrible sadness welled in my stomach, and tears threatened to spill from my eyes, and I blinked them back furiously. Whatever obstacles I faced, I could not forget my grandfather's sacrifice to protect me. I bowed my head in greeting to the man and accepted his offering, vowing to fight for my life. I would not let my grandfather's death go wasted. Temple bells chimed as if welcoming my resolve.

I spotted steps leading to a stream. I sat down on one of them and broke pieces of the coconut flesh to eat. Mothers floated clay lamps on the water, praying for the well-being of their children. Wives placed flowers on the water to wish for a fruitful married life.

Loneliness gripped me as I realized I had no one to pray for. Shame coated my skin a moment later. I had forgotten the kindness of Parimala, her father, and her grandmother. Though the girl cursed me to lead a life of solitude, I could not be ungrateful for the kindness they bestowed on me. Gazing at the sparkling creek, I prayed to the Goddess to guide Parimala to happiness.

A sudden commotion near the entrance signaled the arrival of Princess Malathi and her daughter. Tossing the coconut shell into the water, I rose swiftly to walk toward them. Princess Malathi moved with the grace and elegance of someone of royal birth. Her appearance reminded me that she was the sister of the late king. The more subdued daughter accompanied her. My eyes cast around them, and I found the man with long hair.

When the mother and daughter entered the main sanctum to pray, I approached the man with the long hair. Suppressing my fears that he would detect the boy he knew in me, I smiled at him. "My cousin sent me here. I am Selvi," I said, with a dip in my head.

The man with the long hair gazed at me from head to toe. "You are younger than I imagined."

I made no comment. When the princess walked around the courtyard, the man with the long hair neared her and bent down to whisper in her ear. Her eyes came unerringly to me. I hated to be the center of such attention, especially from someone who intended to kill me, so a shiver ran down my spine. I took a shaky breath to keep my face calm. She muttered something and continued.

With a small gesture of his hand, the man beckoned me closer. "She asked me to bring you to the palace. Follow our carriage."

The warm sun beat down on my head as I walked behind the cart. A light wind kept the day from being oppressive. My stomach growled in hunger as we reached the castle. Alone among the scores of folks doing their daily chores, I hovered near the entrance, waiting for the man.

When ants started crawling up my legs, I brushed them away and switched from one foot to the other. I felt the warmth of the sun climbing overhead in the sky and decided to seek shelter under a tree.

Once, I caught sight of the man with the long hair, but as I ran toward him, he waved me away. "Not now!" I swallowed my annoyance and returned to my spot.

Exhausted, hungry, and irritated, I continued waiting. When the birds started returning to their nests, the man called me. "The princess is waiting." He led, and I followed as he took me through a narrow path into the palace gardens. The servants walking past us barely noticed me as I hastened with my eyes cast down. From somewhere in the castle, the wind carried stray notes of music to my ears.

The man with the long hair pushed open a silent door and led me into a sparsely furnished room. A connecting door on the other side was closed. Oil wicker lamps gave us light. She was waiting for us, wearing a deep blue sari with silver threads.

Our eyes met, and I bowed low to her with my palms clasped. "My lady!"

"I am told you are well-versed in spells," she said.

I nodded humbly. "And incantations and palm reading. I learned from my grandfather. If you have need of me, I would be glad to help," I replied. Such skills were erratic and unreliable, even in ones with years of learning and knowledge. I hoped to use that to my advantage to fake my talent.

"Read my palm," the princess demanded, stretching her hands.

I understood it as a test. I gestured toward the woven mat on the floor. She sat on it, and I lowered myself in front of her. I closed my eyes, bowed my head, and uttered a *mantra*. Then, slowly, I opened my eyes and clasped her right hand.

Her soft skin spoke of her noble upbringing. Her lifeline in her right hand ended abruptly, but the one in her left hand continued. I did not know what that meant. What I wanted to convey was not typically discerned by reading one's palms, but I decided to blend in some psychic abilities. If I could feign one set of mastery, I could fake them all.

"I am sensing strong emotions from you. You seek a girl," I whispered, gazing into the distance.

"Stop," she broke in, and her fears and worries erupted on her face. She dismissed the man with the long hair out of earshot. With an impatient sign, she asked me to continue.

I shut my eyes and traced the lines on her palm. Then I opened my eyes and gazed at her directly. "The girl you seek has a mysterious past. Trouble walks in her heels. She intends to—" I grimaced. "Someone stronger than me is blocking my vision," I mumbled in a weak tone, clutching my head.

Princess Malathi pulled her hands to her side and looked away from me. She drew her breath, and I knew my words had affected her, though I was no closer to solving the mystery of why she sought me.

"I seek an heir, a grandson. You can stay here tonight. A

maid will fetch you food. Do you need to send a message to your family?"

I understood that I would remain a prisoner till I produced results. If her daughter met with any harm, I would face worse punishment. I stood at the lip of the abyss. I flung myself into it. "My husband is away, my lady. I can stay here to serve you."

ATUL

SPRING YEAR 2

I brushed the stallion set aside for Aggabodhi as a gesture of my goodwill, my mind uneasy about our last quarrel. I understood why Aggabodhi despised his brother and resorted to calling him names.

Aggabodhi saw the boy as a usurper of his birthright. I knew why fury coursed through me at his words. His taunts of his brother's low birth rankled me because of my illegitimate birth.

My mother, Queen Meera, loved my father but had married King Atul for the good of the kingdom. She had sacrificed her love at the altar of duty. My father, Rish Vindhya, had served as her bodyguard, spending his days watching a woman he loved in the company of another man.

I could not fathom how he had managed to guard and protect my mother while hiding his love and hurt. While my mother had sacrificed her love for the kingdom, my father had sacrificed himself for his love. Then, Queen Meera and Rish Vindhya, two people who had their emotions tightly leashed for more than a decade, slipped and conceived me. To the world, I was the last son of King Atul, the man who gave me his name. Only a handful knew the truth.

My father was a nobleman, brave, loyal to my mother, and worthy in all ways of her heart. *Yet, I was no prince.* I sensed a note of self-pity in my thoughts and despised it. Nobody but my parents and uncle knew the circumstances of my conception. I knew no taunts as a child for my low birth.

Uncle Jay had loved and cherished me and raised me as his own. When his son had perished, he had crowned me as his heir. There was no cause for the hurt that swirled in my heart. Aggabodhi's words irked me because I deemed myself unworthy of the crown. It opened wounds I had wrought myself.

Aggabodhi arrived near me. "I am leaving," he said sullenly.

"I will saddle your horse," I told him quietly. I found myself taking time, discontent washing through me. I wanted him to apologize for his behavior and his mistrust. I felt soured, even though I knew there was nothing noble about my attitude. My parents sacrificed many things. I should at least rein in my emotions. With effort, I leashed my ill manner. "Bodhi, I still care—" I had difficulty finding the right words to assure him of my loyalty to his cause.

"I know, Brother," he muttered, equally ill at ease. It did not bode well for our mission if we quarreled. I sensed a chasm had opened between us, and I did not know how to bridge the gap.

"Our task is two-fold," Aggabodhi spoke quietly to the horse rather than me. "Outwardly, we will look for Guru Ori's niece, but our hidden assignment is to scout the area and spy on Chief Vikramasinha before their intended meeting."

I nodded, petting the stallion for a few moments. I had ordered my men to do the same, so Chief Jeevahatta's command made sense. However, what interested me was the deception that the chief practiced with his Guru. It told me both men still did not agree on this. I wondered how I could exploit this rift.

"It's unlikely we'll find the girl who has been eluding us for months. If luck favors us, what do you want me to do with the niece?" Aggabodhi asked gravely. I sensed his misgivings pouring out of him.

I had no time to patch things with him. "Send me a message. Then, at the right time, reveal to her your identity. Offer her your protection. My men will escort her to safety." I knew so many things could go wrong with this scheme and put Aggabodhi and Sugandha at risk. But no other bright idea floated into my head.

Aggabodhi said nothing for a while, stewing in silence. The commander called his men to attention. He clasped my arm awkwardly. Despite my earlier irritation, I smiled feebly. "Go safely, Bodhi," I said gruffly. He held the reins and touched his heels to his horse. I watched his retreating back for a few moments before heading to my fake prince. Light stole into the sky, chasing away the darkness.

"Sword," called a female voice. Gowri. I nearly ignored her and walked past. A second urgent call after the first halted my steps.

"My lady," I said cautiously, approaching where she stood under a tree. A sweet smell emanated from the flowers wound into her hair. She held a long peacock feather in her hand. Slowly, she drew the feather across her cheek in a way that might have been accidental, and I turned my gaze away. The sooner I put an end to this, the better. "How can I help?" I asked, keeping my voice neutral.

"My cat is up on that tree," she said, pointing to a branch with her finger.

I looked up and found a brown kitten crouched on the end of a branch, the leaves hiding it partially. "Meow," I called, standing underneath the animal, willing it to jump. The cat glanced at me with bored eyes and then returned to grooming its tail.

"If you lift me, I can reach him," Gowri said, her eyes on my arms as if she already imagined them around her waist.

For a brief moment, temptation flickered in my mind. The warmth of her body pressed against mine lured me. For an instant, I wished I could take what she offered freely. Then I remembered my reality. My body belonged to Malla. I was not free to share it with anyone other than my wives. It would be dishonorable if I acted on my desires. That drove the temptations away.

"Considering our stations, that would not be wise, my lady," I said, trying to remove any sting of rejection in my tone. She scowled. "Please wait here, my lady," I said and returned to the stables.

I rode astride a horse and arrived under the tree. The girl's scowl deepened. Standing on my stirrup, I reached to pick up the kitten. "Here you go, my lady. Your cat is safe," I said, handing her the animal.

Hiding her annoyance, she cuddled the kitten. "Poets will vie to sing songs about your brave deeds today and earlier at the river," she said, not bothering to hide her mockery.

I decided to play along. "I am the prince's bodyguard, and protecting all that he cares about is part of my duty, my lady."

She passed the cat to her companion and strode away. *How could I discourage this infatuation of Gowri's without harming my role or the fake prince?* I considered finding a maid and gossiping with her, maligning Gowri's name in the conversation. I discarded that thought immediately. I could not smear a girl's honor that way. And it would be too risky for the maid, even if I managed to flee.

Better would be to raise the fake prince in her esteem. I had tried and failed to accomplish that with Aggabodhi. With that thought dampening my spirit, I went to locate my new master. I found him seated on the floor, his head bowed, hair falling on his forehead, and an array of carved soldiers and horses arranged in some pattern on the floor. He looked so young that

I realized he should not be courting girls for many years to come. I doubted Gowri still played with her dolls.

When he saw me, he grinned sheepishly. "Chief Jeevahatta said he would take me on this journey across the river. I remembered these wooden toys—sculptures I had," he said.

Reality dawned on me. Whether I approved or not, the chief seemed intent on this alliance between his daughter and the fake prince.

While the fake prince acted like a child, I could not expect Gowri to see him as a man. I would have an easier time pushing a boulder uphill than making him attractive to Gowri. But I should still attempt it. The alternative would be the boulder crushing my feet.

"Do you want to join me?" he asked instead of commanding me.

I felt pity for the boy who had no friends to play with. My cousin Vikram and I would play for hours as children, and due to our closeness in age, we were nearly inseparable. And I had chased away Aggabodhi, the one companion I had gained since my cousin's death.

My heart skipped a beat at having lost a true friend in him. My mind wandered from Aggabodhi to my son in Malla. I did not want my child to suffer this loneliness. When he was older, I would ask my chiefs to send their boys to Akash to foster with him so he could grow with the lads who would one day help him rule.

The fake prince started chewing his fingernails as if he sensed my disapproval. He seemed so small, a child snatched from home and forced to serve Chief Jeevahatta's purpose, with no say in the proceedings.

"My lord, I can teach you how to play Chaturanga. That would be an appropriate game for a prince," I said gently. Aggabodhi's accusations prickled my skin that I favored his brother.

While I did not prefer the fake prince over his brother, I did care for him. Our illegitimate births acted as a bond between us.

The fake prince nodded eagerly, perceiving nothing wrong with a servant offering him this suggestion. Soon, I set a game cloth on a table and used some of his carved soldiers and horses as playing pieces. I started teaching him the game. He found it difficult to grasp at first, but slowly, he caught on to it. After losing two games to me, though I curtailed my moves to the most basic ones, he squirmed in his seat.

I decided he had enough of it. "You played well for a beginner, my lord. In no time, I expect you to beat me," I lied to boost his confidence. His eyes shone, pleased with my compliments.

We went to the training yard and picked dulled practice weapons for our work. The fake prince's wind and endurance had improved over the last few days, but not his fighting. Sweat trickled down my back as I allowed the prince to beat me three times. It took more stamina to lose to him than to win. Still, his grin at the end was a small solace.

That night, the fake prince rested on his pillow, his dark hair slicked back. I walked around the room, snuffing out the lights, except for one, while wondering how to get the fake prince to win over Gowri.

He sat up in his bed. "You are unlike any servant I have encountered here." I was grateful for the darkness as the blood drained out of my face. "You train with me as an equal. You teach me games like a guru. Most servants would have begged my leave to extinguish the lamps."

A wave of wariness swept over me as I castigated myself for my carelessness. Despite occasionally wallowing in self-pity about my birth, my uncle had raised me as a prince, and in Malla, servants leaped to fulfill my every desire. Obedient submission did not come naturally to me.

"Who are you?" the boy asked incredulously.

SUGANDHA

SUMMER YEAR 1

After being outdoors for so long, the four walls oppressed me. A maid opened my locked door and brought in some old rice mixed in with sour yogurt and pickle. Once she placed the leaf plate on the floor, she shut the door behind her, and I heard the bolt lock in place. For a fleeting moment, I wanted to pound on the door, asking them to let me go.

For all the princess knew, I could be a spy. She would check my details before using my service. Selvi did not exist beyond my imagination. *What would happen to me?* With terror clawing my insides, I eyed the meager food. I decided to perish on a full stomach, eating the rice without tasting a morsel.

Then I waited, pacing the floor, hating this imprisonment. Ten steps and then turn. I repeated this for a while, wishing I could feel the breeze on my skin. While my feet traced the steps in the small room, a sudden panic struck me.

The man with the long hair knew me as the priest's nephew. In a boy's disguise, I had told him Selvi was my cousin. He would question the priest about Selvi. I tried hard to breathe, but suddenly, I could not remember how.

Would the priest deny any knowledge of Selvi? The priest had claimed me as his nephew. Whether to protect me or keep me close, I could not tell. At least he was no stranger to falsehoods. I decided I could not worry about the priest. If he claimed to be ignorant of Selvi, the princess would throw me into the dungeon. That would not be any worse than my life since my grandfather's death.

The sounds of the castle dimmed as the night wore on. I realized no summons would arrive that night, so I collapsed onto the mat. Sleep did not want to claim me, and I stared at the ceiling.

I understood my uncle seeking to marry me, though my skin crawled at the thought. But I did not comprehend what threat I posed to the princess for her to pursue my death. I fell into a disturbed sleep of nightmares. A flying arrow aimed for my throat found its target in a swan's neck.

I woke up screaming and sweating. I took several breaths to calm myself. If I had worried a guard outside would rush into my room, this incident dispelled it. No one opened my door. The heat stifled my breath. I sprinkled water on my face and neck from a clay pot and then drank some of the liquid.

The palace stirred to life around me while I stood in the semi-dark room with light sneaking through a sliver of an opening near the ceiling. I could faintly hear the birds calling out to each other.

A spider web hung in one corner, and I watched the spider knitting it with patience. I felt like an insect caught in a web weaved by a skilled master. I spent my time waiting and pacing. After I memorized every blemish on the wall, anger filled my mind. Rage at my uncle consumed me.

Why had he forced my grandfather to curse that ship sailing to Malla? How would the king of Malla react when a vessel of dead bodies arrived on his shore? Was he already on his way to Kashgar to burn us down?

Then, my thoughts jumped to my grandfather. He had not prepared me for these dangers. While he lived, I led a sheltered life with plenty of food to eat in a modest house.

The only worry I had then was whether the weaver would have yarns in the colors I liked for my skirts. While not rich, my grandfather had never denied me yards of cotton fabric around my birthday to stitch into skirts and blouses.

But he had never mentioned Purohit Parivan in the first fifteen years of my life. I did not know why my grandfather had forgotten to mention Purohit Parivan when he told me all the tales of Kashgar royalty or when he had me scribe old scrolls concerning the laws of Kashgar.

My grandfather had taught me how to make ink. Then he had set me to the task every day to copy ruined scrolls, some in tatters. *What was the point of asking me to write about long-forgotten royal births and deaths instead of teaching me to survive?*

In anger, I kicked the brick wall and grimaced as pain shot through my toes. I knew why prisoners went mad in the dungeons. A few days of this, I would start tearing my eyes out.

I plonked down and leaned against the wall. Tears pricked my eyes when I contemplated what awaited me outside these doors. My grandfather's kindly face appeared in my mind. "Child, close your eyes and meditate."

For a moment, I wanted to scream at this image of him in my head. Then, I leashed my temper and shut my eyes. Initially, I found it hard to focus on my breathing. I had a foolish impulse to hiss at the memories crowding my head, useless to me now.

I felt horrible and not calm enough to attempt this. But I did not give up. I let my mind reach out to the river flowing several yards away. I imagined the refreshing water cocooning me in an embrace. The currents pulled me along. Slowly, my breathing steadied. Then, I felt a tiny twitch. It reached for me like a flower bending toward the sun. I allowed it to find me, like a moonbeam casting down through leaves.

Suddenly, the priest with the large mole floated into my head. I sensed rather than saw his hands inside the washing bowl filled with water. "My niece?"

"Selvi," replied a man I could not see. It sounded like the man with the long hair.

The priest asked cautiously. "Why do you ask of her?" A surge of gratitude rose in me as I realized he did not deny her existence.

"Your nephew introduced me to his cousin, Selvi. Where is the boy?"

"You know how lads are at that age. He comes and goes as he pleases. What do you want with Selvi?" asked the priest, still pretending the person I conjured from thin air existed.

"Is she any good at making amulets?"

Please say yes, I prayed.

The priest answered as if he heard my words. "For someone so young, she has a real skill for it." He splashed his face, stepped away from the bowl, and vanished from my mind.

At first, I could see nothing. Nor could I speak. I could no more than breathe. Then came the pain, a blessing to bind my mind to my body. I sighed in relief. Exhausted and disoriented, I let my face sag with weariness. My body ached as if I had fought a battle.

What did I just experience? Did I really listen in on a conversation between the priest and the man with the long hair? How was that even possible? I lurched to my feet and staggered toward the water. Once I assuaged my thirst, I splashed my face. The moisture cleared my blurry vision.

I tried to recall what had happened, and it felt like reflecting on a dream. Only one thing stood prominent in my memory. The priest with the large mole had not betrayed me.

Since my grandfather's death, the strangers who crossed my path deceived me. I knew I had become disillusioned, unable to trust anyone. The priest had spared my life for now. While grateful, I did not have complete faith in him. I carried too many scars to lower the defenses I had built around my heart.

But why did the priest go along with my lie? He did not know who Selvi was. Since I had become embroiled in a royal game, I tried to reason like a spy. *Did the priest gain anything by going along with this? Did he expect to question his nephew when he returned? What would he do when I didn't turn up? Would he raise an alarm?* Before I could pursue this path, a knock sounded on the door.

The same maid who had come yesterday arrived with fresh water and a plate of rice.

"Can I walk around the garden path?" She ignored me while replenishing my pot and left without answering me. When I heard the bolt slide in, I wanted to cry. With difficulty, I dampened my emotions. At least the princess did not send the guards to imprison me. Maybe the priest's responses convinced her to believe my lies. I ate the day-old rice without tasting anything.

Then I waited with all the patience of a five-year-old, gnashing my teeth. I must have fallen asleep out of sheer boredom. When I woke up next, darkness had descended around me. I rose, sandy-eyed, and lurched to my feet. Suppressing a yawn, I stretched my arms overhead.

As I walked toward the water, I stepped on something damp and yielding. I cursed loudly and bent down. The maid had come while I slept and left my food on the floor. I left the banana leaf plate where I found it and walked to the pot. I poured some water on the end of my sari and used that cloth to wipe my face and neck.

Then I returned to the food. I separated the portion touched by my foot and ate the rest. Afterward, the night stretched before me. I longed for fresh wind in my face. Restlessly, I resumed my pacing around the tiny room. A day, then two passed. I lost track of time. My plea to let me go went unheard. My hair grew greasy. Of late, I had become used to that. I was no longer the girl who had a roof over her head.

When I lost all hope of seeing the outside of this room, the door swung open.

"The princess wants to see you," said the man with the long hair. I rose to my feet slowly. His eyes landed on my face and then traveled down. I knew I had lost interest in keeping myself clean. My hair had fallen out of my braid. I'd worn the same clothes for the past few days because I had no others.

He twisted his nose wearily like he could smell the filth I had collected. "There is a servant's entry for the river. Take a bath first. I will ask the maid to fetch a clean sari for you."

As I neared the river, I felt an immense presence. Not threatening but reassuring, like the love of a mother. My throat closed tight at the warmth emanating from her. I had never known my mother. Until then, I did not realize how big a void her absence had created in my life.

Without hesitation, I plunged into the water, imagining I was leaping into my mother's arms. I let it wash my dirt away. I swam with the current like a fish, feeling at home, a calmness in my heart that drew away all my fears.

Slowly, I became aware of the maid who brought me food standing on the shore. I had jumped into the water with my clothes on. With a smile on my face, I stood up, water dripping down from me.

She gasped at seeing me. With my wet clothes and hair clinging to me, my appearance must have given her a fright. I decided to ask for a comb to untangle my hair. It would not do to see the princess in my current disheveled state. I climbed on shore and extended my hand to take the dry clothes she held.

Instead of giving them to me, she whispered, "Mother," and fell at my feet.

ATUL

SPRING YEAR 2

I had misjudged the fake prince. While others saw me as a servant and never past that façade, the boy welcomed me as a friend. That allowed him to plainly see what I should have hidden.

I knew to heed my elders and seek the advice of my council. But, I was groomed to command, not to obey. Uncle Jay had taught me to make decisions and live with the consequences. The lad sensed my upbringing and recognized I lacked the meekness of a servant. I cursed my foolishness in underestimating a child. While adults only saw my well-worn clothes, he saw me.

"My father is a wealthy man," I said, offering him a partial truth. Rish Vindhya hailed from the richest house of Malla. "I am his bastard son," I said as if ripping dead skin off my body. The fake prince flinched at those words. I knew then he carried wounds as deep as mine. "An uncle taught me lettering and more in the hope I could seek a position above my station. But my father could never claim me as his, so I decided to seek my fortune elsewhere." I had twisted the truth like a coir rope.

The fake prince lowered his eyes. His lips trembled like a

baby's as if he were wrestling with some great emotion. I wondered if he would reveal his story to me. I stood still as a statue, waiting.

He let out a sigh, mastering whatever tormented him. Then, gazing at me, he said, "Sword, I am glad we found each other." His command over his emotions surprised me.

I dipped my head, sensing he had the temperament to rule this land. Immediately, I felt guilt for betraying Aggabodhi in my thoughts. The fake prince rested his head on his pillows and closed his eyes. I sensed from his erratic breathing that he lay awake. I had stirred his memories, and he likely found no solace in them.

It was not only his memories that rose to the surface. I was unwittingly back in the past, eight years old, crying into my pillow after one of my mother's visits. For the first sixteen years of my life, I had thought of King Atul as my father. King Atul had died before my birth.

My mother's brother, Uncle Jay, had raised me as a father and had taught me all the duties of a man. Even his love had not completely eliminated my resentment toward my two older brothers, who had stayed at home with my mother, or toward her for sending me away.

Though Uncle Jay had loved me as his own, I had still yearned for my mother. Especially when I had been around Aunt Sudha, and her love for her son had spilled out like a pot overflowing with water. After I had learned the secret about my birth, I knew my mother sent me to Uncle Jay for my protection. But even that knowledge had never healed the wound in my heart.

I wondered if the fake prince knew he was the bastard son of King Rajasuriya. It hurt me to think that Chief Jeevahatta had snatched him from his mother's hands. For an instant, I feared they might have killed her. If the chief planned to set the fake prince on the throne, then killing his mother would put the chief in danger of retaliation when the boy gained power. Once he became king, the fake prince would likely punish anyone who had harmed his mother. Knowing that risk, the chief probably held her in a safe place.

As the moon rose, the boy tossed and turned, tormented by his nightmares. My heart tugged for him. When my men found his mother, I decided I would find a way to unite this boy with her.

The next day, I stifled a yawn as I stood guard in the palace's council room. I had barely managed to get a few hours of sleep last night. I lifted all ten toes to bring my mind to the present.

Afterward, I observed the scene unfolding in front of me. A large rosewood table stood at the center of the space. The fake prince sat in an enormous chair, his feet dangling in the air. Chief Jeevahatta scanned the room, making sure all eyes stayed on him.

"This spring festival, we will celebrate the betrothal of Prince Aggabodhi to my daughter Gowri," he stated and paused. The fake prince shifted in his seat but remained quiet. "After that auspicious occasion, we will cross the Sunkosh River and travel to Singalila," the chief added.

Over the next few days, maids strung flower garlands over entryways. The blooms also found their way into every maiden's hair. The trees themselves greeted the spring by putting forth new blossoms. From the balcony, the fake prince watched the festivities while I stood behind him on guard.

Aggabodhi had mentioned the spring festival to me. Observing what unfolded below us, I realized he had viewed it with the eyes of a child. What I witnessed below was an unabashed celebration of love and renewal of life.

The women swaying in dance to the humming of bees threw red vermillion powder at their lovers. The men smeared sandalwood paste on the arms of the maidens. I sensed normal social restrictions had loosened in this open courting among the unmarried.

Though the day had just begun, the red and yellow colors created the illusion of a setting sun. The fake prince grew listless and retired to his room. I left with him reluctantly, wondering if I had wooed my wife, Vibha, with such merriment, if she would be with a child now.

That evening, we arrived at the garden with the chief. Under a golden sky, a canopy of newly opened blossoms greeted us. The chief's wife and her daughter waited under a mango tree. A dusting of pollen drifted around us on the breeze.

The chief's wife rubbed the tree trunk with sandalwood and adorned it with flowers. "I pray for a fertile growing season," she said. Then, she repeated the same steps with her husband. She rubbed sandalwood on his cheeks and then placed a garland of flowers around his neck. "I pray for your long life," she said to her husband, who applied vermillion powder to her forehead.

The mother turned to her daughter and instructed her to follow her steps. I had avoided looking at Gowri, and now, as she moved forward, I noticed she looked like a budding flower herself.

Apart from a pale pink silk cloth, about the width of my palm, tied around her chest and knotted in the rear, her curvy back remained uncovered from her shoulders to her hips. The flowing silk sari wrapped around her hips dropped to her ankles.

In the gentle breeze, the end of her sari draped across her left shoulder fluttered, exposing her bare midriff. Blue stones glittered around her neck. A matching sparkling gem in her navel drew my eyes, and with difficulty, I pulled my gaze away. With the grace of a dancer, Gowri elegantly smeared the tree with fragrant sandalwood and showered lotus flowers at its trunk. For a moment, I watched her slender fingers and imagined them on my chest.

"By applying sandalwood paste to the prince's forehead, you accept a future union with him," said her mother, bringing me back rudely to the present.

Gowri approached the prince with a smile. As I stood a foot behind him to his right, I could not observe the fake prince's face. But his rigid shoulders and clenched fists told the story of the tension coursing through him.

I kept my eyes firmly on the fake prince's back. Suddenly, I sensed a movement in front of me. Before I could react, Gowri flew toward me. I reached to hold her waist, and she collapsed onto me, her upper body draped over mine.

I felt the softness of her breasts against my chest through the thin silk cloth covering them. With her eyes twinkling, she brushed her fingers across my right cheek, smearing it with sandalwood. Her moist lips, inches away from my face, formed into a smile.

Did the foolish girl think she was binding herself to me? As the crown prince of Malla, I needed my uncle and mother's blessings for any alliances. Even with my inexperience in royal matters, I knew a union with Gowri would better serve Aggabodhi. All this happened in the blink of an eye, and her parents calling her name broke the spell that tethered me to her.

Holding her elbow, I gently pushed her away while my body protested such an action. "My lady," I said with a bow after letting go of her to stand on her own feet.

With a smirk, she applied the tiniest sliver of sandalwood paste on the fake prince's forehead. My heavily coated cheek stood in sharp contrast. The fake prince watched the two of us over his head, confusion clouding his eyes. I avoided looking at the chief, though I sensed his annoyance. Gowri's behavior irked me as well. I wanted to blend in with the other servants, not stand out with a mark on my cheek.

A servant handed a plate loaded with silk saris and jewels.

"Offer this to Gowri to accept a future union with her," snapped the chief.

The fake prince took the plate with trembling hands and extended it to Gowri. She accepted it brusquely and departed with her mother.

The chief lingered for a moment as if he wanted to say something. A servant approached him and whispered in his ear. He left the fake prince and me alone.

"My lord, I have no desires for your betrothed," I said bluntly, not wasting any time.

With a defeated look, the boy glanced at me. "I don't blame you, Sword. There is something about you that makes people want to be friends with you," he said sagely. "Gowri has felt it too."

"I will avoid the lady till we set off on our journey, my lord," I promised. For her sake and mine.

But the lady in question had different ideas on the matter. The day before our departure, a knock sounded on my door. I opened the door, rubbing the sleep out of my eyes. "The prince is seeking you urgently," said a servant. Grabbing my weapon, I followed him in haste, worrying about what caused the fake prince to summon me.

The servant opened a door. "Please follow this path," he said, his index finger pointing toward a dark hall. I paused. *Why would the prince be here?* The man waited for me. If the chief had wanted to kill me, he could have done it in my room. I stepped inside, and the door shut behind me. I followed the dimly lit path to the stairs that led me down. I climbed down the dozen or so steps and halted at the landing.

"In here," whispered a female voice. Another door opened a fraction, and out peeked Gowri.

"My l—"

"Shush," she hissed. Pulling me inside, she closed the door. A single lamp shed meager light on us.

I crossed my arms and stared at Gowri. "It is foolish for us to be together. If your father catches me, I will be beheaded."

"I know that. That is why all the secrecy," Gowri explained as if to a child.

"This is not prudent," I repeated.

"Kiss me before you go," she said at the same time and put her arms around my back.

As her fingers spread fire on my skin, I became aware I had not worn my upper garment since I left in a hurry. I forgot the reason I resisted as her warm body pressed against mine, driving away all other thoughts. She had changed into a cotton sari for the night. I could feel the rise and fall of her chest through the thin material.

I lifted her chin with my hand and leaned in. Without waiting for me, she rose on her toes and touched my lips with hers. Time stood still as I savored her sweet kiss.

SUMMER YEAR 1

I stared at the middle-aged maid lying on the sand, dumbfounded. *Why did she fall at my feet? Why did she call me Mother?*

Before I could get my voice to work to ask her questions, the man with the long hair yelled from a few yards away. "The princess is waiting. Don't dither." I looked up to see him with his back turned to us. Lower-rung women who worked at the castle used this river section, and men typically stayed away from this spot. He broke the accustomed convention by being here.

On hearing him, the maid stirred to life. She wore a clean cotton sari and tiny silver earrings. I squatted down to the ground. "Ma," I called, placing my hand on her shoulder. She peered at me through the tears in her eyes. A dozen questions swirled in my head. "Why did you call me Mother?"

She held my arm and rose to a stand. I moved along with her. She wiped her eyes with the end of her sari. "When you walked out of the river, for a moment, I thought I saw my mother." She wrapped her arms around her thin body as if she grew cold in the warm summer air. "You are only a girl," she said, looking away from me, disappointment lining her slumped shoulders.

I grabbed the dry clothes from her and went behind a tree trunk to change. The maid must be nearsighted if she thought I was her mother. I let go of this strange happening to focus on what I would say to the princess. I wanted to find out why she wanted to murder Ori's niece. For that, I needed to gain her goodwill first. I did not have my grandfather's skills with amulets.

"I can help, Child," a voice whispered in my head. The same benevolent presence I felt in the river. The priest with the large mole called me Child of the River. The swordsmith and my adopted cousin called me Child of the Moon and Water.

I did not know when my life became tangled in mythology. I still felt like the same helpless girl who fled her house in fear. However, even a pretense could sustain me for a few days till I dug out the truth. My heart thudded loudly as a plan formed in my head.

I squeezed the water out of my wet hair. Then, I walked to meet the man with the long hair. With an impatient nod, he strode forward, and I followed behind. I used my fingers to brush my tangled hair and braided it while walking. The man took me back to my room. Someone had swept it clean and changed the water in the pot.

"Wait here," he grunted and left me alone. I rubbed my wrist, wishing I had bangles and earrings to wear. I had fled my house with a pair of each, but I lost them in the Sunkosh River when my boat overturned.

The man came back in a short while and beckoned me toward the garden. Bees buzzed around the flowering shrubs. I paused to snap off a jasmine flower and tucked it into my hair. I had forgotten how to be a girl and what a simple pleasure it was to string a flower garland and weave it in my hair. With a sigh, I rushed to keep up with the man with the long hair.

He took me through a meandering path spilling with new blossoms on either side. The intoxicating fragrance overwhelmed me after days spent in a locked room. Taking a deep breath to fill my insides with the pleasant scent, I scanned ahead. An ornate teak door stood open. The man gestured for me to enter it.

Leaving him outside, I walked in. The princess sat on a swing wide enough for two. With a gentle nudge of her toes, she rocked the wooden plank. The metal chain fastened to the ceiling creaked in the motion. I bowed to her and clasped my hands in front.

The princess had a faraway gaze. "My daughter has stayed barren after two years of marriage. I have offered my prayers to all the temples in Singalila and even some beyond." She paused. I noticed the lines around her mouth and eyes. This matter weighed heavily on her mind. She only had one child herself. I had heard in my village how some families sired like elephants, only one calf at a time. And others bred like dogs with several puppies in a litter. "I need an heir. But I don't want to play with boons and curses. Just like a fire, they burn as much as they illuminate. What can you do for me?"

Sweat trickled down my back, and my tongue stuck to the roof of my mouth. I was no priest or tantrika. I wanted to flee. Instead, I drew strength from the benign presence that comforted me in the river. "I would suggest the couple bathe in the Sunkosh River with me, my lady, while I pray for them," I said, barely hiding my tremors.

I felt like an idiot playing with dangerous weapons without learning how to use them. I had never lain with a man before, so I only vaguely knew what went into making a child. But I knew enough to know that a river bath was not needed.

The princess glanced at me. It took all my courage to meet her gaze politely. "When?" she asked.

"On the next full moon day," I answered. This bought me

some time, but I worried I needed a lifetime, not a few days, to produce a plan that made any sense.

I bargained with the princess to let me roam the gardens. She relented and permitted me access to a small strip by my room that housed herbs. At dawn, while the garden teemed with life, the maid let me out of my room. She avoided looking at me, and I sensed her embarrassment at mistaking me for her mother. I wanted to ask her many questions but did not press any on her.

"I will be back with your food," she said and disappeared.

I stood for a moment under the rising sun, like a sunflower seeking light, letting the gentle rays warm my skin. I perched between the roots of a neem tree and observed the happenings around me.

That early in the morning, only the servants moved around. I could hear the sweep of a broom, the hurried footsteps of a guard, and the creaking of a solid door. I needed to get close to the princess to learn her secrets. That would not happen until I succeeded in her near-impossible task. The princess likely tried all the common herbs, such as Ashwagandha, to treat this problem.

I tried to think back to my grandfather preparing various potions. He had recommended fenugreek for new mothers, but that would not have helped me. My anger bubbled up at him for not teaching me these skills.

I had played with a girl or two who had lived on our street. My grandfather had allowed me to attend dance dramas at the temple with them. These girls had learned to prepare elaborate meals, including sweets that took hours to make.

My grandfather had taught me basic cooking but never beyond that. They had known how to embroider beautiful patterns on their skirts, while I had only learned to mend a tear. If I had had my mother, she would have prepared me for life as a girl. Tears threatened to overflow, and I shut my eyes tight. I reached out to the river, pouring my anguish into her. A sense of calm seeped in.

Each day, the moon grew like a pregnant woman's belly. I smiled resignedly. Even my analogies betrayed my worries. The day that I dreaded arrived soon at my doorstep. I waited for the princess, her daughter, and her son-in-law near the section of the river used by the nobles.

Steps carved out of granite led to the water. Birds returned to their nests as the moon rose in the sky. Wearing pearls that mirrored the moon, the princess arrived with her family. I suppressed my shock at seeing Chief Vikramasinha among them. A thick beard covered his chin, and a faded scar across his shoulder proclaimed him no stranger to battles.

The chief's eyes narrowed as he regarded me. "Is she the one helping us? She looks younger than Parvati."

I remained mute, letting the princess come to my defense. "I am willing to give her a chance," she said. Doubts that plagued my mind echoed in hers. For an instant, I felt guilty about manipulating a mother's concerns, but then I remembered she wanted me dead. I had a right to survive, and I meant her daughter no harm.

Mired in my thoughts, I did not realize the others watched me expectantly, waiting. "Selvi?" the princess uttered my name as a question.

I looked up in alarm like a deer caught in a net and quickly masked my fear. "Please have your daughter and son-in-law follow me," I said, walking toward the water. I stepped into the river, and gentle waves swirled around my ankles, wetting my sari. A soothing sensation reverberated in my heart. I let that tranquility swathe me and gazed at my audience.

The young couple separated from the others and followed me. The man walked one step ahead of his wife, not waiting for her. She stumbled on the damp steps and instinctively threw her arms wide. Teetering for a moment, she steadied herself. Her husband arrived in front of me, not noticing her troubles.

His wife came to a stop a few feet away from him, her chest rising and falling rapidly. "Step into the water, my lady," I said and moved further in. Not looking at each other, they waded in after me.

The three of us stood in chest-high water. I held my arms out, gesturing for them to grasp them. After a slight hesitation, the girl seized my hand first, and then her husband mimicked her. His rougher palm contrasted with her soft grip. I noticed they did not clasp each other's hands.

"Let us take a dip, submerging our heads," I whispered, with no idea how any of this would help them conceive a child. In unison, we dunked into the water.

"Mother, bestow this couple with a child of their own," I prayed silently. A mild current churned around us. We rose with water dripping down our heads. No voice answered my prayer. Disappointment coated my skin, and my stomach squeezed in terror. The couple stared at me expectantly, and I wanted to scream that I was a charlatan.

Controlling my idiotic impulses, I said, "Once more."

"Mother, bring joy into this couple's life by giving them a child to cherish," I appealed. Nothing happened. I had hoped for a sign that someone heard my entreaties.

"Last time," I said, failing to hide the desperation in my voice. I let go of their hands as I immersed myself in the river. *Mother, save me*, I thought.

The girl rose out of the water, coughing. Waves of anguish choked my throat at my failure. Whatever miracle I hoped for did not arrive. Her husband glanced at his wheezing wife as if he had never noticed her before. Wavering for a moment, it appeared like he arrived at a decision. He stepped closer to her and rubbed her back.

I watched them wearily, dejection twisting my stomach.

What did I achieve by getting the three of us wet? Barely hiding my agony, I signaled for them to climb ashore.

On a wet step, the girl slipped again. This time, her husband reached out to grasp her waist to steady her. A quick glance passed between them, and I felt like an intruder into their private universe.

The man did not let go of his wife as they ascended. My heart squeezed at this sight. At least, my actions brought them together. Whatever obstacles they faced, they would be able to withstand them together.

Parimala's curse rang in my ears. "You are doomed to a solitary life." I had broken her heart with my deception and could not fault her for seeking vengeance. But I knew I desired a boy to share my life with. Then, I nearly laughed at my foolishness. My life hung in the balance. I should worry about staying alive first.

With the man still holding his wife, the couple went before me, his wet dhoti clinging to his thighs and her damp sari accentuating her curvy hips.

When we reached the dry shore, Princess Malathi stated, "Parvati will fast for a fortnight—"

Her son-in-law interrupted her. "The priestess asked us to spend the next three days together."

I noticed he called me priestess. His commanding tone caught my attention, and as I looked at him, I saw his gaze fixed on his wife, completely oblivious to everything around him. Yet, it was her adoring regard for him that persuaded me to comply.

"Yes. Spend three days together, just the two of you."

ATUL

SPRING YEAR 2

A vision of my mother floated into my mind, admonishing me for my disregard of my duty. I broke away from Gowri's clutch and took a step back. My body screamed in protest, craving her touch.

"Gowri," I said her name gently. She looked at me like a drunkard under the influence of toddy. I felt no different. "You have no future with me. Forget this ever happened and marry the prince your father has chosen for you."

"He is a child," she snarled as if she contemplated a union with a frog.

"Prince Aggabodhi won't be for long," I said. "If you don't want to marry him, this clandestine meeting is not the way out of your betrothal. Instead, talk to your mother. He deserves better."

I did not wait for her reply. I fled the stubborn girl, like a thief escaping the house he robbed. I knew I lacked the control to deny her again. If she approached me, I would take more than she wanted to give.

I did not want to father a bastard child with her or anyone

else. My feet took me to my room of their own accord. I halted just outside the door, my mind in turmoil. I worried Gowri would send someone after me. They would come looking for me here. I wished to remain undiscovered by her.

I spun around and marched to the river. At the shore, I took my clothes off and plunged in. That night, as everything became intolerable, I swam through the darkness and silence. The cold water did little to extinguish the fire she had kindled.

Memories of my last furtive meeting wafted into my mind. I had left the Malla castle as a prince, swapped clothes with my guard, and returned as him. Rukmini had waited for me in a tiny room connected by the maze of tunnels to the prince's chambers. I had taken the precaution to disguise myself just to be with my wife.

I had refrained from her marriage bed since her pregnancy to ensure I kept peace between the two powerful houses my wives hailed from. Rukmini had borne me a son, heir to the throne. Vibha had remained childless despite our efforts. With only days before my departure to Kashgar, I had longed to spend a night alone with Rukmini.

When I had seen her standing in the semi-dark room lit only by a silver wicker lamp, I had drawn her into my arms with a ravenous hunger. With more than a year of pent-up yearning, I had taken her with a boy's impatience. When I had dropped beside Rukmini, spent of my intense energy, her fingers had traced my cheek.

"My prince, to watch you, someone would think you practiced abstinence," Rukmini had teased me.

"It was worse," I had said, pulling her closer. Even a gardener experienced more pleasure planting his seeds in an arid land. The last few months, the times I had spent with Vibha, my other wife, had become a burden for both of us.

"Worse than me watching you and Vibha together?" she had replied, with a slight reproach in her voice.

I had realized my selfishness in viewing the past only through my needs. With a baby in her stomach and then at her breasts and on her lap, I had forgotten Rukmini was not only a mother. She was my wife.

In thinking about the kingdom, I had forgotten my role as her husband. Instead of answering, I had kissed her gently, trailing from her lips to the base of her throat, with an intent to please. She had come alive at my touch as I had treasured every sensitive part of her, and this time, we had reached the crest together.

Before I had departed Malla, I had mentioned to my uncle about Rukmini and me spending a night together. If she carried my child, I did not want any confusion concerning the father.

Uncle Jay had smiled at me. "Marriage to multiple wives is the first test for princes. Chief Guard Kapil Biha already informed me about your stealth meeting with Rukmini."

I had drawn random shapes on my hip. I had known our spymaster had eyes everywhere. "I am failing abjectly in my test then."

Uncle Jay had said, "Atul, I would not judge you so harshly. You gave a year to Vibha, more than my father ever gave to my stepmother. Neither Vibha nor her noble family can find fault in your behavior. If they deem you undeserving of their allegiance, they can face my wrath."

"It is not their fury I fear," I had muttered. I hated to see the disappointment in Vibha's eyes.

"Let me offer you the counsel I received from your mother. As a young prince unable to keep two wives content, your mother advised me to seek help from your Aunt Aranya to keep your Aunt Sudha happy. I followed your mother's advice, and Aranya has not let me down," he had said.

My mother had indeed provided an elegant solution to my problem. I wished I had turned to her myself. "Uncle Jay, Vibha has been depressed, and I have struggled to keep her cheerful. Rukmini can be my ally in this."

I had discussed this matter with Rukmini while I had bid farewell to her and my son. I had asked her to keep Vibha company to ensure my childless wife remained loyal to me. Rukmini's eyes had widened as if I had asked her to be my queen. In some ways, it had felt like a predecessor to that question. She had promised to befriend Vibha.

I swam across the river, pushing my body to cross the swift currents to calm the turmoil in my mind. I missed them all sorely, even Vibha.

"**Protect her,**" a voice pleaded in my head.

"My men are looking for her," I thought. I had enough trouble with girls. I almost did not want to add Sugandha to my pile of worries.

The phantom voice appeared to have heard my musing. "**Her life is in danger,**" it echoed. Then, for the first time since I started hearing these voices, an image flashed in my mind. Someone hid among the leaves on a tree trunk, parting the branches to peek down. They turned, and eyes shaped like two fish pierced my heart.

I came up gasping for breath with no energy for another stroke. My guard, Dayalu, stepped from behind a tree trunk. Seeing me struggle, he jumped in and swam to me. He dragged me to the shore, and I collapsed on the wet sand. Coughing racked my chest. A splitting headache throbbed in my head. Dayalu squatted beside me, rubbing my back to expel any water I consumed. He rubbed my feet, bringing warmth to my cold and weary limbs. His fingers, deft and practiced, kneaded the soles and arches, rekindling my numb extremities.

As life returned to my sore legs, I waved him off and sat up with my head between my palms. It hurt to open my eyes. He hovered nearby, understanding my desire for silence. After a few deep breaths, I stood shakily. I took a tentative step and then another to where my clothes lay. Dayalu stood close, watching me as a father would observe his child take his first steps. I draped my dhoti over my wet body.

"I lost you for a few moments tonight," Dayalu said, with no trace of any annoyance. If I had the same conversation with the fake prince as his sham guard, my irritation would shine through.

"Gowri sent for me," I replied.

"I don't like you taking these risks. If something happened, I would be too far to protect you." He sounded concerned and not irritated with his errant prince. I knew he and my other guard had befriended the palace servants and maids to gain access to places I frequented.

"Have you lost faith in my skills?" I jested, squeezing the water out of my hair.

"On a battlefield, facing a dozen men, I would have no doubts that you could take them all down. Alone in a tunnel, a slender knife can slice your throat," he whispered.

Uncle Jay ruled Malla, and I had fathered a son. *Was my life that valuable anymore?* I thought rashly. "If something happened to me, aid Aggabodhi in retaking the throne," I said.

"If something happened to you, the five of us, guards sworn to protect you with our lives, will have to meet our deaths too," my guard reminded me. Five men, sworn to me, Prince Atul, Heir to Malla, to guard me with their lives. After being in Kashgar for over twenty days, I needed to remind myself of my name and title. Their oath let me take considerable risks, knowing they shielded me with their bodies.

I could not be callous with the lives of my men. "My life just became more precious to me," I said. After we met Chief Vikramasinha, I decided to reveal myself to both chiefs. Aggabodhi had the backing of the Magadha armies. That would be a powerful reason to crown him. An alliance with Magadha also meant new trading opportunities. Rugs from Padi, spices from Saral, and gold from Malla would be welcome in Kashgar. Kashgar traders could ship silk to Magadha.

"There is some time before dawn. If you want to sleep, I can stand watch," the young man offered.

I stifled a yawn and nodded. He spread his shawl on some dry grass. "Are you married, Dayalu?" I asked as I rested on it.

His head swiveled from side to side like an owl's, scanning our surroundings. "No, my lo—." He caught himself from calling me lord. "My mother has found a girl for me. When we return to Malla, with your consent, I want to visit my village for a fortnight to marry her."

"Are you not going to invite me to your wedding?" I asked.

"I w-w-would be honored," he stuttered.

I shut my eyes with a smile. My last thought was about the person with the eyes shaped like a fish. *Who were they?*

A young person cupped their hands, plunging them into the cold stream. Water dripped down their chin as they drank it greedily. Through a hazy cloud, I noticed the matted hair, dirt under the fingernails, and torn clothes. The air around me vibrated with a strange energy. Like a prey detecting its target, the same dark piercing eyes from earlier found me, sensing my presence.

I tried to flee, but I could not move. Something held me in place.

"Who are you?" echoed that voice.

I tried to speak. However, no sound came out. A hand came out and grabbed my throat, choking the life out of me—a girl's hand from the size of it. "No-Not your enemy," I stuttered.

She let go.

~

I opened my eyes, gasping for breath. My guard hovered beside me, his hand on my shoulder.

SUGANDHA

FALL YEAR 1

I strolled through the garden as the sun peeked over the distant hills. The early morning dew caught the rays and glinted like gemstones. Like the dew, my heart gleamed with gratitude for the roof over my head and food in my stomach.

Then, some gray clouds floated in to block my light. I had not made much progress in learning about why Princess Malathi wanted to kill me—five days had passed since the meaningless river bath. Parvati could start her monthly flow anytime now. Once that happened, Princess Malathi would kick me out of the castle, and I would become homeless again.

My feet took me to the kitchen as they had the past few days. The aroma of black pepper and turmeric wafted in the air as I entered the large room. I took a deep breath, letting my eyes adjust to the semi-dark room.

Two wooden stoves blazed in a corner, and the cook stirred one of the large bronze pots perched on top of the fire. The cook's mother leaned against the wall and offered instructions to which no one seemed to pay attention.

I grabbed the vegetable cutter, an instrument with a curved

blade set into a wooden base. I settled beside the mother, one leg folded on the base to hold the blade in place and the other stretched forward. Using both hands, I sliced a gourd with the sharp blade. The older woman reminded me of my grandfather. However, I did not seek her today because I yearned for my grandfather. I sought her to get some answers to my burning questions.

"Selvi?" asked the cook's mother, peering at me through her clouded eyes.

"Yes, Ma," I said, keeping my eyes on the vegetable. I nearly cut my finger yesterday when I got distracted by one of the helpers dropping a hot pot of ghee. "You promised to tell me about your life in Tipti," I said, feeling guilty about using her.

She sighed with contentment. "I grew up in a small village and had never set foot outside it. My father married me off at fifteen to a twenty-year-old man from a neighboring village." Fifteen? I was sixteen now. I quickly glanced at her, trying to imagine her younger self through the wrinkles that drew a tapestry across her countenance and failed.

"I traveled in an oxen cart to his village with all my belongings packed in a jute sack. After spending a few days with me, my husband returned to work in Tipti while I stayed with his family in their thatched-roof house. My husband promised to send for me, but my mother-in-law liked having me with her. Her grown daughter had married and left her home. While my father-in-law and my husband's two younger brothers worked in the field, she did all the household chores alone. She appreciated having another female in the house. She taught me how to cook, and soon, I prepared all the family meals. My husband would visit me during the festivals, but with four others living in the tiny house, we never had any privacy." The older woman chuckled at this memory. "Anytime my husband tried to kiss me, his mother or father or one of his brothers would stumble upon us. We brewed creative ways to be together."

My mind traveled to my days with Parimala while I had pretended to be her fiancée. Her house had held one small room with a door. The rest were open spaces. I had struggled to find a quiet spot to change, always worrying someone would see me unclothed and discover I was a girl. Even now, weeks later, the mere thought of those days caused a knot in my stomach.

"When both his brothers were married, and their wives came to live with us, I begged my mother-in-law to let me go live with my husband. With two other daughters-in-law to order around, she finally gave in. Four years after my wedding, I arrived in Tipti feeling like a new bride. My husband worked in the stables and lived behind them in a small windowless room." She waved her hand around the kitchen, and I could see the blue veins that traced an intricate pattern under her paper-thin skin. "You could fit three such rooms in this kitchen. After spending years with six other people, it felt like a mansion to me." She paused, lost in her thoughts.

While I loved hearing her story, I wanted to learn more about Princess Malathi, so I directed the conversation. "Is that where you met the princess?"

"Hmm. King Jayadheer's grandchildren, King Rajasuriya and Princess Malathi, were little children then. While most royals ignored me, King Jayadheer's second wife always treated me with kindness. She came to visit me soon after I arrived in the city. I still remember seeing the queen for the first time. She looked like a goddess in her lotus pink sari and delicate pearl jewels. Something about her kind face caused me to pour my heart out, and she sensed my loneliness. She found me a job as the cook's helper. She always asked after my husband and daughter when she visited the kitchen. Once, when my daughter fell ill, she sent me an herbal tea that cured her. Working in the palace kitchen were some of my happiest days." She halted with the corners of her mouth lifted.

"The princess, Ma," I prompted after waiting for her to resume her tale.

"The princess?"

"When did you first meet the princess?" I repeated my question.

"I had seen her from afar a few times. One day, the cook sent me to the princess' chamber with a plate of freshly prepared milk sweets. I barely uttered a few words to the young princess. I lingered in her room with my mouth open, dazed by the large rosewood bed, silk sheets, and open airy windows." She sounded like how I had felt when I first arrived in this city.

"Then King Jayadheer died, and his oldest son, Kulashekara, came to power. Soon after, the king's half-brother, Prince Bhaskara, also died, and a pall hung over the city."

"How did King Kulashekara's brother die?" I asked, grabbing an eggplant to slice.

"Hush," she said in a loud whisper. Then she leaned in and spoke in a voice still clearly audible to anyone paying attention. As usual, the cook and her helpers ignored her mother. "Many rumors swirled around the prince's death. Some insisted the king himself murdered his half-brother. Some claimed the king's stepmother cursed her stepson after the incident. Even before this, some had called the queen-mother a *tantrika, a magician.* They also said she had practiced black magic. I only sensed kindness from her." It would have helped me to learn some tantras and mantras.

"Even the king's little niece was not spared."

"The old king killed his little niece?" I gasped. I judged my Uncle Ori harshly for wanting to marry me. The old king's actions appeared vile.

"She was just a toothless baby," said the cook's mother. *How could a king, a man entrusted to keep us safe, kill his own niece?*

"The veil over the city finally lifted when the old king crowned the young prince Rajasuriya as his heir. The prince rode through the city on a white horse, his golden crown shining." She paused to yell at her daughter about adding salt to the stew. The cook muttered under her breath.

"Why did you leave Tipti, Ma?" I asked.

"A few years later, my husband died of a snake bite. The foolish man did not see where he stepped. Princess Malathi married Chief Vikramasinha shortly after, though his father was still chief then. King Kulashekara wanted to send some helpers with the princess. I had become a good cook by then and agreed to accompany her to Singalila. I have lived here ever since."

Nothing I heard today brought me closer to finding the reason why Princess Malathi wanted to kill me. I left the kitchen mired in my thoughts and nearly bumped into the man with the long hair. I halted just in time and regarded him.

"I have been looking all over for you. Where have you been?" he asked curtly.

"In the kitchen. Cutting vegetables," I said in a wounded voice.

"Princess Malathi wants to see you," he said, starting to walk without waiting for me. I nearly ran to keep up with him.

"How is Lady Parvati doing?"

He shrugged his shoulders. I abandoned my desire to ask him more questions and remained silent.

He escorted me to the same room as before and departed. I found the princess perched on the swing, her head leaning against the iron chain that attached the swing to the ceiling as if the weight of the world rested on her shoulders. I gazed at her face as though the lines on her forehead would reveal the answers to my questions.

"Selvi, we have given the couple enough time," she said, wrinkling her nose. I guessed whatever act they needed to perform to conceive a child revolted her. I worried if the deed hurt her daughter and wished I was not so ignorant. At least

Lady Parvati need not worry about lack of privacy. She likely had her own chamber. "What do we do next?" asked the princess.

I felt foolish because I had no idea how to help Parvati conceive a child. To mask my embarrassment, I mumbled, "Let me meditate, my lady."

Before she could examine my unfitness, I dropped onto the floor. Sitting with my legs crossed, I shut my eyes and focused on the river. I imagined the water enveloping me like a mother's womb. Peace settled over me. I sensed Parvati floating on the river, her hand frequently touching her stomach. A vision of a pregnant Parvati in tears pierced my mind. Pain shot through me, and I opened my eyes, gasping for breath. I did not know why the lady cried. But I seized upon the other image I saw, that of pregnant Parvati.

"What happened? What did you see?" The princess hauled herself off the swing and crouched near me.

I could not stop the tremors in my fingers, so I clenched them into a fist. I allowed myself to smile. "Please allow me to wash Lady Parvati's feet. I believe we will hear some good news soon."

In the ensuing month, I met with Princess Malathi and her daughter frequently. I learned Lady Parvati's monthly flow was late, and a cautious optimism filled the castle. The princess trusted me more and more, and I prescribed harmless remedies for her daughter, like ginger broth to ward off nausea or saffron milk to keep the baby healthy.

One day, after the midday meal, I entered the kitchen, looking for some coconut oil. I saw the cook's mother in her usual corner. I greeted her.

Her face brightened. "Selvi, I have not seen you in many days."

"Yes, Ma," I mumbled, feeling guilty for not visiting her.

"Can you fetch me some water?"

I filled a small clay pot with water and brought it to her.

"Come sit with me. I can tell you one of my stories," the older woman said, patting the space beside her. Like the newly arrived young bride in the city, the older woman was lonely. I settled beside her and let her talk while my mind wandered.

A sudden thought occurred to me. When she paused in the middle of her tale about preparing Parvati's wedding feast, I asked, "Did you ever meet Purohit Parivan while you lived in Tipti?"

"Purohit Parivan? Why, I have not thought of him in decades," she said with a faraway gaze. "He was a favorite of King Jayadheer, who never even bathed without asking him. King Jayadheer was childless for many years, and Purohit Parivan found him his second bride. After the king's marriage, both queens gave birth to a boy in quick succession. King Jayadheer always praised Purohit Parivan for saving the kingdom from being heirless and made him his royal guru. His beautiful wife and their son frequented the palace gardens. She was a skilled healer and used the herbs we grew for her potions."

"What happened to the priest after King Jayadheer's death?" I wondered why my grandfather wanted me to find this priest and how he could have helped me.

"In the days after the king's death, rumors flew in the kitchen. Maids who served the royals always stopped to share the latest news with the cook. I heard Purohit Parivan favored Prince Bhaskara over his brother, King Kulashekara. Purohit Parivan no longer held sway over the new king, and they constantly battled over what to do. Then, after Prince Bhaskara died, Purohit Parivan left the capital and retired to a remote village in the north."

The vision from my dreams drifted into my mind. In that vision, Priest Parivan had visited my grandfather with a baby. *Who was the child he delivered into my grandfather's safekeeping? Did it happen before or after King Jayadheer's death?*

"The king's stepmother, Queen Sugandha, disappeared from Tipti as well. Some said she had gone with Purohit Parivan."

My heart nearly stopped on hearing the queen's name. It was common for folks to name their children and grandchildren after the royal family. But I grasped at this first tenuous connection I heard between Princess Malathi and me. *Did she hate me because I shared her step-grandmother's name?*

ATUL

SPRING YEAR 2

"My prince, we have a long way ahead of us today. A chariot would be better," I said, trying to dissuade the fake prince from traveling by horse.

"No, Gowri is coming to send me off. I want her to see me ride on a horse," the boy said with a sheepish grin.

Curse that girl. I thought I had seen the last of Gowri yesterday. I would have to hide from her this morning, though I hoped she would not try anything stupid in the presence of her father.

I went to the stables and found the gentlest horse for the fake prince. Chief Jeevahatta and the fake prince arrived first in the courtyard. While waiting for his wife, the chief walked among his men, leaving the boy alone.

Standing by himself, his shoulders hunched and misery writ large on his face, he appeared less like a prince and more like a lonely young child. I was tempted to approach the boy but stayed concealed among the other guards, keen to avoid Gowri.

The lady of the house and her daughter arrived with *arati* plates, the traditional way to send off loved ones. The lady waved the silver plate holding turmeric water around her husband's face to ward off evil and applied a tilak, a vermilion paste, to his forehead.

The fake prince fidgeted with a loose thread on his upper garment while Gowri repeated her mother's action. After she smeared the tilak on the fake prince's forehead, her eyes searched the crowd gathered in the courtyard. I ducked behind another man.

The fake prince chose that moment to approach his horse and call out to me. "Sword," he said in a feeble voice.

Resigned that Gowri would see me, I separated from others and proceeded toward the boy. I helped him mount the horse and handed him the reins. Gowri drew closer, her anklet bells ringing her presence.

"Bring him back safely to me," she spoke to the horse, stroking its mane.

"Don't worry, Gowri. No harm will come to me with Sword guarding me," said the fake prince.

I sensed her eyes on me but kept my gaze on the horse. "My mind is at peace with someone *strong* like him by your side," she said, emphasizing strong. "Sword, I have something for the prince. I left it in my room. Come with me to get it."

"Go with her," squeaked the fake prince.

I cursed the day I donned this disguise and followed her to the castle. She glanced at me coyly through the corner of her eye while she ascended the steps. As her long braided hair swayed with her hips, I knew I had to put an end to her infatuation with me. When I stepped inside the room, she firmly shut the door behind me and strode toward me.

I could feel her warm breath as her index finger traced my bottom lip. "What are you doing?" I asked, tired of her games.

"Making you ready to receive my message," she laughed. Her hand cupped my cheek. I knew she treated me like a toy to play with and discard.

I decided to shock her to her senses. So, I clasped her waist and pulled her against me. I could sense her heartbeat against mine. Her eyes gazed at me with a mixture of fear and excitement. Fool.

I crushed my lips against hers while I pulled my knife out. Underneath her sari, she wore a tight-fitting cloth band that covered her chest and was tied behind her back. Using the tip of the blade, I traced her spine. When I reached the knot behind her back, I cut through it. As the garment slipped, she placed her hand over the cloth to hold it in place and stepped back from me.

I sheathed my knife and moved toward her. "Stop," she said.

I ignored her and traced her spine with my finger from her neck to her hips. She gasped loudly. "Isn't this what you wanted last night?" I said. She swayed toward me, her chest rising and falling. *Did her mother not teach her anything?* I uttered a threat I had no intention of carrying out. "If I put a child in you, will the prince still marry you?"

"Child?" she mumbled, parting her lips. The mole above her lips beckoned me like a beacon. If I were not careful, she would bring me ruin.

I kissed her roughly while pinching the soft skin of her waist. That should leave a bruise.

"You are hurting me."

"I am only getting started. You will know real pain in nine months when you give birth," I said, giving her a fierce grin.

I could see her face change from confusion to panic. She retreated from me. "Leave. Else, I will call the guards."

Before she changed her mind, I opened the door and disappeared. On the stairs, I halted and raked my fingers through my hair. I despised myself for treating her poorly, but I hoped I drove Gowri away from me forever. If word reached my mother on how I treated Gowri, she would slap me for behaving like a brute. I would face the consequences of my actions soon enough.

When I reached the courtyard, I found the others ready to leave. I jumped onto my saddle and nudged the mare with my thighs. The horse, waiting impatiently to stretch her legs, took off.

I scanned my surroundings and found Guru Ori riding beside Chief Jeevahatta. He seemed comfortable handling his large stallion. The fake prince, on the other hand, squirmed in his seat as if ants were crawling in his saddle. Only after we crossed the castle gates did I slow down to approach the fake prince.

He greeted me with a scowl. From how he leaned in on his seat, I sensed his discomfort. I slowed my mare down to an easy trot. "What took you so long? What did Gowri give you?"

Curse that girl. I racked my head for an appropriate response. "She reminded me to keep you safe, my lord," I mumbled.

"How long is our journey today?"

"It is only a short ride to the river. We should reach the shores by day's end," I answered.

His scowl deepened. I doubted he would last all day long on his saddle, but I did not want to recommend the chariot ride yet. His horse followed mine, so I kept the boy occupied with mindless chatter.

When the sun rose overhead, we halted. When I helped the fake prince down, he nearly collapsed into my arms. I led him to a shady spot under the trees. His servant brought him his meal.

As he picked at his food, the fake prince asked, "Once we cross the river, how far is Tipti?"

"It will take several days by horse, my lord," I answered.

The boy's eyes clouded. I guessed the reason. "Is that where your mo—" I nearly said mother and halted just in time. The fake prince was not aware that I knew the truth about him. The real Aggabodhi's mother died years ago. Though the fake prince's mother likely still lived, he had mentioned her as his caretaker. "Is that where the woman who took care of you lives?"

He nodded, drawing circles in the rice. I had asked my men to find his mother, but I had no news yet.

"My prince, it is hot, and I am tired. If you ride in the chariot, I can accompany you," I said. I knew his pride would not allow him to ride the chariot for his own relief.

His eyes brightened. "I will grant you this favor. Prepare the chariot for my journey," he said. I dipped my head and went to make the arrangements. The rest of our journey passed uneventfully in the comfort of the chariot, and we arrived on the shores of the mighty River Sunkosh. The droughts of the last few years had reduced her water levels, but I marveled at how she still raced like a girl eager to meet her lover.

We camped beside the water that night and rose with the sun at dawn. Several boats lined up to take us across.

Chief Jeevahatta's guard commander gathered us. "Once we cross the river, we enter the Singalila region. I want you to be on high alert and guard the prince every moment."

We dispersed, and I armed myself with a bow and arrow and boarded the prince's boat. "How far will an arrow shot from that bow reach?" asked the fake prince.

"As far as the enemy's chest," I replied, scanning the horizon.

"Enemy? This is my kingdom. All its men should be loyal to me," said the fake prince.

"Yes, my lord. But my duty is to be prepared."

The fake prince stayed quiet, watching the waves crash against our boat.

"Baseborn prince, I welcome you," echoed a voice in my head. Shocked, I looked around. No one on that boat addressed me. The people who knew the truth about my birth lived in Magadha.

"Your secret is safe with me," whispered the voice. I glanced at the prince to see if he heard it, too. He watched a duck catch a fish.

"**As long as you help Sugandha**," it warned. Not that girl again, I thought grimly. A huge wave came from nowhere and drenched us. The fake prince screamed. The two boatmen struggled to keep the rocking boat afloat.

I wiped the water from my face and approached the fake prince. I draped my arm over his shoulder to keep him calm. *Who are you, and why do you want me to help Sugandha?* I asked silently.

"**I can drown you in a single wave**," the voice threatened.

Who would aid the girl then?

The strange voice chuckled, and no one else appeared to hear it. "**Find her, Prophesied Prince**," whispered the voice. Prophesied? I felt like a man thrust into a musical play, not knowing any of his lines. Just like it arrived, the voice vanished without a trace.

We reached the other side safely, and a familiar face ran toward me. "Brother," exclaimed Aggabodhi as I disembarked. But he stood awkwardly rather than approach me.

I glanced at him while I helped the prince off the boat. Only a little remained of the eager boy who had left Malla with me. After I settled the fake prince with his servants, I moved toward Aggabodhi.

"No broken nose or black eye. That's a good sign. I was worried you might have picked a fight with anyone who looked at you the wrong way."

"I am glad to see you too," he said snidely.

I punched his arm, and he grinned sheepishly.

I dragged Aggabodhi to a quiet spot. "Tell me everything you know," I said.

"Chief Vikramasinha has arrived with a small army of men."

I absorbed the news. "That may not mean he is planning any

offensive against Chief Jeevahatta. A show of strength could be an effective deterrent as well."

"You think he has brought additional men to prevent Jeevahatta from attacking," Aggabodhi said with a frown.

"That is one possibility. I will find out more when I meet him later."

That evening, I accompanied the fake prince to a small gathering in Chief Vikramasinha's tent. As I entered behind the fake prince, I glanced at the men gathered in the room. In my experience, men fell into two groups: prey or hunter.

Chief Vikramasinha held himself like a hunter. I had learned about the death of his wife, Princess Malathi, soon after I arrived in this kingdom. He did not look like a man still mourning her death. I guessed the younger man beside him to be his son-in-law.

Upon seeing us, Chief Jeevahatta peeled away from the others and approached the fake prince. Holding his elbow, the chief guided the boy back to them. "Prince Aggabodhi, son of King Rajasuriya," he said, and I carefully watched the others.

Chief Vikramasinha studied the boy, his face a mask. "My nephew has not grown for the last few years," he remarked. Few in his group chuckled.

His eyes swept the room. "I have held Prince Aggabodhi in my arms. He would be sixteen if he lived. It is traitorous to claim his identity," he said, glaring at the fake prince. The boy nearly withered under his menacing look.

"Wait here, everything I stated is true," snarled Chief Jeevahatta.

"My lord, you forgot to mention the boy is the bastard son of our king," said one of the men with Chief Vikramasinha. I nearly flinched on hearing that word, so I understood why the fake prince reacted as if someone had whipped him.

"Trueborn or not, he carries the king's blood. He even looks like his father," snapped Chief Jeevahatta. I carried the queen's blood. *Was that sufficient for me to rule Malla?*

Guru Ori cleared his throat. All eyes turned toward the tall man in saffron robes. "We are entrusted with an important duty. We need to decide who will rule this mighty kingdom. Let us put aside our differences and think about the welfare of this kingdom."

Another man with a large and grotesque mole on his cheek spoke up. "Princess Malathi's trueborn heirs have precedence over the bastard."

"Purohit Vasudev," greeted Guru Ori. "Do you have any word of my niece?" A hushed silence fell upon the room, and the man addressed as Purohit Vasudev swallowed twice but remained silent. The image of two fish-shaped eyes floated into my memory.

"I heard the news that your niece went missing, and you have been looking for her for over a year. I understand the loss of a loved one. I am still mourning the death of my wife, Princess Malathi. I hope your niece is safe. My wife would have insisted I aid you in your search. I promise to help you find her," answered Chief Vikramasinha.

Guru Ori gazed at him, his eyes narrowed. My mind wandered as the words of the voice I heard in the river echoed in my head. *With all these others seeking her, how would I find this girl?*

Chief Vikramasinha said something about a dance drama to celebrate his wife's life, and we dispersed.

On the way to his tent, the fake prince whimpered. "My lord," I said, stopping beside him while ensuring we were out of earshot of others.

"I am the king's son," he said, tears brimming in his eyes.

"I don't doubt that, my lord," I said, wishing I could comfort him better. I knew how much it hurt to be deemed unworthy.

Though, in my case, I did most of the self-assessment. "You can make your father proud by acting as his son." I tried to find the right words that would get him to take two steps forward. The wind tugged gently at our dhotis.

"He never acknowledged me," he said, his head hung low. *Why did I ever believe our situations were alike?* I had never doubted my mother's love for me or my uncle's. Even my birth father kept his distance from me out of love. His father had abandoned the poor boy in front of me.

"Mothers are better anyway. Make her proud of you." I realized why my mother had sent me to her brother. Not just to keep me safe but also to protect me from any rumors about my birth. I had never been subjected to the kind of slight the fake prince faced today. I hoped to make her proud by placing the right ruler on the Kashgar throne.

Thinking about his mother, the fake prince straightened his shoulders and wiped his eyes. We resumed our walk to his tent.

"You are a good man," he said. If only he knew the secrets I harbored. Another guard came to relieve me. "No, I want Sword to accompany me to the feast," the fake prince said, dismissing him.

As twilight descended, I escorted the fake prince to a meadow dotted with flaming torches. Insects danced around the light like drunken sailors. He sat next to Chief Jeevahatta, and I stood behind him.

While the servants brought the food, a drama troupe enacted a musical play for the audience. Though I had studied the Kashgar language, I did not follow everything sung in the poetic verses. The play depicted the story of a woman who rose to life from the river and married a king. Maybe the woman was the river in human form. She promised to come to the aid of the people in their dire need. Light and shadows played on Guru Ori's face, and his brows knitted together as the play progressed.

In the middle of the feast, a messenger approached Chief Jeevahatta, and I tilted my head to hear what he said. "Malla ships were spotted a few miles from our coast, my lord."

247

SUGANDHA

END OF YEAR 1

"Selvi, come quick!" exclaimed the man with the long hair standing outside my door.

I adjusted my saree and hastened after him. "What is the matter?" I asked, worrying Parvati had taken ill.

The man with the long hair shrugged his shoulders. After living in the castle for over four months, I should know he never answered my questions.

We hurried through bright halls filled with sunshine and stopped in front of two large wooden doors. The man with the long hair muttered in the ears of the guard outside. The guard opened the door, and I saw a few women gathered inside.

"They are expecting you," said the man with the long hair.

I stepped into the room, a tight knot twisting my stomach, and the door shut behind me. I had never grown comfortable in my life as a healer. Dispensing advice on matters I knew nothing about made me ill.

"Selvi," called Princess Malathi from beside a large bed that dominated the room. A smile played on her lips, and my breath struggled to return to normal. I walked toward her, noticing two other women standing beside her. I knew them both. One was Parvati's maid, and the other a midwife. Parvati reclined on the bed, her hands on her stomach and a content look on her face.

"The baby has quickened," said Princess Malathi, placing her hand on her daughter's belly. Watching the princess gaze at her daughter with tenderness tugged my heart. I never knew my mother.

"Do you want to feel the baby?" asked Parvati from the bed, a shy grin lifting her lips.

I nodded and leaned in to touch her stomach. All eyes turned toward me. I perceived nothing under my fingers. Panic gripped my throat.

"Here," said Parvati and moved my hand to the top right corner of her bulge.

I sensed tiny flutters like the flapping of butterfly wings. I beamed at the pregnant woman. I had heard that after the quickening, the risk of losing the baby diminished. Parvati was around the four-month mark of her pregnancy. That gave me five to six months in this castle. I knew I had grown complacent in the past few months, but with a full stomach, any dangers I had discerned seemed distant.

"Tell me if it is a boy or a girl," she asked.

The subsided panic raised its head again. I snatched my hand back. "I will meditate on it, my lady," I said, keeping the tremors out of my voice.

While I bathed in the river the next day, I reached out to the pregnant woman. I sensed her humming a song to her baby. A pleasant sensation filled my heart as I imagined my mother singing me a lullaby.

Then my vision darkened, and Parvati sobbed. Terror gripped my neck, and I pushed through the images. Parvati held a baby to her chest, cooing softly. Soon, she placed the baby on the floor and unraveled the cloth swaddle. A baby boy. The heir the princess wanted.

Suddenly, my vision changed. I saw another baby through the fog. A faceless baby girl reached toward me with her arms stretched, and my heart squeezed tight. I came up gasping as all my breath left me.

A sharp headache pierced my skull, leaving me disoriented. With difficulty, I climbed out of the water and grabbed my clothes. As I draped the sari, I tried to picture the infant I saw, but the image slipped out of my mind like sand slipping through my fingers.

All I could do that day was crawl up on my mat and wait for the pain to subside. When I woke up, darkness swirled around me. I still felt too worn to move, so I curled up and went back to sleep.

The next day, as I returned from the kitchen, I heard the familiar laughter of Parvati's husband. My feet took me in the direction of the sound. I came across the young couple standing under a mango tree, the husband holding a bow in one hand and gazing affectionately at his wife. I could see Parvati's tiny bulge through her sari. The tree bore some late-season fruits.

My feet crunched on some dry leaves, and the couple turned in unison.

"Selvi, where did you disappear yesterday?" asked Parvati.

"I had taken ill, my lady," I said.

"Did you meditate on my child?" she asked expectantly.

The vision of the baby boy on her lap floated into my mind. Then, another drifted in from a distant past. Once, when I was about ten, my grandfather had woken me up at dawn and taken me to practice archery.

Deprived of sleep, I had acted like a stubborn child, resisting to learn. When he had lost his patience with me, I had dropped my bow and walked away. When he had sought me later, I had complained about learning a skill I would never use. "What use is archery for a wife and mother?" I had repeated words I had heard others use, not understanding them completely.

Shocked, my grandfather had stood in silence. Then, slowly, he had touched my head. "My child, I hope your destiny allows you to be a wife and mother. Nothing would bring me more happiness." My kind grandfather had never pressed me to learn again until I had sought him myself and begged him to teach me.

I had not clasped a bow in over a year but held my hand out to the husband. "I will use my arrow test. If I hit a mango fruit, then it will be a boy. If the arrow reaches the leaves, it will be a girl."

Curious, the husband handed me the bow and an arrow. I nocked the arrow and regarded the stem of a mango above my head. I shut my eyes and said a quick prayer. Then, with my gaze firmly on the mango, I released the arrow. It flew into the air, striking the mango stem and tearing it from the branch.

The fruit fell toward the ground, and the husband dove to catch it. He held the green mango in his palms, a wondrous look on his face. "A son," he whispered as he spun to face his wife.

She smiled. "A son."

I felt like an intruder in their private celebration. I leaned the bow on a tree trunk and left them alone.

"Selvi, tell my mother," Parvati called over her shoulder.

On hearing the news, the princess removed a coral necklace around her neck and gave it to me. I rubbed the soft pink corals between my fingers. I had never possessed much jewelry and lost even the few trinkets I had in the river. "Ask the cook to prepare a feast for all," she said, a content look on her face. With her husband, Chief Vikramasinha, away on some political matter, she planned a visit to a temple of Goddess Earth to pray for the health of her daughter. This temple was situated on the other side of the river, so we gathered on the shores.

The river glittered like a diamond necklace. "Water levels are low because of our lack of rain. If we don't get a good downpour, our crops will fail," someone uttered.

I climbed aboard a boat with some of Parvati's companions. The flowers that adorned all our hair filled the vessel with a sweet fragrance. Once the boat floated on its way, these unmarried girls turned toward me.

"Tell us, Selvi. How come someone with your tantric talents doesn't have a child yet?" asked one of them while twisting her long braid.

"Even with my magic, you still need a husband," I giggled, momentarily forgetting I pretended to be a married woman. Recovering quickly, I said, "My husband is on a pilgrimage. He will return home soon."

"Can you find me a husband, Selvi? With broad shoulders I can bury my face in," said another, a dreamy look in her eyes.

Parimala's curse echoed in my head. *"You are doomed to a solitary life."*

I gulped my anguish. "It is better to find a boy the old-fashioned way." Suddenly, a vision of a ship wafted into my mind. A young man stood at the bow, staring into the distance. There was something about his features that reminded me of a well-tempered sword. A dull ache crept into my head like a snake slithering into a dark hole, and I shut my eyes tightly.

The girls started gossiping about eligible boys, and I let the rocking boat soothe me.

As the boat neared the shore, I opened my eyes to gaze at the pyramidal tower of a temple. I had pictured a temple similar in size to the river Goddess one I visited in Singalila. A much smaller Earth Goddess temple appeared in front of me.

The temple priest received the princess warmly and took us inside. We walked through a square hall adorned with carved pillars. I stopped to regard the sculpture of a cow and her calf on one side of a pillar. Lush grass grew at their feet.

I marveled at how the sculptor had depicted a gentle breeze causing the grass to flutter. The small inner sanctum housed the goddess idol seated on the backs of four elephants, each representing one direction.

The priest lit an oil-wicker lamp and waved it around the deity's face, chanting ancient *mantras*. "My lady, the goddess will bless you with a healthy grandson," he said, offering the lamp to the princess. Princess Malathi cupped her hands over the flame and touched her palms to her eyes, signifying her acceptance of the divine blessing.

I left the others and wandered outside. Sitting on a dry rock, I watched the boats ferrying people and goods across the river. Everyone had a purpose, including the Sunkosh River. She wanted to reach the ocean and let him envelop her in his arms.

I moved through life without any purpose beyond my survival. A row of ants crawled in a single line toward a hole at the bottom of the rock. Even these ants engaged in meaningful work every day.

Sadness engulfed my throat. I knew the time had come to leave Chief Vikramasinha's castle. The cook's mother had mentioned Purohit Parivan's village. Even if the priest was dead, I could go to his village. Someone alive might remember his stories.

"Selvi, the princess wants you," somebody called. I glanced up and saw everyone getting ready to depart. Like moving through a dream, I stood up and walked toward the princess.

"My lady," I bowed.

"Selvi, join me on my boat," she said. Gray billowing clouds gathered on the horizon. So far this monsoon season, it had rained like tears coming out of a toddler's eyes. Light rain one moment and then clear skies the next. I hoped these clouds would fill our waterways.

When the boatman helped me climb in, he peered at my face. His brows furrowed while he opened and closed his mouth a few times. Giving his head a firm shake, he started rowing.

The princess watched the water and stayed quiet. When we

approached the middle of the river, she raised her hand. The boatman stopped rowing and kept us spinning in place. The other boats continued. The first raindrops fell gently, kissing my skin, and a light breeze rustled our clothes.

Princess Malathi gazed at me. "Selvi, you helped my daughter conceive a child and saved Kashgar. There is a bigger menace threatening our kingdom. I need to find Ori's niece."

"Ori!" exclaimed the boatman.

The princess glared at him.

"Apologies, my lady. I remembered who this girl was."

With eyes narrowed, the princess observed me. All color fled my face. The sky darkened ominously. "Selvi?"

"No, this girl is too young to be her. But I know who this girl looks like," the man said.

"Who does she remind you of?" asked the princess impatiently.

"Ori's sister, my lady. Many years ago, I rowed her and her husband across these waters." Thunder rumbled like war drums while jagged bolts of lightning streaked across the sky, illuminating the face of the princess.

"She looks like Ori's sister? Who are you?" Princess Malathi asked me, her brows drawn together. The sky opened its gates, and the rain poured down. I remained silent. But she read the answer on the fear playing across my face. "You are her, Ori's niece, the girl ushering in our ruin." Her face darkened. "Kill her," she screamed at the boatman, and thunderclaps drowned her voice.

"No," I said, standing up. Rage pounded my heart like the huge waves battering our boat—enough of the royals destroying the lives of innocent people. I would not be a victim.

The boat's bow plunged, causing a cascade of water to wash over the deck. The river churned the boat relentlessly as if it echoed my will to survive. The vessel's wooden hull creaked and groaned, and the boatman clung to his oar, trying desperately to maintain control. I could not let them live. They knew my secrets. A monstrous wave capsized the craft and threw us into the embrace of the mighty river.

The current twirled us around like leaves. I saw the boatman come up for air before I sank. *Drown them,* I thought. Let my secret perish with them.

ATUL

SPRING YEAR 2

When Chief Jeevahatta heard the message about the Malla ships on his shores, he peered at the messenger with his mouth open. However, I doubted the words had caused his heart to race as fast as mine. I wanted to gather all my men and vanish from here. Yet, I stood rooted to the ground like a tree trunk.

"Ships?" whispered Chief Jeevahatta, finally finding his voice.

The messenger nodded.

The chief waved the messenger away and scratched his chin. With my index finger, I drew circles on my waist and scanned the room. Apart from the chief, everyone else appeared to be enjoying the feast. I could not leave now. It would raise suspicion. When my duty ended tonight, I would slip away with Aggabodhi.

I watched the chief closely as he beckoned one of his men. "Tell Chief Vikramasinha I want to meet him after this play ends."

The man scurried away while the chief tapped his fingers on

the table. It seemed an eternity before the drama ended. I escorted the tired fake prince back to his tent.

"Did you see how the river goddess defended the king?" the fake prince asked while slipping under the covers on his bed.

With other things on my mind, I nodded grimly. I barely watched the play after the messenger arrived carrying his dire news.

"My mother performed as the river Goddess once," the boy whispered, no longer hiding from the truth.

I glanced at him, wondering what would happen if the truth about my birth came out. "What is your name?" I asked, not wanting to think of him as the fake prince anymore.

"Dipankara," he whispered.

"Prince Dipankara, I am honored to serve you," I said truthfully. His eyes misted on hearing my words. Soon, his breathing settled into a steady rhythm as sleep claimed him.

Once another guard relieved me, I marched to find Aggabodhi.

He sat staring into a diminishing fire. "Bodhi," I called.

"Brother," he said and stood up.

He followed me to a quiet spot. "What did my uncle Vikramasinha say about my bastard brother?"

I wrinkled my nose at how he described his brother. The boy was not at fault for the behavior of his parents. Aggabodhi moved restlessly, shifting from one foot to another. The latest news about Malla ships had crowded all else out of my mind. I tried to recollect what had happened earlier that day. "Your uncle immediately realized your brother was too young to be you."

Aggabodhi chuckled while rubbing his palms. "What did Chief Jeevahatta say to that?"

"He accepted the truth and said Dipankara was a son of the late king."

"Dipankara," he spit out the name as if condemning his brother. "Bastard son," he repeated that hideous term.

Another time, I would have admonished him, but I had more pressing matters to discuss. "Listen, Bodhi. A messenger brought the news that he saw Malla ships on the shores of Kashgar. We cannot stay here any longer. Be ready to leave in a few moments. I will get my guards, and we will join the rest of my men camped a few miles from here."

Aggabodhi gripped my elbow and pulled me toward him. "Atul, I cannot leave now. I will reveal myself to my uncle. With him and you on my side, I can capture the throne."

"No, Bodhi. This is not the right time. I am here with only two guards. If the chiefs decide to capture us, we cannot fight back. Let us leave tonight. Once we are safe, I can send a messenger to both the chiefs, and we can meet them as princes with our royal ensemble."

Aggabodhi let go of me. "You are right," he said.

"Get ready to leave and meet me here," I said and went looking for my personal guards. Dayalu and Pusha found me before I stumbled upon them. I told them what I heard at the feast. "Time for us to flee." After agreeing to meet them by a banyan tree a few yards from the end of our campsite, I collected my belongings. I returned to the place where Aggabodhi and I spoke and waited.

Suddenly, I saw a figure sneak toward Dipankara's tent. A figure that looked remarkably like Aggabodhi. With a sense of foreboding, I saw him halt outside the tent. I promised to protect that boy. I could not let Aggabodhi harm his own brother.

I walked purposefully toward the tent as if I were still guarding Dipankara. When I lifted the tent opening and entered, Aggabodhi clamped his hand over the mouth of the man protecting his half-brother. Before I took a step in, Aggabodhi plunged his dagger into the man's chest and let him fall to the ground.

He removed his weapon from the slack body and looked up as I entered. Our eyes locked, and I tried hard to keep my horror masked. "Brother, help me finish this pretender, and we can leave," Aggabodhi said.

I drew my sword out, my anxiety building. "You call me your brother. How can I let you kill yours, that too, a blood brother?"

Aggabodhi's lips twisted into a menacing smile. "I knew you wanted to protect this weak and pathetic lad. You lack the ruthlessness to be a ruler, Atul."

"Bodhi, don't do this. He can become a valuable ally when you rule this land. Escape with me."

Instead of listening, Aggabodhi ran toward the sleeping boy with the dagger dripping with blood. I ran after him. Dipankara woke up at the commotion. "Sword," he whispered from his bed.

Aggabodhi jabbed his weapon, and I caught the sharp end with my blade. Aggabodhi pulled out his sword with his other hand and swiped at Dipankara. He ripped the silk sheets while I dived to shield Dipankara.

"Get off the bed," I screamed and vaulted onto the bed. Dipankara rolled awkwardly. Aggabodhi's blade plunged into the boy's arm, and he cried.

I kicked Aggabodhi's chest, and he stumbled back. "Do you know how many times I have been tempted to kill Ori? But I held back for your sake. Don't spoil everything we have worked for. Let us leave now while we can."

Instead of answering, Aggabodhi thrust his dagger at me. I shifted aside and attacked him. While Dipankara sobbed, Aggabodhi and I danced around the room. Pots dropped to the floor, breaking into pieces. Pillows spilled out their feathers, which floated in the air.

In the dimly lit room, we cast long shadows on the wall. We knew each other's moves well, having trained side by side.

Aggabodhi's initial strikes were cautious, and I parried them, the ring of metal on metal echoing in the night air.

For a brief moment, as Aggabodhi spun, he left his chest exposed to me. I hesitated to maim him, our shared history lingering in the air. When he landed, he stuck my shoulder with his sword, drawing blood. Pain flared down my back.

Curse this fool. Using my height to my advantage, I swept my arm in a powerful arc and landed a crushing blow to his head. Aggabodhi, momentarily disoriented, staggered back.

I heard the sound of rushing footsteps. "Go," I whispered to him. Glaring at me with hatred, he delivered a burst of strikes. I sidestepped his attacks.

"Catch that man. He tried to kill me. If not for Sword's bravery, I would be dead," cried Dipankara.

As two other soldiers approached us, I darted around Aggabodhi and muttered in his ears, "Don't do anything stupid. I will come to rescue you."

He glared at me as I pointed my blade at his chest. "Drop your weapons. No harm will come to you."

With a growl, Aggabodhi let go of his weapons. Holding him on each side, they dragged him away. In a flurry of activity, a healer arrived to patch us up. Before I could slip away, Chief Jeevahatta entered the tent.

"Uncle Jeevahatta," whimpered Dipankara.

The chief patted Dipankara's head awkwardly.

"Are you the one who saved him?"

"Yes, he nearly died for me," gushed Dipankara. "Who was that man who hurt me?"

"He is claiming to be Prince Aggabodhi and has demanded to see Chief Vikramasinha," the chief sighed.

"Prince Aggabodhi? My brother?" mumbled Dipankara.

I had planned everything meticulously for months, and that idiot had unraveled everything in a day.

Making some excuses about needing to rest, I left the tent

and headed toward some bushes. Making sure I was alone, I crawled through them on my knees, putting some distance between the camp and me. Once I felt safe, I rose to my feet and crept to the banyan tree. My guards ran toward me. "Prince Atul, you are hurt," said Dayalu, gazing at my shoulder wrapped in a bloody cloth.

"Jeevahatta's men captured Aggabodhi," I said and gave them the details.

"Do we go back and rescue him?"

"No," I said with a heavy heart. "They outnumber us, and I won't risk our lives." And I was still mad at the reckless prince for putting our mission in danger.

With that, the three of us walked into the night.

SUGANDHA

WINTER YEAR 2

I sank down and down, letting the water take me home. A school of fish gathered around me and pushed me up. Maybe I dreamt that part. My head broke the surface, and I gasped for breath. Like the air filling my body, my memories came rushing back in. I had killed the princess and the boatman. Pain ripped my heart, and I could not bear to see another sunrise. I let go.

Water surrounded me like a blanket. I wanted to rest at the bottom of the river on the fine sand that felt like silk. A bird dragged me to the top, its beak clutching the back of my neck. Did I dream that too? A flutter of wings caused my eyes to open. The world seemed to blur at the edges as exhaustion threatened to overwhelm my senses. I blinked a few times and noticed a pale light filling the horizon. The scent of wet foliage wafted through the air. My ear appeared to rest on something moist and slippery. I shifted slowly to glance at lotus leaves.

A tiny bubble popped on the surface, and a thought burst into my head. Maybe the princess and the boatman had survived and washed ashore. That view gave me the strength to scan my surroundings. I was in some body of water, nestled among lotus plants.

When I gazed up, I could see pink buds starting to bloom. A shimmer danced at the corner of my vision. I turned my neck with effort. Swan! The rising sun illuminated its gold-tipped feathers. The bird cocked its head to one side and stared at me.

"I am glad to see you," I murmured. Taking a deep breath, I swam toward the shore. The swan floated along. I collapsed on the wet sand, gulping in the air. After a few moments, I sat up. I was several yards away from where we should have landed.

How much time had passed since the storm? We should have landed during twilight, so at least one night had passed. I saw no search activities on the river bank. That appeared strange. I would have expected Chief Vikramasinha's men to scour the area during daylight.

I stood up and wobbled on my feet. Feeling lightheaded, I dropped onto my knees. Hunger and thirst became my relentless companions as my empty stomach churned. I dragged myself to the water, weariness echoing in each step. I cupped my hands and gulped the water down, letting the liquid nourish my body. Satiated, I rolled onto my side.

I could not go into the village as a girl. Like the boatman, others might recognize me. I hid among some bushes, waiting for the washerwomen to bring clothes to wash. The swan swam in the river, and I drew comfort from its presence. Soon, two women walked to the river, bearing a sack of dirty clothes. Leaving most of the clothes on the shore, they carried one or two pieces into the water to clean.

If I could distract them, I could sneak in and steal some clothes. As if hearing my thoughts, the swan floated next to the women, flapping its wings. As the washerwomen tried to get away from the hissing swan, I crept in with a smile on my face and stole a dhoti and an upper garment. A bird that read my mind could come in handy.

Donning the disguise of a boy, I approached the two women. "Is that bird troubling you?" I asked.

The swan stared at us from a few feet away. The women eyed it cautiously. "We must be close to its nest," one of them murmured. "We will go to another spot tomorrow."

I stood silently, struggling to inquire about Princess Malathi. One of the women brought up a related subject. "Since the storm, even the river creatures are agitated."

"What happened to the princess?" I asked and instantly regretted being so direct in my questioning.

The woman wrung the water out of a sari and tossed the garment on her shoulder. "They found her lifeless body last night. Her poor daughter paced the shores for two days, hoping to find her mother alive."

Waves of nausea threatened to overwhelm me. I bit my lips to control it. I was a monster that killed mothers.

"Are you okay, lad?" she asked, gazing at my face.

I nodded, unable to form any words. Tears filled my eyes. I staggered away from the river, drowning in grief. I found an isolated area and collapsed on the ground. Two days? I had been unconscious for longer than I imagined.

The swan pecked at me with its beak. "Leave me. I only bring death and ruin. I don't deserve your kindness," I mumbled. Voices drifted in the air, and reluctantly, I sat up. "Where do I go?" I whispered. The bird tugged at my dhoti. "You have a place in mind?" I asked and rose. That was when I heard the cries coming from the river.

I ran toward the water and saw people on the shore screaming. I scanned the water and found some dark heads swimming around. They did not appear to be in trouble. I searched the shores again. A woman sobbed while beating her chest.

"What happened?" I asked.

"My son," she hiccupped. "He is only four. The cursed river has claimed him like it swallowed those three people." The river had swallowed only two people. I had survived for an unknown reason.

"Help me find the child," I prayed and dived in. I opened my eyes and peered through the churning water. Two feet kicked up the currents, muddying the water. Something beckoned me—deeper—and I followed that tiny ray of light.

I found a small body facing down on the river's bottom. *No. Please let him be alive.* I lifted the limp body gently and held him against my chest. I felt a trifling spark of life clinging to his cold body.

"Mother, help me save him," I pleaded as I kicked my legs with all the force I could muster. Loud yells greeted me as I broke the surface. Someone grabbed the child from my hands and passed him to his mother.

I heard the whimper of a child as I rose out of the water. He will live. I turned to leave. "Wait," a woman called.

I halted. "You saved my boy," the mother said, approaching me. She clutched the child to her body like he was the most precious thing. Jealousy clawed my throat. I wished for a mother who would tell me what to do. "I have not seen you before," she continued.

"I am a traveler on my way to see my family," I lied easily.

"Let me give you some food and dry clothes," she said warmly. I wanted to decline, but my empty stomach growled in anticipation.

I accepted her hospitality and followed her home. She took me to a modest single-room hut. "My husband has gone to the market to sell our goat," she said, settling the boy on the floor. Lying on his side, he stretched his hand, pointing to something. I followed his fingers and found a wooden toy. I picked it up. An elephant carved out of teak nestled in my palm, its trunk chipped at the end. I placed it in the boy's hand. He made a trumpeting sound while moving the toy in the air. While his movements were sluggish, I felt hope that he would make a full recovery.

His mother scooped some day-old rice into a bowl, poured sour buttermilk over it, and handed me the dish. I mixed the rice with my fingers and gulped the food down.

She rummaged in an old trunk and took out a worn but clean dhoti. "You can change into this," she said.

Looking at her meager possessions, I knew her husband did not have many clothes to spare. Her generosity overwhelmed me. I shook my head. "That is not needed, Sister. My clothes will dry in the sun."

She thanked me profusely for saving her son's life. I accepted her gratitude with reluctance, knowing I had taken two lives. Wishing her well, I wandered the countryside with no set destination in mind.

Days passed in a blur. One evening, as the sun set, I peeked into an old barn. Smelling of manure and hay, it appeared abandoned. Rat feces dotted the floor, and spider webs hung from the ceiling.

I spotted an old broom leaning against the wall. I swept the floor clean and dusted off the webs. I made a bed out of hay. Placing the broom beside me, I fell into a disturbed sleep, dreaming of my faceless mother. Her melodious lullaby turned into an odious hiss and startled me awake. Wiping the crust off my eyes, I looked around in the dim moonlight. A cobra stood ready to strike.

Wielding the broom as a weapon, I tried to scare the snake away. Instead of slithering away, it attacked me. I took off at a run and sprinted into the meadow outside. My guardian swan flew in and attacked the beast. I joined the fight. The swan pecked at the snake's eyes, blinding him. The sun loomed on the horizon when it crawled away in defeat. Exhausted, I stroked the bird's neck.

I found work as a cowherd in a nearby village. All able-bodied young men appeared to have joined one of the two chiefs' armies, so the farmer hired me eagerly. After a peaceful day in the meadow, I slept among the cows that night. Loud moos woke me up. I found a calf dead on the ground and a snake crawling toward me. Terror gripped me as I ran out as fast as my feet could carry me.

I did not know what I was running toward. But with every pounding step I took against the hard ground, I feared I would not reach it. I made my way up over a mound, frightening cows grazing on pastures as I leaped over a fence on the way down.

When my lungs burned and I lost all feeling in my feet, I stopped and leaned against a wall. My heart pounded against my sweat-dampened chest while I caught my breath. A snake slithered through a hole under the brick wall. A sense of dread pervaded my mind. I knew I had to flee before the snake struck me. Yet I could not move. My heart beat so hard I thought I would collapse where I stood. I held onto the wall and slid down on wobbly knees. I huddled against the wall with my hands drawn over my head, waiting for the bite. Then, I saw a flash and nearly screamed.

A mongoose caught the snake in its long, curved claws. When the animal dragged the half-dead snake to its den, I followed. Mongooses were the natural predators of snakes and should offer me some protection. The animal entered a crevice under a tree, and I climbed up the trunk.

I peeked through the leaves, and suddenly, a face loomed near me. I turned to catch a glimpse of the young man from my vision—the one who reminded me of a well-tempered sword. I reached out to touch his face and only caught the air. Nervously, I let go of the branches, and he vanished in the blink of an eye.

Who was this man? Why did snakes chase me? I only had questions and no answers.

When thirst pricked my throat, I looked around—carefully—

before sliding down the tree. I broke a long branch off to use as a weapon and walked to the nearest stream. I cupped my hands and plunged them into the cold stream. Bringing the liquid to my mouth, I drank deeply. Suddenly, I felt someone watching me. I glanced around and saw no one.

On a vague intuition, I stepped into the water. The tempered sword young man emerged as a ghost with shimmering edges. He appeared to be lying on the ground with his eyes closed. *Was he dreaming about me in his sleep?*

"Who are you?" I asked. He remained mute. I wondered if he was a sorcerer who invoked a curse to send snakes after me. Anger coursed through me, and I grabbed his throat.

Shocked by my action, he choked out, "No-Not your enemy."

I let go, and he disappeared. A stabbing pain hit my temple. I shut my eyes till the ache subsided.

I did not know if a day or a week had passed. In a confusing blur, snakes swooped at me without mercy. They fell onto my back from treetops. I found no respite from the beasts, and every sound made me jump.

I eyed everything suspiciously. I was afraid I was losing my mind. A tremor ravaged my body. Tired and in pain, I staggered to the river, my safe haven. On the sandy shore, I found an empty boat. My worn body begged me to halt. I climbed into the craft and rested my head on the plank. The last sound I heard was an ominous hiss.

ATUL

SPRING YEAR 2

I heard the sound of hooves and paused. "If Aggabodhi blurted out our mission, the chiefs will send men to capture me."

Dayalu, my guard, drew his sword. "Please leave from here, my lord. We will stay and fight," he said.

"I have a better idea. Let us climb these trees and hide among the leaves. I don't want to risk our lives without knowing who these men are."

My guards sheathed their weapons. Holding onto a branch with both my hands, I hauled myself up onto a sturdy limb of the tree. Scaling further up, I nestled among the leaves and peeked down.

In the moonlight, I saw four horse-mounted riders halt under the trees. The horses, their breaths warm and heavy, pawed at the soft earth—a symphony of snorts and whinnies filled the air. A smaller animal sniffed the ground. They had brought a hound to track me. It was risky, but I decided to act while I had the element of surprise on my side.

Drawing my dagger, I flew down the trunk and landed on top of a horse standing underneath me. The rider and his mount smelled of an odd mixture of hay, sweat, and dirt. Before the rider could react, I pushed him off the saddle.

I held the reins and coaxed the horse a few feet away as the unhorsed rider staggered back a few steps and fell on his stomach. The other three men rounded up to face me. At that instant, my guards leaped down from the trees with a piercing battle cry.

Dayalu sliced a man's neck as he landed on the ground. My guard rolled to the side and bounced to his feet. In the blink of an eye, Dayalu pulled the leg of the man he had injured and unsaddled the rider. The rider's limp body hit the ground, his arms and legs stretched at an odd angle. I doubted he would live to see another daylight. One down, three left.

I leaned back to draw my sword from the sheath at my hip while simultaneously pulling the stallion's reins. The horse reared its head, and I brought its hooves down on one of the two remaining riders.

The man slipped off his saddle while his horse ran away from the chaos. The strike jostled his grip on his sword, and it fell with a clang and skittered away. The whinnying of the horses mingled with the loud barking of the hound to create a cacophony of noise. The last mounted rider rushed at me before I could react. He swiped his sword and tore a gash through my arm.

As blood oozed out of the wound, I heard a loud cry and turned to watch my other guard, Pusha, meet the pointy end of a spear. Pusha crashed to the ground and twitched. His opponent, the man I had first unhorsed, marched to my dying guard's side. I wanted to rush to my guard's side and pull him atop my horse. But I had enemies of my own to contend with.

The sole rider, still on horseback, maneuvered his horse to face me. "Prince Atul, I have instructions to capture you. No harm will come to you or your men if you surrender."

I steered around him. "I will let you leave in peace. Tell the chiefs I will return as Prince Atul, Crown Prince of Malla."

The man I knocked to the ground earlier held the end of the spear protruding from Pusha and twisted it, plunging it deeper into the heart of the man sworn to die for me. With a whimper, my guard perished. The man turned to me. "You don't make the dem—"

Before he could finish his sentence, I rode forward, hoisted my blade high, and slashed his throat. As his scream rushed into my ears, I realized I had killed my first man. I glanced at the blood dripping from my sword and gripped the hilt tightly.

I only felt rage at the death of my guard and no remorse for killing the savage. Dayalu swung his sword at the other warrior still on his feet, and the clash of metal echoed in the air. While the two fought fiercely, I faced the lone rider. "Unless you wish to die at my hands, return to your lord."

Before our eyes, Dayalu sank his sword into his opponent and kicked him to the ground. As the lone rider shuffled his horse around, I blocked his path. "Leave on foot," I ordered. After one glance at me, the man dismounted, called the hound to him, and walked the way he had come.

Dayalu grabbed the reins of one of the horses and placed Pusha's body on it. While he mounted the other horse, I seized the fourth horse. Watching our backs, we thundered across the terrain, pushing the weary horses.

We kept a lookout as we made our way through a mist that rose from the river and blanketed us. The night and mist made it seem like we were passing through a cave. We picked our way carefully through the darkness and sprinted whenever the fog shifted to allow the moon to illuminate the way.

The sky lightened as we halted by the river. "Let me look at your arm, my lord," Dayalu said.

I glanced at it. The blood had clotted around the rip. I allowed him to tie a cloth around it. "The cut is not deep and will heal on its own. We have another problem. Dayalu, we stand out on these horses. We have to travel by foot," I remarked, watching the dark blue night sky change to gray.

"What do we do with Pusha, my lord?" Dayalu asked, pointing to the corpse of the man who had vowed to protect me with his life.

"Strip him of any personal belongings. His mother will treasure those. Then let us give him a river burial," I said, choking down my grief.

"You died a warrior's death with a sword in your hands," said Dayalu as we carried the body into the water.

"Your sacrifice will not go to waste. I will strive to be worthy of it," I whispered as we let the river carry the dead body. I knew Dayalu gazed at me as I wiped my eyes. Without glancing at him, I marched to the horses. Their whinnying greeted me. Rubbing their manes, I set them loose. They dashed back south to their master.

Under the cover of the fog that rose from the river, Dayalu and I walked north. "Your height puts you at a disadvantage, my lord. Those hunting for us can easily spot you."

"Do you know any *mantra* to shrink me?" I jested. A strange cold had clutched my heart from the death of my guard and the man I had killed. I kept moving, afraid my horror at these deaths would freeze me in place.

"I stay away from magic, my prince. But I know a trick or two to disguise you. A coating of ash on your hair to age you, and then if you hunch—"

"Make me look older. But I am not going to pretend to be a hunchback or a stooped old man," I said vehemently. I let Dayalu sprinkle ash on the hair on my head and face while I kept my eyes closed. Worry about losing Dayalu plagued me. Then, a way to keep him alive popped into my head. "The chiefs won't harm me. That would risk a war with Magadha, and they can ill afford that. But you, on the other hand, will wear a bright target on your forehead if you accompany me. I am not going to risk your life. Let us split up."

Dayalu protested. "My lord, I cannot protect you if I abandon you."

I ignored his objection. "I can hide my height by folding myself into a boat. I will row up the river, and you can travel by foot. We can meet again by nightfall."

"My lord, I can find us a boat. If you crouch inside the boat and hide, I can row."

I shook my head. "No more concealing myself. Also, the chiefs would not expect me to be alone." Dayalu gazed at my face and realized the futility of arguing with me. Soon, I perched on a wooden plank and rowed up the river. I sensed Dayalu watching me from the shore but disregarded his attention.

Instead, I inhaled the crisp morning air and watched the sun rise over some distant mountains. My mind raced with questions. *How would I free Aggabodhi? Did he even want to be rescued? Would Chief Jeevahatta back Aggabodhi instead of his half-brother?* And Chief Vikramasinha had a daughter with her own claim to the throne. In the midst of this, memories of the strange river girl and her fish-shaped eyes wafted in. *Who was she?*

The mist hanging over the river cleared, and I saw a swan gliding on the water. Its feathers, white as snow, transformed the greenery around me to the color of a pearl. Its beak, red as a coral, changed the color of the water around it. Then, I noticed the gold-tipped wings, a bird unlike any I had seen before. Boldly, it turned to look at me.

As I watched, the bird waded toward me and flew into the boat. While I gazed at it in wonder, the bird tugged my dhoti with its beak. Recovering from my initial shock at seeing the swan up close, I tried to shoo the bird away.

Then, something strange happened. A large wave overturned my boat and tossed me into the river. For a moment, I could not tell up from down. Then the voice—eerie yet familiar—spoke in my head. **"Follow the swan"**.

Curse these mystical voices. *Didn't the voice speak to me while we had traveled by water yesterday? Why couldn't it do the same today instead of getting me soaking wet?* I surfaced, gasping for breath.

A gentle wind tossed my boat, and the swan drifted beside it. Wearily, I climbed into the craft. Reaching across the water, I grabbed the oar floating nearby and started rowing again. "Lead me," I said, feeling like an idiot for talking to a bird.

The swan glided ahead. I followed grudgingly, muttering under my breath. Sweat trickled down my back as the sun climbed higher. My stomach grumbled, and I tried to recollect my last meal. I remembered some porridge I ate yesterday morning. Last night, all I did was watch others eat.

We approached a forested area surrounded by trees. The swan waded onto the shore and waited. In a foul mood, I leaped out and dragged the boat onto the gravel. That was when I saw the other craft resting a few feet inland.

Gripping the hilt of my sword, I strode toward that vessel. Inside, I found the girl—dressed in a boy's clothes—who had haunted me this past month.

I stood frozen, gazing at her until the swan squawked loudly. Coming out of my stupor, I noticed the bluish tint on her lips. She hadn't made any movement since I arrived. Panicking that I had come too late, I rushed to her side and grasped her wrist. I sensed a faint pulse.

Worried about losing someone else that day, I bent down and picked up her limp body in my arms. Guided by some instinct, I marched to the river. Clutching her tightly, I trudged in till I stood in chest-high water.

Fear raked my mind as I steeled myself and submerged with her. For an eternity, nothing happened. Then, a swift current pulled us in and churned us around—faster and faster. I held onto the girl, forgetting to breathe. Everything went completely still as I watched something dark approach us. The beast resembled a snake but was also unlike any I had seen on land. My heart raced as I watched the creature bite her ankle. A scream of pure terror rose up my throat.

Then the girl in my arms opened her eyes.

SUGANDHA

SPRING YEAR 2

I was on fire while snakes twisted around every part of my body, leaving me breathless. I was dying—by drowning in dark water.

A hand closed around my waist. I sensed my beating heart—wait—I heard more than one heart.

I opened my eyes and gazed at brows knitted together with concern. The young man I had seen in my dreams held me tightly. *Was I dead, and had I reached the abode of divine beings?* Before I could react, he kicked his feet and broke through the surface of the water, shattering my illusions about his divinity.

He waded out of the river, his grip as powerful as his stare. My heart hammered when I realized a strange man held me in his arms. I jumped out and faced him. I was not particularly small, but he seemed imposingly tall. Mustering my courage, I threw my question at him. "Who are you?"

He looked amused for a brief moment, and then a mask went up on his face. "Who am I? Did you send those visions to a stranger?"

I looked at him, confused. "What visions?"

His eyes narrowed while we stared at each other awkwardly. "Sugandha—" he started.

I nearly leaped out of my skin. *How did he know my name?* My body crouched into a defensive posture. "Who sent you?"

He observed every move of mine. "Who sent me? Weren't you asking me to find you? Protect you?"

His words made no sense to me. I straightened my shoulders. "Tell me your story from the beginning."

Matching my action, he drew himself to his full height and towered over me. "Never mind my story. Why do you need my protection?" he asked.

"I don't need your protection," I said defiantly.

We glared at each other. I did not wilt beneath his steely stare. He took a step toward me. "I am sorry about my questions. Especially after your near-death experience."

I did not expect him to apologize, so I had no response.

"I am just trying to understand—" He gestured vaguely at me.

A wave of tiredness rolled through me. I tucked my chin to my chest to stop the trembling that threatened to erupt.

"Are you okay?" He took another step toward me.

I was too weary to form words, so I just nodded. I wanted him to leave me alone. Instead, he held my elbow and guided me to a dry spot. As I sat down, he left my side. I bent my knees and placed my head between them, waiting for the dizziness to dissipate.

He returned with a half coconut shell filled with water. A part of my mind, still capable of thinking, wondered where he got half a coconut shell.

"Drink," he said in a voice accustomed to being obeyed. I guided his hands to my face and sipped the liquid. Strength returned to my limbs as I breathed in and out.

He crouched beside me. I realized that I had not thanked

him for saving my life. "I must appear as an ungrateful boor. I do appreciate your actions."

"What happened to you?" He genuinely sounded like he cared.

"Snakes have been chasing me for days. Finally, one succeeded in catching me," I said, sneaking a peek at him out of the corner of my eye. He stared at the river, but the furrow of his brow told me he listened attentively.

"When I found you, it looked like someone had poisoned you. A snake bite would explain the bluish tint on your skin. But why would they hunt you?"

"I suspect someone cursed me to be haunted by these reptiles," I mumbled. If snakes continued to seek me, I would put his life in danger as well. "Look, I will be fine after some rest. You can leave now."

He did not say anything for a while. Then he fixed me with a curious look. "Why is Guru Ori looking for you?"

Shocked by his question, I froze with my mouth open. Finally, I found my voice. "What? Guru Ori?" My words came out in a jumble.

He was quiet for a beat. "I know you are Sugandha, Guru Ori's niece." He paused as if waiting for my confirmation. I nodded slowly, hoping he could tell me more about myself. "I know your uncle is intent on finding you. But you have evaded him because of a protective spell."

I gasped out loud on hearing this. "How do you know about the spell?"

He shrugged his shoulders. "I witnessed a priest trying to seek you. He nearly died in his attempt."

"What else do you know about me?"

"I heard voices urging me to find and shield you from harm. I know I sound mad," he said with a crooked grin.

"You did not go mad," I answered.

He waited for me to continue.

"I saw you too—in my visions." I lifted my eyes to the blue sky. For some unknown reason, I felt compelled to talk to him. "My grandfather's final act was to cast a blessing on me, to hide me from my uncle." My chest tightened as I relived those memories.

He waited without saying anything. "I don't know why my uncle seeks me. I don't know why Princess Malathi wanted me dead. Now, I will never find out because I killed her." A heaviness pressed against my chest, and I could hardly breathe.

"If she planned to kill you, there is nothing wrong with defending yourself. You wanted to live," he said gently.

"I don't know. Maybe I could have escaped without murdering her and another innocent man," I said. My body threatened to seize up in guilt.

"I killed my first man yesterday," he said, sounding as if he was thinking out loud. "I understand what you are going through," he added, his finger drawing circles on the sand.

We fell silent again. The world around us came alive. Birds sang as they left their nests, looking for prey. Boats slid past us carrying vegetables and fruits.

"I am sorry about this," I said.

"Sorry?"

"For bringing you into my messy world. I will deal with whatever happens. You don't have to worry about me."

Suddenly, I heard voices—real ones, not the ones I usually perceived in my head. A few men with weapons drawn approached us. Fear clutched my throat. *Ori's men?*

"There he is," yelled one of them, pointing at us. I assumed the 'he' meant me because I still wore the garments of a man. We both hopped to our feet and faced them. The tall man beside me—I did not even know his name—drew his sword. Then, an arrow flew out of nowhere, slicing through the air, and lodged itself in his chest. He stumbled backward, tumbling through the air.

I caught his arm and dragged him to the river. I plunged into the water, pulling him along while muttering a prayer. If Ori's men were after me, I had endangered the tall man's life. But how did Ori's men find me while my grandfather's blessing protected me?

Maybe it was Chief Vikramasinha's men looking for Princess Malathi's murderer? Two dark creatures slithered to my side, guiding me deeper. Trusting these river animals, I followed them to an underground cave.

The walls of the cave glowed in the darkness. In the dim light, I saw an enormous, three-hooded snake watching me. I wish I had paid attention when my grandfather told me stories about Nagas, a semi-divine serpent race. All I remembered was that they dwelled under bodies of water.

"Sugandha, welcome to *Nagaloka*, my abode. I am Princess Ulipi," spoke the nagin. I recollected how my grandfather addressed a male naga as just a naga and a female one as a nagin. Her body glistened like a green emerald.

Despite the dark surroundings, she radiated warmth and comfort. I recalled a story of Nagas helping a mortal, so I sought her aid. "Princess Ulipi, I am indebted to this young man for saving my life. I implore you; please assist me in bringing him back to life."

"Come with me," said the princess and glided inside. Mesmerized by everything around me, I would have spent hours exploring if not for the man in my arms. I could feel the warmth seeping out of him, so I knew I only had a short time to restore him.

"We will carry him," said a naga. I moved away to let the four snakes—single-hooded—curl their giant tails around the tall man's body and lift him. They placed him on a rock bench. A two-hooded being pulled out the arrow from his chest and covered his wound with a pungent-smelling mixture.

"I will give him an elixir known as *nava pashana*, made from nine deadly poisons," said the two-hooded snake.

"Poison?"

"Snakes, our land cousins, will continue to hunt for you. When this young man brought you to the river earlier, one of the Nagas infused our venom into you. That will shield you from many poisons, including venomous snake bites. You need the help of this young man to save the Kashgar kingdom. This elixir will protect him from snake bites, too. And help him survive underwater for a day. In some mortals, it will even enhance their strength," answered the princess.

I stood dazed by her response. *Save Kashgar? What did she mean by that?* Then, a strange question arose in me. "How am I breathing in this underwater cave?"

Princess Ulipi laughed softly. "Because you are a child of the river."

ATUL

SPRING YEAR 2

Someone yanked me out of the cold water and pulled me through the muddy bank. I tried to roll onto my side, but excruciating pain stabbed me, so I gave up and stayed motionless. Next, when my eyes opened, I gazed at a starry sky. My head felt too heavy to move, so I closed my eyes. A hand brushed my forehead, making me feel oddly warm and safe.

A shadow swept over me, and I blinked my eyes open. "My lord," said Dayalu, kneeling beside me.

I pushed onto my hands and knees and coughed up the river water. "What happened?" I asked in a hoarse voice. "How did you find me?" I scanned the surroundings, looking for Sugandha, and was disappointed not to see her. I had hoped to learn more about her and why she haunted me.

"I saw Chief Vikramasinha's men and followed them. They led me to you. Before I could warn you, they shot an arrow in your chest. A boy—a stranger—plunged into the river with you. The men who sought you waited for some time along the shores of the river. They left, thinking you were dead. I continued my search for you. By nightfall, I had nearly given up hope when the same boy surfaced, pulling you along. I helped him bring you ashore," Dayalu recounted his tale.

I touched the spot on my chest, pierced by the arrow. Apart from a fading scar, the wound had healed completely. I knew no human could have mended the injury so quickly. "Where is the boy?" I asked, glad I had not imagined Sugandha.

"I am here," she called from behind the trees. I turned, and she emerged from the shadows, appearing like a mystical nymph despite the man's garments she wore. "This man claimed to be your servant, so I left you in his care while I fetched food." She held some bananas and mangoes in a makeshift cloth bag.

"Dayalu is more than my servant," I answered while gazing at Sugandha. I had many questions for her, including how she had mended me. But my stomach growled in hunger and demanded my immediate attention. I approached her.

Sugandha handed me a ripe mango and some bananas. I peeled the golden skin of the mango with my teeth and bit into the sweet flesh. Juice dripped down my chin as I scraped every bit of the fruit clinging to the pit and tossed the seed. I ate two bananas and drank the river water before feeling mildly satiated.

Wiping my face, I looked at Sugandha. "I am indebted to you for saving my life."

"I know a way you can repay me," she said with a pointed glance at Dayalu.

"Give us a moment alone," I said. Dayalu scanned the area and moved out of earshot. "How did you cure me?"

Sugandha gazed at the morning sky. "I did not. The nagas healed you with their powers and potions."

"Nagas?" I had read about the mythical serpents in stories and poems and wondered if she jested.

She shrugged as if she herself could not believe these creatures existed.

"Where did you find these snakes?" I teased.

"They are more than snakes. Their princess has a three-hooded head, and her body is as wide as a banyan tree trunk and longer than the ship you traveled here on."

"Ship?"

"In one of my visions, I saw you on a ship." My curiosity aroused, and I waited for her to continue the tale. "One of the nagas had bitten me earlier, and his venom had acted as an antidote to the snake bite I had suffered."

I remembered the strange creature I had seen yesterday while I had held her limp body. "I saw a snake-like creature sink its teeth into your ankle, and you recovered soon after," I said.

Taking that as a sign of my belief in her, she continued. "I found their cave abode underneath this river. They treated your wound and—" she paused, looking uncertain. I remained silent.

"As I had suspected, someone had cast a curse and set the snakes upon me. The nagas gave you an elixir—*nava pashana*—made of nine poisons to protect you from snake bites."

"Elixir?" I mumbled, pondering on her revelations. *How did I get mired in this land of mythology, surrounded by creatures and mantras that I had assumed only existed in tales?*

Her eyes met mine, and my confusion reflected in hers. "I didn't know the nagas existed until yesterday." She bit her lower lip as she puzzled over the events. "Somehow, my life has intertwined with these otherworldly beings. Now, I've drawn you into this web."

"Me?"

Her eyes gazed into mine. "The naga princess foresaw my need for you. She said I need your assistance to save Kashgar. From whom or what, I don't know. Also, I don't know why the princess thought a lonely girl like me, who could barely save herself, could save this land."

There was something mysterious about the girl in front of me. I sensed she was no ordinary person. But, I had traveled to Kashgar to seat Prince Aggabodhi on the throne. It appeared imprudent to forsake that mission, even if Aggabodhi's actions tempted me to abandon him.

Yet, something kept me tethered to this girl. I had felt the tug since the first day I bathed in the river. However, as the crown prince of Malla, I had a duty to protect my kingdom. I did not know what was in the best interest of my land. With my mind in turmoil, I replied, "I am a mere mortal with no ability to cast curses or blessings. I am not sure I can be of much help to you."

Her lips quivered as if overcome by some terrible emotion. I resisted the urge to comfort her. I did not know her—at all—to provide any solace. "My grandfather died a year ago—offering me his protection as his last act. Since then, I have been trying to survive. But events beyond my control keep thwarting my efforts to live. I am going to the village of Purohit Parivan to seek some answers. I know I am asking too much, but can you accompany me on this journey?" She clenched her fists as if the effort to seek my assistance weighed her down.

"Tell me everything that has happened since your grandfather's death," I ordered, still contemplating her request.

She sighed. "I will start with the events of that day. My uncle Ori forced my grandfather to curse a ship from Magadha." My body tensed at this revelation, but I held my tongue. My anger at Ori grew manyfold when I learned how he had used his father to kill the Malla men. With occasional pauses, she narrated the strangest tale.

"I don't know why my uncle is seeking me. Nor do I understand why Princess Malathi wanted me dead. I have an odd connection to the river that manifests as an ability to manipulate water. I have no idea how to control this skill. And instead of using this erratic power to help others, I have drowned two people. You must think me a freak—a monster," she said, a shiver running through her.

"Sugandha, I find you many things—astounding, bewitching, courageous—but a monster isn't one of them." A crow flew overhead, its wings flapping to gain altitude. As she glanced at the bird, I gazed at her vibrant cheek, covered with freckles. I knew then I had to accompany her on her quest, though I could not explain why. "I will go with you," I said, surprising myself. "Whether I like it or not, we are in this together."

She smiled but then grew pensive. "I still don't understand many things. I don't know what mysteries await me. I feel a pull of something strange yet beautiful. Something old that exists beyond our memories. Your life would be in constant danger." She hugged her arms more tightly against herself, trying to fight off whatever demons haunted her.

The way she talked openly about her problems gained my trust. I decided to share my story with her. "Your uncle started a war with my kingdom when he used your grandfather to curse my ship."

"Your ship? Who are you?" she asked softly.

I stopped directly in front of her. "I am Prince Atul, Crown Prince of Malla. I am determined to punish Ori for his deeds and seat the rightful heir on the Kashgar throne. I will help you figure out why Ori is after you. Then, together, we can right his wrongs."

Her skin shimmered in the sun, and her eyes shone brightly. "Let us leave now. I found a boat for us," she said.

"Give me a moment to confer with Dayalu," I said. Without waiting for her response, I marched toward my guard. Part of my mind reflected on my remarkable recovery from my arrow wound. The nagas must have vast knowledge of medicines.

I wondered if the Malla healers who had come with me could learn from them. Dayalu watched me approach and waited patiently. "Dayalu, go to our men. Dispatch Malla soldiers to find out what happened to Aggabodhi. He is still under Malla protection, so I want to keep him safe. If Chief Vikramasinha thinks I am dead, let us continue that pretense. Let some soldiers return to our ships off the coast. Ask our ships to sail south as if they are returning to Magadha. I am going to Purohit Parivan's village. Follow me there with just my four other sworn guards."

"With Pusha dead, we are down one. Do you want to choose a new man, my lord?"

I swallowed. "I trust you to choose the right man."

He protested about leaving me alone, but I commanded him to depart. Then, Sugandha and I headed toward the boat she had hidden. Without a thought, I hoisted the wooden craft on my head and marched toward the water.

"How did you do that?" she asked.

"Do what?" I asked, confused by her question.

"Lift the wooden boat above your head. It would take at least two men to pick up this boat," she said, eyeing me curiously. I halted, realizing the boat felt as light as a wooden plank. "The elixir has infused you with strength," she said.

I felt the same as before, though I knew I should not be able to raise the wooden craft so easily.

I set the vessel down. "Come here," I said. "Let me see if you feel different in my arms."

Sugandha turned red, reminding me that a pretty girl existed beneath the tangled hair and grimy face. "Wh-what?" she stuttered.

"I carried you to the river yesterday. If I have truly gained superior strength, you should feel lighter."

She shook her head. "I am an unmarried girl. I am not letting you carry me."

"Yes, that would be unwise. But traveling together, in this small boat—" Before I finished, she started laughing. I joined her in merriment.

"Okay, I will allow you to carry me. For a brief moment. Don't forget my powers. I could drown you with the flick of my fingers."

For an instant, images of my cousin drowning in the ocean

drifted into my memory. I pushed those away. "Yes, I am quivering in fear," I said in a mocking tone. I bent my knees and lifted her, holding her shoulders and knees. "You are light as a feather."

"And earlier?" she asked with a twinkle in her eyes.

I set her down gently. "I am married to two women. I would be a fool to answer that."

"Married?" she asked.

"Yes. Just now, you felt as light as my son."

Her eyebrows lifted in surprise. "How old is your child?" she asked as we resumed our march toward the river.

"He is a year old," I answered with a sigh, an ache spreading in my stomach. I missed my family.

She seemed to sense my longing. "You will return to him soon with superhuman might."

"How do you know this power does not fade?" I asked.

She frowned. "I don't," she answered.

Nothing about this land made sense—least of all this girl and my desire to travel with her. I lowered the vessel into the water and held out my hand. Sugandha grasped it and climbed into the boat. I got in and grabbed the oars. The swan with gold-tipped wings landed next to our boat.

"You are back!" I exclaimed.

"You know my bird," Sugandha said, surprised. The swan looked at both of us and glided forward. The water sparkled like diamonds.

"This bird is your savior. Yesterday, it guided me to you. I found you unconscious and carried you to the river. If I had come any later, death would have claimed its victim. The river and its inhabitants worked their magic to bring you back to life."

Her gaze darted between the bird and me. "I am not without friends," she said, blinking her eyes.

"Do you have a name for this bird?"

"No," she answered slowly. "Is it my place to name him? I think it is a male bird." The bird appeared to understand our conversation and turned to look at her with a tilt to its head. Without waiting for my reply, she continued, "Hamsa."

"Fitting name for a swan," I said, smiling. "What do I call you? Sugandha hardly seems an appropriate name for a boy."

She laughed gleefully, very unlike a lad. "Call me Nanda."

I remembered Dipankara's name for me. He called me Sword. Sugandha could not call me that, but I had a better name. "And you can call me Asi," I said. Asi, per ancient legends, was the primordial sword created to defeat evil and restore dharma. It seemed an apt name for this land of myth.

I hoped the divine beings here would use me as their weapon to revive the Kashgar kingdom to its former glory. I knew my desire sprang from my need for approbation. Restoring Kashgar would attest to my prowess to rule Malla.

She eyed me intently. "When I first saw you in my vision, I thought you looked like a tempered sword."

I beamed at her and started rowing north. "Nanda, let us seek the truth about you."

END OF CHILD OF THE RIVER

ALSO BY ANNA BUSHI

Sign-up for my Newsletter at AnnaBushi.com to get my new release notifications.

Swayamvara Romance Series is a Historical Romance series based on the ancient Indian custom, *Swayamvara*. During a Swayamvara, a bride chooses her groom from the assembled suitors. Each book in my series will be a stand-alone romance novel about a royal couple.

King in Hiding: In ancient India, King Dushyant captures Princess Lalitha's father on the battlefield, but finds himself captivated by her. Without revealing his identity, he offers to escort her on the journey home to her kingdom — and Lalitha feels an undeniable pull towards her mysterious escort. But what happens when the truth comes out? An unforgettable romance full of duty, love, and honor!

Land of Magadha trilogy

Based on medieval India, this is the story of royal siblings: Princess Meera and Prince Jay. The epic trilogy follows the Malla siblings over three decades as they face upheaval and downfalls, uncover treason and royal secrets, and experience shattered hearts. With the voices of their ancestors screaming in their heads, can they guard the kingdom entrusted to them?

Heir to Malla - Book 1

In medieval Magadha, a young princess stands alone between the

throne and an enemy horde.

Raised in ancient Indian tradition, Princess Meera neither wields a sword nor wears the crown. She is content to let her father and brother manage the affairs of the court. She performs her duties and knows her place.

When her brother disappears in enemy territory, her kingdom is left without an heir. As princes vie for her hand to capture the throne, her only use seems to lie in her ability to give birth to a son to wear the crown.

Afraid for her people's future and her brother's life, Meera can no longer accept her traditional role. As she fights to guard her heart and keep her kingdom safe, she struggles to navigate the royal game of chess without becoming a pawn.

Can she save what she holds most dear, or is her brother's disappearance a harbinger of worse to come?

This royal Indian saga weaves a tale of destiny and danger, forbidden love and courtly intrigue.

Heir to Malla is the first book in the epic Land of Magadha trilogy.

<u>War of the Three Kings</u> - Book 2

Jay promised not to kill him a decade ago. Now he stands between Jay and the throne.

Crown Prince Jay has grown into a legend with all his triumphs on the battlefield. While he is away helping a neighboring king, Jay is unaware of a new enemy who has emerged back home.

Jay fought with Nakul many years ago, but he believes the bitter past is behind them. Unknown to Jay, Nakul covets his crown. With chaos brewing in his realm and the lives of his people in peril, Jay stands exposed to danger as he cannot tell friend from foe.

Neither is Jay aware of the grave secret that binds him and Nakul together. Plunging into a conflict that might result in destruction, is he ready to pay the price for triumph? His failure would result in death—his and the kingdom he vowed to protect.

Malla siblings, Meera and Jay, return to face the consequences of their actions in War of the Three Kings, the second book in the epic trilogy, Land of Magadha.

Perfect for fans of historical fiction like Wolf Hall and Ponniyin Selvan or lovers of fantasy like Baahubali and The Lost Queen.

<u>Burden of the Crown</u> - Book 3

Blinded by despair, they fail to see the foe plotting their ruin.

His people revere him for the prosperity he has ushered. His enemies cower on hearing his name. Then, disaster strikes King Jay. He drowns in grief, forgetting his duty as a king.

When tragedy strikes, Meera thinks it is punishment for her past mistakes. One, in particular, rattles her. When she sets out to right her wrongs, she doesn't know if she can make up for the biggest mistake of all.

Anger festers in Jay's heart, threatening to ruin all he holds dear. The pain Meera inflicted on the one who captured her heart haunts her. A dangerous enemy seeking to seize the throne uses this opportunity to cause chaos in the kingdom.

Their foe has anticipated their moves to stay two steps ahead. Will the siblings heed the troubling signs? Or will they cause the downfall of their kingdom?

Burden of the Crown concludes the epic trilogy, Land of Magadha. Malla siblings face their gravest threat yet in their mission to protect their kingdom.

ACKNOWLEDGMENTS

From the age-old tales of the Mahabharata to the magical realms of Lord of the Rings by JRR Tolkien, Farseer Trilogy by Robin Hobb, Chorus of Dragons by Jenn Lyons, Mistborn by Brandon Sanderson, Song of Ice and Fire by GRR Martin, and many more, I love to escape into the world of mythology and magic.

I've always marveled at the brilliance of these authors who conjure entire new universes from the figment of their imagination. I owe a debt of gratitude to fantasy authors for inspiring me to embark on my storytelling journey.

My sincere thanks to Mary and Priya for journeying alongside Sugandha and Atul as I penned their tale. Your invaluable feedback has been instrumental in strengthening this novel.

I am immensely grateful to Christa Yelich for her editorial guidance on this novel, and to Toni Cox for meticulously proofreading this story.

Special thanks to Mia Harris for transforming my rough sketches into a beautiful Map of Kashgar.

My heartfelt gratitude goes out to my fellow local authors: Dhara Parekh, Theresa Halvorsen, Chris Bannor, Celeste Barclay, Dennis K. Crosby, Leslie Ferguson, and Jolie Tunnell.

Your dedication and creativity are a constant source of inspiration for me.

Big thanks to my mom for being my dedicated reader and supporter, and to Ranga for also taking the time to read all my books. Your encouragement means the world to me!

Special thanks to JR Jean for all the social media shoutouts! Your support is truly appreciated. A big shoutout to Meera, an incredible artist, for your unwavering support.

To my dear husband and daughters, your patience and understanding while I write, even during our vacations, mean everything to me. I couldn't pursue this passion without your unwavering support.

To my amazing friends, you are my biggest cheerleaders, and I'm so grateful for your unwavering support. To my father, brother and extended family, your kind words and encouragement mean the world to me.

Most importantly, to all the readers who have supported me by purchasing my books, your unwavering enthusiasm has been my guiding light through every twist and turn of this journey. I am deeply grateful to each and every one of you.

ABOUT THE AUTHOR

The stories I read growing up inspired me to write. I am interested in medieval India and within that society, examining the human heart in conflict. I like to place my female characters in difficult situations and see how they learn to survive with no actual power. And watch my male characters fall in love while fighting for king and land. I love exploring the struggle between love and duty.

I live in California with my family. Visit me at annabushi.com to learn about upcoming books.

Thank you for reading! If you enjoyed this book, I would love it if you let your friends know so they can experience the adventures of Atul and Sugandha. You can also leave a review so that other readers know what they're getting into when they pick up this book!

facebook.com/annabushibook
instagram.com/anna.bushi.book
amazon.com/author/annabushi